DREAMS IN BLACK STATIC

AMBROSE IBSEN

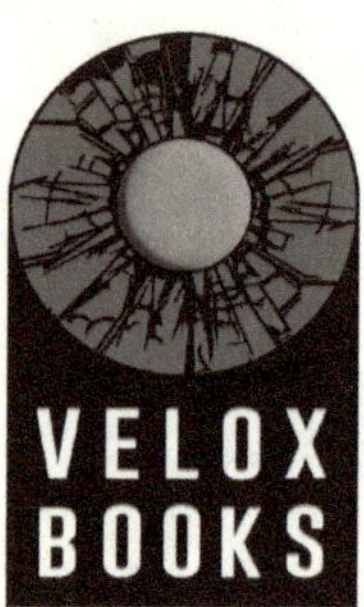

Published by arrangement with the author.

YOU'RE READING ANOTHER TERRIFYING COLLECTION FROM

FOLLOW VELOX TO KEEP THE NIGHTMARES COMING:

CONTENTS

ME AND MR. RAY

Everyone over a certain age has a first memory of the VHS tape. Mine? I was at my grandmother's house, watching a pastor for some megachurch on TV. He was waving a tape around and talking about how, thanks to technology, we could now find God on a tape. "Through this new medium, we have a remarkably powerful tool for spreading the Gospel!" he announced to riotous applause.

What didn't occur to me then, but now seems only too obvious, was that one could find the devil on a tape, too.

Ray and I had grown up together. Our parents had bought up houses in the same subdivision and we'd been classmates at the same private school. We'd shared the same hobbies, sipped from the same garden hoses; we'd been photographed together so many times that our families jokingly referred to us as brothers. He'd always been a little taller, and his hair was darker than mine, but to hear others tell it, Ray and I even *looked* the part of siblings.

When my bachelor's in computer science failed to open any worthwhile doors and Ray's scholarships dried up—after four staggered semesters and as many changes to his major—we became restless, the two of us. In our little hometown, where our old schoolmates were already cleaning up and venturing into adulthood, we carried about us the stench of failure. Tired of dodging questions about our futures, we set out for a new life in the city. We sought jobs, secured our first apartment and held out hope that the best was still ahead of us.

Looking back on it, I don't know what it was either of us expected. The much-discussed "future" never seemed to arrive, only one "today" after another. Through them all, we only grew a little older, a little more set in our ways, and clung harder to the same security blankets. Rather than striking out into the world and growing, we continuously regressed, mythologizing the past in favor of new experiences. Our days became dull, ritualized things intended to keep alive the spirit of times long-passed—the spirit of days, we would often agree, that had been "better" than these we presently trudged through. We cleared our mid-twenties together, yearning all the while for a return to the kinder, quieter years of our shared boyhood.

Sometimes, when things are quiet and the smell of the night breeze is just-so, or the field behind the nearby elementary school glows with clouds of fireflies, I'm reminded of those old times, and I long for them still.

But there are other nights, too—nights where I find myself walking through the city with a chill running down my spine despite the summer heat; nights when something seems about to emerge from the inscrutable mess of shadow that fills out the alleys and byways. On such walks, I remember *that* night—the night we sat side-to-side, peering into the black static—and each time, the old dread roosts in me like a fever I can't break.

Ray was never a tidy guy.

Upon moving in, he'd selected the smaller of our apartment unit's two rooms, and in our years of living together I don't think he ever cracked the small window in it even once, leading to a perpetual stuffiness he seemed to enjoy—or, at least, did not feel moved to prevent. Till I took them down myself, the gingham print curtains I'd helped him hang in said window had never been moved an inch.

The room, perhaps ten-by-fifteen feet of beige carpet and eggshell-colored walls, had space enough for his sagging queen-sized bed in one corner, a lumpy futon across from it, a TV stand and a dresser. It did *not* have sufficient room for the three packed bookshelves, the stacks of old videotapes that stood in for footrests or coffee tables, the piles of VCRs, LaserDisc players and vintage video game consoles all in varying states of disrepair, and yet Ray managed to *find* room for them, cluttering up all the open floor space till one felt half-smothered by the hoard. The use of any single device—even the old box TV with its duct-taped remote—required the careful navigation of a Gordian knot of power cords, and brought with it odd, high-pitched tones and a smell like burning dust.

It was afternoon when I awoke on the floor of his room, queasy from the glut of pizza I'd scarfed down late in the night. I panned about the dim, the only source of light being the bluish flickers of the TV. Sore and groggy, having had only a balled-up sweatshirt for a pillow, I turned and found Ray had already been up awhile. He was outstretched across the futon, watching the cheesy 90s fitness tape he'd put on the night before. A curly haired host clapped and thrust his hips in time with a tuneless soft rock number while overweight extras in pastel jumpsuits panted in the background. The graininess of the tape, coupled with the recurring sonic artifacts, gave the whole thing a dream-like feel so that I wasn't even sure I'd fully awakened till Ray spoke aloud.

"Ready to go, Silvio? It's two-for-one day. I've been waiting all week," he said, crossing his thin legs and stretching. He hadn't changed out of his uniform—the ratty jeans and red polo with the Stefano's Pizza logo on the back—after work the previous afternoon, and odds were good that he'd keep on wearing it till his next shift on Monday.

For a time, I simply stared at the TV screen, rubbing my stomach and fighting back a succession of yawns. "It's two-for-one day? Already?"

"Yeah, man!" he replied. "I can't wait to dig in. You want to go?"

Two Fridays a month, the only remaining video store in our area—the old Spectrum Video nestled in the shop district downtown—offered a two-for-one promotion, and two Fridays a month, the two of us would spend an hour there, rummaging through piles of secondhand tapes in search of treasures and lugging home armfuls. Unless one of us worked, our weekends were spent watching the haul over pizza or Chinese takeout. It was a nostalgic ritual of ours; a throwback to the sleepovers we'd had as elementary school kids in the mid-90s and just about the only thing the two of us looked forward to from day to day.

I rubbed the back of my neck, twisting this way and that to rid it of a niggling crick, then nodded. "As a matter of fact, I'd love to, Mr. Ray."

"Remember that comic shop we used to walk to after school, back in junior high?" I asked.

"Monarch's?"

"That's the one!"

"You know they tore it down, right? Replaced it with a vape shop, of all things!" Ray shooed off a curious fly, adding, "Last time I went home to visit mom and dad, I happened to drive by. I barely recognized the street. School's still there, but that's about it."

"Say, what about that soft serve place near the park? Was *that* still there? Remember how good that place was? I doubt there's a spot in this whole city that has ice cream as rich as that little place back home did. They were always so generous with the toppings, too."

"Soft serve these days doesn't taste like theirs did. It's all so artificial—cloying. It's barely even real food! Leave it in the sun and it doesn't melt! I can't stand the stuff. Back then, they used to make it *right.*"

"For sure. Man, running over for a cone or a slushie after an afternoon on the playground was the best, wasn't it?"

Ray nodded. "Pretty sure that place is gone, though. Unless I'm mistaken, it's a payday loan outfit now."

"Huh... no kidding..." I muttered, a little crestfallen. "That reminds me, last time I went back home, I had to run to the grocery store on Westfield. Remember the video rental place near the freeway? In the shopping center? It'd been empty for a few years, but recently a chain salon moved in. It was so strange to see it that way. Whoever worked on the building cut a lot of corners—you can still tell where the tape return slot was!"

"Ah, yeah. Those were some good times. Everyone in town would stop in there on Friday or Saturday night—it was basically a local tradition." Ray motioned further down the street, where the shops became more numerous and clusters of pedestrians began popping up. "At least we've still got Spectrum. I don't know what I'd do without it."

Spectrum Video is a literal hole in the wall. You have to walk half a mile into the bustling downtown strip, navigating heaps of kitschy shops and cafes to find it. A very small neon sign leads the way into an alley linking Main Street to a rear parking lot, and a little way down a brick-floored corridor, on the right, across from a janky arcade, is the front door. The shop is run by an old Korean guy named Hoon who's in the habit of wearing Hawaiian shirts and shaking hands with everyone who comes in the door. Ray and

I must be his biggest regulars and just about the only people in town who are still interested in VHS tapes, and over the years we've gotten to know him reasonably well. It was he who first referred to my roommate as "*Mr. Ray*", and the nickname stuck as an in-joke between the two of us.

At Spectrum, the dull green carpeting is threadbare and dusky with grime, the drop ceiling is dusty and water-spotted, and there's no bathroom. The inoperable box TVs anchored to the walls look as though they haven't played a screener in over a decade and have spent their years of retirement slumping in the grubby crook over the horror/thriller section. Hoon offers the usual moviegoing snacks near the register—microwave popcorn in cardboard buckets, overpriced boxes of candy and cans of soda—though you can tell by the washed-out wrappers that it's all well past its sell-by date.

Tapes make up only a small portion of Spectrum's floor space. Our beloved dead format had ceded all its ground to newer disc-based media over the years, and it's mainly DVDs and Blu-Rays which fill out the bulk of the shop now. A corner in the rear of the store, beyond the piles of NES cartridges and Playstation games with broken jewel cases, homes Spectrum's two bookshelves of VHS tapes, and despite the precipitous decline of the format in the past fifteen years, the stock is refreshed with surprising regularity. Hoon will purchase lots of secondhand tapes from sellers for a pittance, or claim free collections listed on Craigslist by locals desperate to offload them, and it was from these semi-regular infusions that Ray and I had come across some of our most treasured finds.

We walked into the shop and engaged in our usual banter with Hoon. He was wearing a silky button-down with an eye-catching pink lei motif, and for reasons unknown to us had his sunglasses on despite the dimness. Of Spectrum Video's eight or ten ceiling lights, only about five actually functioned, and the hue of these all varied depending on what bulbs he'd been able to find on sale.

"Lots of new tapes in," he said, shaking our hands and motioning to the back. "Some new lots from around town. Hit an estate sale. Got a donation, too. Hopefully some good stuff for you boys." He then spent several minutes showing us some of the other acquisitions he'd recently made. With all the flair of a master showman, he displayed for us a handful of vintage Casio watches from behind the counter and an allegedly functional Commodore 64. These exhibitions of recent purchases were always accompanied by almost legendary descriptions of his haggling prowess. Once, when Ray and I had come by late, near close, and there'd been no other shoppers in the store, he'd shown us a handgun he'd pawned off of someone, and had insisted that we both hold it before lecturing us for twenty minutes on proper trigger control—a skill he claimed to have mastered after studying Dolph Lundgren's *oeuvre*.

Hoon released us after waxing nostalgic about the Commodore, and Ray and I started through the store, making a beeline for the back corner. Sure enough, the bookshelves were teeming with tapes, and we began rifling through the unsorted mass at once.

Disney films with well-grubbed clamshells were abundant in this newest influx of stock, as were eighties kung-fu flicks with dubious—almost certainly bootlegged—packaging. There were also a few tapes of a particular Japanese cartoon Ray and I had both been fond of in the 90s, which I pointed out to a wry reply of, "They should have stopped after Frieza."

Ray happened upon a stack of Harmony Korine films between the ten or twenty copies of *As Good As It Gets* and eagerly set them aside. You couldn't scan any of the shelves without coming across at least a couple of the two-cassette box sets of *Titanic*, and there were so many *Forest Gumps* you could have built a table out of them. A half hour of searching brought my yield to a mere three tapes; a cheesy Spanish instruction tape, a Jackie Chan film and some early 90s made-for-TV movie about monster spiders.

Ray spent another twenty minutes perusing the shelves. He'd already picked up everything he was planning to buy but was driven to keep scanning the titles on offer so as to prolong the thrill of the hunt. Spending time in this stuffy back corner of the store, surrounded by tapes and other ephemera, was one of life's great joys for him, and he stood there a long while like a moth drawn to a bulb.

"Look at all of these," he said, pointing at the stock. There was something child-like in his movements, in his tone. "There's stuff on some of these tapes, the obscure ones, that hardly anyone's ever seen—stuff that no one's thought about in years and years." His eyes were distant; though he was working over the rows of tapes, it was clear his mind was elsewhere, in a far-off place. "That's the magic of a dead format, man. These days you can rip a movie in Blu-ray quality and put it on every hard drive in the world. File-sharing and such makes videos immortal in a way. But not these babies," he said, giving one of the tapes in his hand a shake. "There are forgotten things on these tapes. They're like ancient scrolls, you know? There's stuff on these just waiting to be discovered, but if they degrade or break, it'll be gone forever. These tapes are just as transient as we are." When his thoughtful soliloquy was through, he basked in the corner a few moments longer, then motioned to the front. "Want to grab some stir-fry on the way back?" he asked, holding out the cluster of tapes in his arms. "We'll need some fuel to get through these."

"Only if you're picking up the tab, Mr. Ray."

We walked out of Spectrum three dollars lighter, with a combined total of nine VHS tapes, and then started back through the dim alley toward a small Chinese takeout place called Golden Kitchen, from which we'd ordered many times. As usual, we bought more food than we could comfortably eat and hauled the payload back home. Ray, gem that he was, paid for the meal. "Next time it'll be your treat, yeah?"

"Of course," I replied.

Unbeknownst to me at the time, that was the last meal we'd ever share.

—w/\/—w/\/—

The afternoon and evening played out like they'd done hundreds of times before.

We got back to the apartment and headed straight for Ray's room. He started up the TV, which loosed its troubling, high-pitched whine, and we carefully balanced our styrofoam clamshells of stir fry and crab rangoon on a pile of busted VCRs that answered for a coffee table in his packed quarters. A pound of greasy noodles and a two-liter of ice cold Coke between us, we made it through a choppy, rough-grained version of *Battles Without Honor or Humanity* and agreed that the hideous resolution of the tape added a much-welcome veneer of grit and authenticity to the film. When that was through, Ray got up for a bathroom break and entrusted the next pick to me. "Surprise me," he said, pointing to the stack of tapes I'd brought back from Spectrum.

Having only the three to choose from, I decided to give the made-for-TV film a go and eased the tape out of its tattered cardboard sleeve. The black shell felt cold and brittle in my hands, and in the low blue glow of the TV I inspected the reels within for mold. The tape looked well and clean enough, though I noticed something strange as I examined it—something that I had somehow missed back at the store.

If in fact this tape was a copy of the low-budget movie advertised on the cover, there was no trace of this to be found on the tape itself. It was a plain black tape of the commonest sort, with a white adhesive label on the front that bore no identifying marks whatsoever. I turned it in my hands, disappointed in myself for not having more thoroughly studied the thing in-store. *Oh, man, looks like I accidentally bought a dud. I should have looked at the tape before buying it—this is just someone's cast-off blank.*

But my disappointment was blunted at another discovery, which inspired a pique of curiosity. The recording tab had been broken off, which told me that the tape had been used at some point. Though I still had no clue as to its contents, I was now certain that the tape was *not* a mere blank.

I had left the video store believing I'd purchased a tacky made-for-TV thriller I could fall asleep to; instead, I'd come away with something else altogether—something that promised *real* intrigue. Now and then, our nets had dredged up little treasures like this one. Sometimes people would get their tapes mixed up, donating footage of their kids' Sweet Sixteen to the local Goodwill where they'd meant to drop off *Batman Forever.* Other times, people would record over portions of VHS movies, and years later, having bought them secondhand, you'd find yourself watching early 90s commercials during *Top Gun*, or home movies at the tail end of *The Shining.* There was no telling what we'd find on this unmarked tape, and the prospect was thrilling.

Ray returned some minutes later, plopping down onto the futon. "What'd you pick?"

I handed him the tape. "Looks like I accidentally scooped something up. There's a blank label on it, tab's busted. I think we've got a live one here!"

He waggled his eyebrows, grinning. "Could be someone's wedding, a football game—no telling!" Ray got up and fed the tape into the VCR. Returning to the sofa, he manipulated the unresponsive duct-taped remote until the tired player finally saw it fit to rewind the thing, and after several seconds, the telltale *click* was heard. He leveled the remote at the TV and pressed *Play*. "Let's see what we've got here..."

The two of us leaned in and watched very closely as the screen flickered to life.

—w∿—w∿—

There is no simple way to describe what we found on that tape, and to this day I can't tell you where or when it was recorded, nor by whom. For hours afterward, late into the evening, Ray and I discussed precisely these things, but our theory-crafting brought us no closer to the truth. Instead, our fevered speculation about the tape only served to reinforce the strange footage in our memories, and to incite in us a spine-tingling chill I am not ashamed to admit still plagues me latterly.

In a word, the tape's contents were dream-like. I hope you'll excuse me for using such a cliché, but years of sustained—almost *maniacal*—reflection have brought me no closer to an apt descriptor than this. Perhaps it was merely the aural hiss and the severe visual artifact haunting the footage that made it seem so, but I almost felt I was watching a literal nightmare unfold. I am no stranger to horror films, even experimental ones, but nothing else I have ever glimpsed in waking life has so uncannily captured the heart-rattling heights of hypnopompic terror as this.

The set—if it can even be called that—is heavily shadowed. Very little color exists in the whole of the "film", which is of three minutes and fifteen seconds' length, but it is not in black and white. Rather, it appears to have been shot on a cheap camera, and in the dead of night without the aid of a light. As such, there are precious few certainties to be found in the footage, and the unplumbed dim stirs with doubtful shadows. It is the type of recording one might feel compelled to watch multiple times in the interest of gleaning new insights, though Ray and I watched it only three times that night—for despite the hateful pull of our curiosity, neither one of us could bring ourselves to watch it a fourth.

The entirety of the short piece takes place within what appears to be a sitting room. Various shapes ebb and flow from sight, giving the impression of an armoire, a sofa and other expected bits of furniture in the background. But it is to the upper left of the screen that one's eyes are quickly led, for in that corner, moving furtively in the black tableau, is a human form. One's discovery of the figure—which appears to sway gently frontward and backward in a high back chair—coincides with a pained, almost choking sob.

At first hearing it, Ray and I both agreed the voice of the weeper was aged and feminine, and rather unnerved at what was unfolding on-screen, he wondered aloud if we hadn't stumbled upon a snuff film. We continued watching through hooded lids as the figure came very gradually into sharper focus. The camerawork was smooth and slow—unnaturally so for something we presumed had been shot with a handheld camcorder—and as more of the swaying sitter came into view, more questions arose.

Something seemed to flutter about the figure's lolling head.

"Is that a trash bag?" dared Ray, squeezing the remote tightly in his fist.

The camera continued its slow approach, and after a few moments, the appearance of a pale, withered face within the shadows clued me in on the nature of the fluttering material. "It's a veil," I said, pointing at the screen.

Second by second, the screen was being filled by the form of an old woman rocking back and forth in a chair. Dressed in black and wearing what looked to be a mourning veil, the bony outlines of her aged face were left blurred by the sway of the fabric, and her tormented weeping grew steadily in volume.

"What... what is this?" I remember Ray asking, one hand over his mouth as though he were on the brink of being ill.

I, too, felt a curious nausea coming over me as I watched the footage. Nothing had yet occurred to warrant such a reaction, of course—but sitting in Ray's dark, stuffy room and watching that ghostly pale face slowly take up more and more of the screen left my guts churning. We felt, I think, that we'd happened across something truly private—something that should never have been filmed in the first place, and where usually we felt nothing but amusement at discovering such obscurities as this one, we now found ourselves terribly unnerved.

In the last ten or fifteen seconds of film before the screen cut to black, the cameraman ceased his advance toward the weeping woman and merely remained stationed some few feet away. At this proximity, the dreaminess of the scene reached its zenith, with the veiled figure blurring into the surrounding darkness. It was only thanks to a shaft of moonlight, perhaps drifting in from some window off-screen, that we could make out the glow of the woman's skin under the veil—and it was this feeble light which gave us the final, terrible look at what lay beneath.

The woman's body hitched forward very slightly and her face entered—for an instant—into sharp relief.

Behind the veil was indeed the face of an old woman—crooked nose, sagging chin and silver hair much in evidence. Startlingly however, there were no eyes in her sockets, and no tongue visible behind her wagging lips. Instead, dark, shimmering ribbons erupted from each orifice along with her sobs, pooling in her lap.

From her eyes and mouth, the woman was spewing a torrent of unspooled video tape.

In the final seconds, the subject ceased her crying; instead, she began to laugh—quietly, ominously—and rose suddenly from the chair.

At the end, the room was bathed in darkness and I recall that we both settled against the futon with a shudder. It was Ray who eventually broke the tense silence, regarding the television with an uncommon scowl. "That didn't look fake to me," was all he said.

I didn't reply, merely nodded, because I had been thinking the same thing.

—ʍ\/ʍ—

Ray inspected the tape like a zoologist cataloguing a new animal; he flipped open the guard panel, took a thorough look at the insides as if expecting it to differ from the hundreds of other tapes he'd owned over the years. It was, in the end, the same genus as all the rest.

"What *is* this?" he half-demanded after chewing his nails down to the quick.

"A prank," I offered. "An elaborate one."

He shook his head furiously, unconvinced, and dropped the tape onto the carpet. "I don't buy it." With a wild look in his eye, he added, "It's too *authentic*, Silvio."

I don't mean to make it sound like I wasn't unsettled by what we'd seen on the tape; I was—and I *still am*—but more than the footage, Ray's rapid shift in demeanor had me on edge. Over the course of our three viewings he'd become supremely agitated—more agitated than I'd ever seen him before.

"Well, what about it?" I tossed my shoulders. "It's real. Fine. So, what? You want to try and show it to someone else? Maybe we could ask around online, or—"

"Oh, no," he shot back. "I don't think so."

"You don't want to show it to anyone else?"

Ray sat on the question a moment, then finally replied, "What good would it do? The only one who could possibly point us in the direction of its maker is Hoon—and that's if he even remembers what lot this random tape came from." He grit his teeth as he went on, picking up the tape and staring at it. "This doesn't feel like something we should spread around. You and I shouldn't have seen it, probably. Showing it to other people just rubs me the wrong way."

I laughed then, though in retrospect perhaps I shouldn't have. "What, do you think the tape's dangerous or something?" I yanked it out of his hands and gave it a cursory study of my own, quite cavalier in my tone and handling of the thing, though the memory of what it contained struck me once more and I hurriedly dropped it back into Ray's lap.

"Didn't... didn't it bother you?" he chanced, plucking up the tape and setting it gingerly atop the VCR. "Didn't you feel something as we watched it?"

"Sure," I said, and I did my best to appear unfazed, though the kneading of my earlobes between my fingers till they grew red and sore betrayed something of my true unease. "It's eerie. What about you?"

Ray was silent for a long while. It was an unnatural silence for a man who rarely had trouble speaking his mind. "I feel... as though something has its claws in me," he uttered, and he appeared poised to elaborate on his feelings with a knit brow and closed fists, but the words wouldn't come and he eventually abandoned the effort as futile. "I'm tired," he added with a convincing sigh. "I'm gonna crash."

Without our realizing it, the bizarre footage had soured our cherished weekend ritual. I tried to salvage things, to put on something else to watch, but Ray had no interest in the other tapes we'd bought. Instead, he bid me a good night and sank back against the futon.

I didn't know what time it was when I heard the sliding door to the balcony grinding open, only that the sun hadn't risen.

The grating noise of that door sliding along its dusty track jostled me awake at once. It was a distinctive sound, not to mention a rare one, for except on days when I burned popcorn it always remained shut. Ray was terrified of heights and never set foot on our little balcony, so at hearing the door slide open I was more than a little startled. My first thought was that an intruder had crept up the fire escape and had somehow popped the lock. We lived five floors up, though break-ins of this kind were not unheard of, and we ourselves had witnessed skulkers scaling the fire escapes of adjacent buildings in search of unlocked doors and easy marks.

I stepped out of bed and, hugging the wall, began through the dark hallway, toward the living room. There, I discovered the balcony door was indeed open, though I saw something most unexpected as I snuck further in.

Ray was sitting on the balcony, draped in a blanket and staring wistfully into the twilight. The scene beyond the railing was dominated by the sky-piercing bulk of the Keenan Building—an empty, 38-floor skyscraper abandoned since the late 80s—which limited the reach of the moonlight and draped a fuzzy blanket of darkness across our building and everything else that fell within its prodigious shadow. The structure was an eyesore, discolored by age and neglect; and for the citizenry, it was a painful reminder of more successful eras in the city's history. Despite its being the single most noticeable fixture in the skyline, it was treated with a forced, almost superstitious disregard. Joggers would go out of their way to avoid running past it, and despite its decades of abandonment, it lured neither criminals nor squatters. Ray and I both had gotten used to the sight of it, had even made a sort of peace with it, as every building that fell within its shade enjoyed lower rents for the trouble.

Ray was sitting on the grating, one arm hanging loosely from the weathered rails, staring at the Keenan with such intensity I wondered if he hadn't spied something in one of its vast, dusty windows.

Before I could ask him what he was up to, he turned a little toward me, his eyes moist and hooded, and uttered, "Everything is changing, Silvio."

The night air was chill. It didn't seem to bother him, though I couldn't help but shiver as I paused at the threshold. "What do you mean?"

The hand perched upon the rail like a jittery bird pointed a finger into the distance. "Have you noticed the skyline?" asked Ray, swallowing very hard and turning back to the tower. "Things are changing all around us. Familiar shapes are being worn down and new ones are starting to spring up. New lights come on every night, while at the same time others go dim and burn out for good."

I took a step onto the balcony and panned about. Our vantage point offered only a limited view of the city; whatever wasn't blocked out by the abandoned monolith behind our building was shielded from view by other large structures. To hear him talk about changes to the city's skyline made it seem as though his vantage point was different—higher up than my own. "Well, sure," I said. "Things change, man. And since when do *you* keep up with the view, huh? I don't think I've ever seen you out here on the balcony before. You scared me half to death when you opened the door. I thought we were getting burgled."

Ray snickered. For all I know, he really was looking down upon the world from some other place, much higher up. "You don't get it. The city—the *world*—as it exists *now*... it's just a dying format. No one knows it yet, but all of this is just tumbling into obsolescence." Here, he turned slightly, leering at me with one wild eye. "You and I? We're just old tapes festering on a shelf, Silvio. Forgotten footage—ephemera."

Drawn out of bed in a panic, I hadn't been prepared for this kind of existential talk and had little to add to the conversation. Thinking back on it, I only wanted to shuffle off to bed and leave Ray to his brooding, but I remained there awhile longer instead and played the part of sounding board as he aired his thoughts. Come morning, he'd be his chipper self again, no longer weighed down by whatever it was that presently seemed so burdensome. That was always what happened when Ray got into one of his philosophical jags—I'd seen it play out a million times, though as I stood there groggily I was unsure what had triggered this particular episode.

Ray continued, head low. "What has it all amounted to? We burned out back home and moved here, to the city. But what's come of it? We spend all of our time looking backward to the highlight reel. Is that all there is? If we're videotapes, you and I... why would anyone watch past those early scenes? If anything, they would probably just fast-forward through *these* parts, right?" He shrugged, then laughed with an eerie suddenness in spite of himself. "What kind of ending could you possibly hope for with such a weak middle?"

"Relax, man," I said, leaning against the railing, hands in my pockets. "It's not all that bad. Things could be better, but we're hanging in there, right?"

Ray didn't respond. Instead, he stared up at the black tower, hands clasped in his lap and shoulders subtly quaking.

"What are you looking at?" I asked, scanning the upper reaches of the dark skyscraper with a frown.

"Everyone in town *hates* that place," said Ray, nodding at the pitiable building. "But do you know *why* they hate it? It isn't just because it's worn-out and ugly. It's because it reminds them of how much better things were, once upon a time. The people who built it were optimists; it's a monument to their hopes for the future. But if those architects could see it now—if those city planners could have seen what a miserable sight it would become—they would never have built it. They would have put something intentionally unsightly there instead—a landfill, maybe. They could have piled mounds of rotting garbage thirty-eight stories high and the people in this city would be happier with the stench than they are with the sight of this thing, with all its unrealized potential." He cracked a sad smile and lowered his head. "Some days, I feel like this tower, Silvio."

We went back and forth awhile longer. I commiserated with him while trying to urge him back inside, but he refused me time and again, remaining seated on the balcony and staring up at the Keenan's black borders with something like longing.

Before I finally threw in the towel and shambled back to bed, Ray asked me one last question. Drinking in the night air, he posed, "If there was some way to go back to those old days, Silvio—a way to return to them, so that you could live in them forever and never leave... would you do it?"

Tired as I was, I replied more harshly than I should have. "No," I said, and I did it with unreasonable haste, having given the question little thought.

Ray grunted and gave a feeble nod, appearing deflated for my answer. He said nothing more as I started back into the apartment, but he didn't really have to. I already knew what his reply to that question would have been had I posed it to him.

I first realized something was wrong upon waking.

It was a few minutes past ten in the morning when I rolled out of bed, though I'd been up at least a half hour, sitting up and listening to the persistent rain against my window. The forecast hadn't said anything about rain, and where usually I found the sound of it soothing, the noise of unexpected showers only left me feeling agitated, out of the loop. There is something particularly coarse about waking to the unforeseen.

Perhaps what'd *really* put me on edge was the fact that, in my time spent listening, I'd heard *only* the rain—nothing more.

Where I am a chronic over-sleeper, Ray was a morning person. Rare was the day that he didn't beat me out of bed by a couple of hours. The sounds of his putzing around the apartment, fixing a meal in the kitchen or watching TV in his room, were daily standbys of mine, but on this late, grey morning I heard only the patter of rain. I recalled his outburst on the balcony the night before and decided he must've tuckered himself out good and proper, but with each passing minute the weight of the unusual silence grew, and I finally rose with a mind toward checking up on him.

I hobbled out of my room and started for Ray's, only to find the door ajar and a faint, bluish light flickering across the floor just inside. *Oh, he's watching some TV*, I thought with what seemed at the time an incommensurate relief. I pushed open the door and uttered a groggy "Good morning", but as the door swung open, revealing an empty bed and futon, I was faced only with a mumbling TV set, its screen a jumble of white static.

I guess he did beat me out of bed this morning, thought I, and I passed from his room toward the kitchen, where I expected to find him munching some cereal or making coffee. The kitchen, though, was unoccupied—and I spent only an instant peering into it, as my attention was drawn instead to the open balcony door in the living room. The smell of warm rain flooded the space richly from the open door, and the edge of the carpet had grown damp. I started across the room immediately, complaining, "Dude, if you're gonna stand out there, at least close the door! If the carpet gets moldy they'll take it out of our deposit!"

My words passed across the room, out onto the balcony, and were carried off by a whistling breeze, unheard. There was no one on the fire escape, and nothing much of consequence to be seen there save a familiar blanket left matted to the grating by rain.

Dumbstruck, I stood at the door a long while, staring at the dripping scenery. No matter how long I stared, Ray didn't emerge from the mist.

After idling in the living room some minutes, I shut and locked the sliding door and knew I was alone in the apartment—and that I'd almost certainly been alone there for some hours. There was something in the air of the place that assured me it was so—a choking stuffiness that even the rain and breeze couldn't chase away.

"Maybe he went out," I said aloud, and I wandered back to his room, where the TV was still spitting out a blizzard's worth of visual snow. It wasn't like Ray to leave his TV on when he wasn't using it—but then, it wasn't like him to step out in the mornings suddenly without saying something, either. Even on mornings when he had to work the opening shift at the pizzeria, he usually thumped on my door to let me know he was leaving, and I knew for a fact that he wasn't scheduled to work that day.

For the first time in some hours, I recalled how we'd spent the previous evening—the awful tape we'd watched—and for the first time in said hours I felt a nauseous fear welling up in my gut. The surprise at finding my ordinarily predictable roommate absent this morning, coupled with my brief recollection of the bizarre footage we'd accidentally stumbled upon, led me to somehow conflate the two events in my mind, and to wonder—perhaps foolishly—whether Ray's absence and the wretched tape were in some way related. *Did he watch it again? Is that why the TV's still on? Where could he have gone?*

I couldn't picture Ray braving another viewing of the tape solo, but knelt down to inspect the VCR nonetheless. The rickety device proved empty. I had trouble remembering what we'd done with the tape the night before, and I rifled through several piles about the room in search of it—though it was all fruitless.

Ray wasn't home, and the tape was missing in action, too. It seemed apparent to me that they'd gone to the same place, though where that might've been I hadn't the slightest.

—w\/\—w\/\—

Despite the strangeness of the situation, I assured myself that nothing was wrong. I theorized that Ray had gone downstairs to check the mail or take out the garbage, and that he'd be back up at any moment—except that his only pair of shoes was sitting by the door and the waste bin in the kitchen remained half-full. When several minutes passed, I sought out my phone and decided to shoot him a text message. I parked myself on the living room sofa and tapped out the most nonchalant thing I could think of. *What're you up to?* I expected a quick reply—a funny one, taking me to task for being a paranoid nag.

What I did not expect was to hear the chittering of his phone issuing from inside the apartment. I followed its noisy vibrations all the way to the bookshelf nearest his bed, where I found his cell rumbling beside his keys and wallet.

Up to that point, I'd been baffled at Ray's absence, though I'd done a good job of staving off what seemed like unnecessary panic. But wherever Ray had gone, it was now clear he'd set off there without his shoes, keys, phone or wallet. In fact, the *only* thing he'd seemingly taken with him had been that awful tape. It was at that moment, staring down at his rattling phone, that I truly began to court fear.

Where could he have gone? Is he just messing around—hiding? I peered into every closet and nook in the apartment, but found no sign of Ray anywhere. *What did he get up to after you went to bed?* When last I'd seen him, he'd been sitting on the balcony with a blanket wrapped around his shoulders, so I wandered back to the sliding door in search of some clue.

I paced out into the rain and picked up the sodden blanket, and as I did so, glancing past the thin railing, a terrible thought occurred to me. With blanket in hand, I stepped across the fire escape and scanned the world below with bated breath, but thankfully the sidewalks were empty and the gory sight I'd begun entertaining remained nothing but a dark joke. *Of course he didn't jump,* I thought. *He was really worked up last night, but he wasn't suicidal.* Guilt stole over me as I peered beyond the rails; I wondered if he was angry with me—if I shouldn't have spent more time with him, listened to him patiently during his tirade.

I backed off of the balcony but kept staring out into the rain. Looming ahead of me like a black tombstone was the shell of the Keenan Building, the silent monolith Ray had found so fetching during his nocturnal ramblings. I scanned it, window by window, searching for whatever it was he'd seen in it, but found only tons of inexpressive glass and concrete. I was momentarily distracted by daydreams of what the forsaken building was like on the inside, what its shadowed halls held—and I half-wondered if the same questions hadn't entered my roommate's mind the night previous, leading him to an impromptu trespass.

There is no fixture in the whole of downtown that wholly escapes association with the Keenan Building; even those homes and businesses that are not stationed immediately within its impressive shadow are in some way drawn into its gravitational pull. Its position as city epicenter had always been self-evident, though as I left the complex and walked along the sidewalk in the skyscraper's shade, I felt as though the whole of the Earth turned with the Keenan for an axis.

One tends to avert their eyes as they walk past the thing in much the same way the superstitious will hold their breath in passing a graveyard. It is only natural that something so blighted should be eschewed at every opportunity—but as I walked to a late lunch, I overrode the impulse to ignore it and instead gave it more attention than I'd ever done in our few years of acquaintance.

She had been played with by the elements, roughed up by time, but even on the day the ribbon had been cut one would have been hard-pressed to describe the Keenan as a "pretty" building. It was a brutalist construction, its thirty-eight stories of grey-black concrete offering nothing in the way of decorative flourishes. Its windows were dark—though as I walked past I couldn't be sure whether to attribute the gloom of the panes to the building's lack of lighting, or to some quality in the glass itself—and squinting through them, though I knew nothing of its interior layout, I got the impression that the structure's aesthetic sterility continued within.

An etching near the front doors of the building—fixed shut by a knot of chains—gave a construction date of 1957. In its almost thirty years of operation, I knew the Keenan had homed several small shops. Speaking with locals, you would sometimes pick up bits and pieces of the building's history, and in this way I had a working idea of what the tower had been like in its prime. A pharmacy had been located on its ground floor, as had a credit union. Some of the upper floors had been occupied by a local news station, though a merger with one of the major networks had led to massive reshuffling, and when the dust had settled the local arm of said network had been amputated, leaving those levels of the Keenan suddenly vacant. The vacancies rolled downward from there; office rents increased to make up for the loss of revenue and renters on other floors broke their leases. In the space of thirty-odd years, the building had gone from bustling city center to ghost town; in the space of the *next* thirty, which were marked by periods of rolling recession, none had moved to fill the vacancies and the tower had remained a sore spot in the public consciousness.

The night before, Ray had scrutinized the building with curious intensity—had even expressed a kind of kinship with it. "*Some days, I feel like this tower.*" I'd never known him to have an interest in the thing; we'd discussed it no more or less than any other feature in our surroundings. Living in the shade of the Keenan was a daily reality for us; despite its size and reputation, it had become, over the course of countless days, just another brushstroke in the scenery. But last night, to Ray, it had suddenly seemed like so much more. In his strange mood, he'd been called out to the balcony to stare at it—heedless of his usual fear of heights. What had been the draw?

I paused before the massive tower, looking through the glass of its long-chained doors, and I couldn't help imagining my roommate stumbling through its dark halls, barefoot. *Is that where he went?* I thought. *Did he go in there to look for something?* I had no evidence that this was the case—no grounds whatsoever to suspect he'd broken into the abandoned skyscraper except that he'd stared longingly at it the night before in his brooding—and yet I almost thought I could *hear* the clopping of bare feet echoing from some unlit space beyond that door as I stood at gaze.

Though I had fled the apartment on the pretense of seeking out a meal, I passed several restaurants in my wandering, each of them more unappealing than the last. The truth was that I'd only gone out to escape the apartment, whose air had been fouled by my hours of hand-wringing and pacing. I hoped, almost certainly in vain, that I would return in the evening, bone-tired, and find Ray in the living room, back from his excursion.

Bright sunlight began to ooze through breaks in the cloud cover, drawing up the standing water in the streets and adding an almost intolerable thickness to the air. The sidewalks were cluttered with pedestrians and the roads choked with cars, superadding exhaust and exhalation to the already pungent tang of the city air. I ambled, half-choked, past the iron palisade of a government building and then paused a moment beneath the awning of a shuttered convenience store in search of cooler air to sup. Horns blared in the distance, and the maddening click of crosswalk signals, coupled with the never-ending staccato of hurried steps, coalesced into a noise I could have mistaken for the city's heart.

I looked up the street and back down the way I'd come, feeling suddenly lost and having little memory of the ground I'd hitherto covered. Only the Keenan rising up to my back felt familiar to me, and as I eyed it from beneath the awning, wiping the sweat from my brow, it looked back at me with its myriad glass eyes. I turned away, continued staggering deeper into town, determined to put the black monolith behind me.

But as I have said, all the city is arranged with the Keenan for its nucleus, and it was only a matter of some few minutes before I met it again. I had bought a sandwich and fries from a street vendor that would ultimately go uneaten, and despite the terrible humidity I chose the "scenic" route back to the apartment, which led me up Brixton Avenue, past the outer gate of a small metro park and a succession of tottering parking garages. It was here, on this meandering path, that I had hoped to get my head straight.

Instead, I was reunited with the Keenan. Emerging from a bank of shops, I could not help passing the building's southern face, and my gaze, not moored to anything of substance, was naturally drawn to its striking bulk. Of particular interest were its great doors, fastened tightly with chains as the others had been. I noticed something different about this set—something that made me halt on the sidewalk and take a few measured steps toward the abandoned structure. The thick metal handles were festooned with a knot of chains, yes—but something else, fluttering about those rust-flecked links, caught my attention.

I paced closer to the building, standing within a stone's throw, and noticed that several tangles of reflective black material had been woven into the links of the securing chain, almost like streamers. The luster and dimensions of this material were too familiar to me to dismiss it as a mere party streamer, though; I leaned in closer and confirmed my suspicions.

A mass of video tape had become tangled there.

The presence of tape on these door handles could be nothing but strange coincidence—that was what I told myself as I shuddered at discovering it, anyway—but what a coincidence it was. I tried imagining what odd circumstances could have led to the tape's entanglement there, but was hampered by intrusive thoughts—thoughts of Ray's dreamy expression as he'd moped on the balcony the night previous, visions of him wandering out of our apartment in the pre-dawn gloom, soaked by the rain, ripping the guts out of that accursed tape and weaving them around the door handle toward ends unseen.

Maybe Ray *had* left the tape there for my benefit—as a signpost that would steer me to him.

Or maybe the ribbons had grown tangled there for no rhyme or reason. Everywhere I turned I could point out other instances of the city's filth. Perhaps this discarded tape was no different from the syringes strewn about the curb, or the cans and bottles jettisoned by passing motorists.

I returned to an empty apartment and resumed my vigil.

With others out and about, seeking to enjoy their Saturday afternoon, the bumps and mutterings of the tenants in neighboring units had been reduced to nothing. This imparted an otherworldly quiet to the apartment I found execrable. No sooner had I returned home did I wish to flee back into the city; yet, knowing better than to expect consolation from the outside world, I surrendered instead to the silence and marched to the shower. When I emerged, I stationed myself on Ray's futon and stared at the lunch I'd bought till it had grown too cold to bother with.

It was in sitting there that I first laughed that day—laughed, because I realized how insubstantial and pitiable a thing our existence in the city really was. I had nothing else to fill my time with; no errands, no other friends to meet. Instead, I was confined to this apartment, waiting for Ray like a mother sitting up for her teenager who'd been out past curfew. And like a mother, I kept on fretting, sure with every passing minute that something truly terrible had happened.

The afternoon rolled aside to reveal the first stirrings of evening. I retrieved Ray's phone and thumbed through his recent calls and texts in the hopes of finding some clue as to his whereabouts. This invasion of privacy yielded nothing, however; his most recent call had been to his boss at Stefano's a few hours before his last shift, and the last text message he'd sent had been to *me*, a few evenings prior.

More and more it seemed as though Ray had been plucked from the balcony late in the night—spirited away somewhere without a trace. If he *had* ventured somewhere of his own volition, then he'd gone to enormous lengths not to disclose the barest hint of his destination. And that simply wasn't like him. My imagination conjured images of him sitting on that balcony, buried in the shadow of the Keenan and gradually fading into it, till nothing of him remained—visions of him being absorbed completely into the ether.

I rose with sore legs, hobbling off to the kitchen in search of a stiff drink. Ray's room was gloomy at every hour, and was doubly so now that the sun had set, but as I exited and began crossing into the kitchen, I found a pleasant moonlight drifting in through the parted blinds of the balcony door.

There was something else, too.

Cast hazily upon the glass of the door by the powdery moonlight was the shadow of a lurker on the fire escape. Owing to the interference of the blinds, and to the figure's seeming distance to the door, a clear description of this unwelcome visitor was not possible—though the figure's crooked posture and utter stillness transmitted a hint of intimidation that I took to be quite intentional. I froze there, several paces from the kitchen, staring at the door and waiting for the shadow to make its move. How long it had waited there I couldn't guess, for I hadn't heard even the faintest step upon the metal grating while brooding in Ray's room. Was the figure aware of *my* presence? Was it merely biding its time, waiting to slip in at the most opportune moment?

Was it Ray?

No. At a glance I felt quite certain that the figure prowling on the balcony was anyone but Ray.

With all the silence I could muster, I started through the living room and approached the balcony door. When I had come within arm's reach of it, I sidled up to the adjacent wall and carefully pushed aside one of the dusty blinds. Through this small opening I peered out onto the balcony narrowly, chest heaving. Accustomed as my eyes were to the interior darkness, I found the pale moonlight rather harsh, and it took a few seconds for my vision to adjust to the brightness. When it had, I surveyed the whole of the balcony.

And I found it unoccupied.

I stepped back and took in the whole pane, looking for the shadow that had been projected there only an instant prior but finding no trace of it. Incredulous, I tugged up the blinds with such force that the mechanism nearly tumbled from the mount on the wall, giving me an unencumbered view of the fire escape and the black skyscraper beyond.

Someone had come up onto the balcony, loitered there a short while, and had subsequently fled in the space of an instant—and they'd done it all without a sound.

Terribly shaken, I unlocked the door and slid it aside, marching noisily onto the fire escape and hoping to find some shape in retreat through the lower levels. Instead, I was greeted only by a warm summer wind. The evening proved impeccably still and quiet.

I had been sitting too long in the darkness and my eyes had gotten the better of me; that was the only explanation I could think of as I paced about the rectangular enclosure, hands gripping the rails. I had almost completed a full circuit when, with a start, I nudged something with my foot. I knelt down to examine the thing I'd nearly trampled and felt my heart become lodged in my throat. My first thought was to wonder how this object could have gotten there, but as I panned about the balcony in a daze, I realized I knew well enough how it had been done. Someone had only moments ago left it behind—hand-delivered it.

The object left sitting on the balcony was an unmarked videotape. It was a common brand, black plastic with a white label, though whether it was *the* tape—the one Ray and I had watched the night before, and which had since gone missing along with him—remained to be seen. I picked it up, though not without some trepidation, and my doing so coincided with an errant glimpse at the slumbering Kennan building. In one of its windows I spied something that stood out starkly against the darkness that reigned within its halls.

Someone had been watching me from one of those far-off windows, roughly opposite my balcony. The tape in my hand rattled as I witnessed the shape of that distant watcher fall out of focus. Never before had I seen anyone inside that building. I could not say that the figure in that window and the one glimpsed on my balcony had been the same, but I was well and convinced enough that it was the case—and more than that, that this unmarked videotape had been intended as a message.

I hastened back inside, locking the balcony door and drawing the blinds. The tape—a mysterious and unwelcome thing—exuded a psychical foulness, and upon tossing it onto the sofa I promptly wiped my hands on my pant legs as though to rid them of a spiritual griminess. My journey back to calm was further delayed by a flash of bluish light which suddenly entered my field of vision. The oft-heard warble of Ray's TV accompanied this burst of light, and the glow oozed from his doorway in rolling waves across the carpet. I mashed every light switch I could find while making my way toward the hall and braving a look into Ray's room.

The television and VCR had started up; the former was host to a jittery blue screen awaiting further prompts, and the latter had begun to whir and click. I batted on the lights and—when I was sure I was alone in the room—examined the VCR more closely. It had been set to "record", though no tape had been inserted yet.

My pulse pounded so loudly in my ears that I could scarcely hear the high-pitched whine of the TV and the groan of the laboring tape player. Reaching into the dusty knot of cords on the floor, I yanked a handful of them free at random and watched as both devices powered down with a staticky wheeze.

—ᴡᴧᴡ—ᴡᴧᴡ—

The tape was a blank. I knew it because the recording tab was still in place. I studied it in the light of the kitchen over a glass of Ray's whiskey. The inside of the tape appeared very clean; in fact, as a whole, it looked as though it had only just come out of the shrink wrap. Something I did not do as I paced the floors that next couple of hours was to put it into the VCR, however.

I had retrieved the puzzling little delivery from the balcony only to be greeted by the flickering of Ray's old TV. It had powered up all on its own, and the VCR had struggled to record as if prompted by an unseen hand. It seemed as though someone had brought me the tape in the hopes that I might record something—something transmitted through the very air, something that spoke to and awakened the two devices. What shape that broadcast might've taken was beyond guessing.

Now and then, as I walked woozy circuits around the kitchen and living room, I would pause at the balcony door and steal a peek through the blinds. Then, with grit teeth, I would scan the windows of the Keenan one by one. Each and every time I came away with the impression of being watched from within that dark hulk. The source of this feeling seemed to come from a different window each time, and on no occasion did I manage a prolonged look at the owner of the eyes that dissected me from afar. There *were* vague stirrings though—glimpses of nebulous things in its dusty windows that shouldn't have been there.

It seemed clear enough that someone was trying to get my attention. Whether or not that someone was Ray I hadn't yet decided, but there could be little doubt that it had worked; my thoughts were now centered on that eerie ruin behind the apartment, and already I had begun to consider a visit.

Earlier in the day, I had walked past it and found its doors tethered with old videotape. This, too, had been a sign—an attempt to win my attention and lure me to the building. When it had failed, someone had moved to more overt gestures, setting foot on my balcony.

I could not simply wait around for the next overture.

I stepped into my shoes and rummaged around in the closet for a flashlight. Downing the remainder of my glass, I took one last look through the blinds. This time, the Keenan was still and contemplative. This only added to my resolve—made it easier to dismiss those earlier glimpses as mere imagination—and I left the apartment with the hopes that I would soon be reunited with my missing roommate and have all my questions answered.

Once, as kids, Ray and I got picked up by the cops.

On an evening in early summer, the two of us had gone for an aimless bike ride, and had made it as far as our elementary school by sundown. With very little traffic to worry about and in no hurry to return home, we rode circuits around the school parking lot for a time, and discovered on our third or fourth pass that one of the exterior doors had been left propped, possibly by a careless janitor.

For nearly an hour we explored the dark building and rode our bikes through its halls. We relaxed in the faculty lounge, inspected the food our teachers had left in the staff refrigerator and even played around in the vice principal's office before the night-shift custodian heard the commotion and called the police. A pair of local cops threw us in cuffs and jammed our bikes into the trunk of their cruiser, screaming at us all the way home. We avoided trespassing charges by a hair's breadth, though we both faced in-school suspensions and were grounded for weeks after.

I was reminded of that night as I paced around the Keenan, looking for some way inside. I couldn't count on some hare-brained janitor leaving a door propped open this time, and I had no partner to explore with. I was alone—though not quite so alone as I would've liked, for each time I dizzied myself by looking up at the skyscraper's towering facade, I felt eyes on me. Motorists were few along the main road; pedestrians fewer. There could be no doubt that the gaze that fell upon me issued from the monolith. I could only hope that they were friendly eyes peering down at me—Ray's.

For my route of ingress I was drawn to the building's southern face. It had been there that I had hours ago spied tangles of unspooled tape drawn tightly around the door handles; and it was there that I presently found the chains around said handles slack and the knot of tape forged into something of a messy bow. It was obvious that the hardware on the door had very recently been messed with—not altogether removed, but sufficiently loosened to allow the doors to open a fair width. Such an opening would admit a man roughly my size without much trouble. The way ahead had been cleared to me, an invitation extended.

But by whom?

As much as I would have liked to imagine Ray plotting this entire mess as a prank, I couldn't really believe that to be the case. I had been drawn out of my apartment by the beckoning of some audacious presence within the Keenan; whether Ray would be found within the building, or whether the strangeness issuing from it had anything to do with his absence, I couldn't yet say.

I tried the door; the chains kept it from opening completely, but there was space enough for me to wriggle into the opening if I set about the task at the right angle, and with a strategic sucking-in of the paunch. But I didn't enter—not at once. Instead, at my first glance of the darkness that dwelt beyond the threshold, I stepped backward and nearly tumbled down the three or four concrete steps leading back to the street.

Poets have ascribed much to darkness, have over the years saddled it with human characteristics it could not in reality possess; and yet, I tell you the darkness in that building *lived.* It surged from the doorway like blood from a wound, proving blacker than the not-insubstantial gloom my eyes had grown accustomed to. Though intangible it possessed an undeniable weight—the weight of something highly pressurized and seeking escape. The door clanged shut and I stood in trembling terror of it.

The reason I did not turn and run—the reason I would, after some minutes of ridiculous self-talk, rush headlong into that pulsating darkness—was that I had glimpsed something in my initial trying of the door. A red polo shirt with the logo for Stefano's Pizza had been discarded, quite intentionally, it seemed, just inside the entryway. I was, despite my fright, seized by gladness at the find. *It's Ray's! It's got to be! He's in here after all!* The notion that my roommate was holed up somewhere in the Keenan, that my period of anxious waiting might soon end, served to steel my resolve.

With the utmost solemnity, I eventually opened the door as far as the chains would allow and squeezed myself through the opening. On setting foot within the Keenan, as the door swung shut behind me and I was utterly buried in the powder-like darkness, I imagined myself *consumed* by it—envisioned the chained doors as the uncooperative lips of a dying man and my own body as a dose of medicine pushed through them, set to travel throughout his system and to confront the ailment that had rendered him ill.

The air was stuffy, scented with the worst of the city. It was as though the Keenan had sat quietly all these years, assimilating what it could of its surroundings through its pores. The thick air I waded through was heavy with the scents of today and yesterday—and it was just barely possible that I would encounter more primordial air as I ventured deeper in. Upon entering I'd taken up the discarded polo, clutching it in one hand while the other wielded the flashlight. The LEDs brought into focus corridors and lobbies which, beneath the grime of decades, were of the most banal and predictable designs imaginable.

And yet, my meager light could only uncover so much with each sweep, and I never quite escaped the queasy fear that something truly diabolical dwelt just beyond the reach of its jittery scope. The mere turning of a corner in this building was to confront the unknown and phantasmagoric; each time I found my way into a new section, I never knew what shape it would take—whether I would be faced with more twentieth-century brutalism garbed in innocuous late-eighties décor or a scene from Dante. I never once mistook the refusal of these surroundings to morph into the latter as proof that they *could not*—only that the Keenan had stayed its hand. If there *were* horrors to be found in this building, I felt confident that they would be revealed to me in due time.

I don't mean to give the impression that my exploration of the building was rooted in sound planning. I stepped blindly, as a fool might step, from room to room and passage to passage, with an eye toward signs of Ray alone. At various moments I might have chosen to stop, to better examine the setting and to deduce, however foggily, my position in the night-black monolith, but the sum total of my interaction with each quadrant was to search for any hint that the owner of this familiar shirt had passed through, and to move on when I found none. This journey brought me to no few dead-ends, to no shortage of cloistered corners where the stench of abandonment waxed nauseatingly—and it was after these many fits and starts that I finally stumbled upon that next clue I had so eagerly sought.

At the end of a long hall I arrived before a door that would have been unremarkable enough but for one arresting detail. Its chipped surface had been plastered in unspooled video tape; lengths of the shimmery stuff had been wrapped around the door from all sides and clung to it like vines.

How strange it was to have found the sort of sign I'd sought, only to recoil from it in the sighting. I eyed the effusion of tape growing through its seams, the brownish-black coils that stood out from the degraded wooden paneling like knotty veins on the back of an aged hand, and was stricken by fear; and even as I was nearly overcome by that fear I knew very well that I had no choice but to open the door and to go where it led.

I did so, stepping timidly into what I now saw was a stairwell. Flights both ascending and descending met me as I stood shivering on the first-floor landing, but it was to the upper levels that I would ultimately climb, for I noticed the dusty metal handrail leading upward was wreathed in still more tape. These ribbons had been placed here as a guide, intended to draw me in certain directions toward I knew not what. I cursed the finding of this new signpost despite its necessity and took the steps two at a time, my aggressive trek upward serving to fill the confines of the stairwell with the echoes of what sounded like a legion.

I climbed two floors and still the tape on the railing persisted.

Another two—then four—saw no change in the presence of the tape along the rail.

I was being drawn upward, very high up, and as I trudged and panted I wondered what awaited me above. I tried recalling what businesses the Keenan had housed in its heyday and remembered that its uppermost floors had once been dominated by a local news station. Having climbed something like a dozen flights and slowing due to a soreness in my calves, I began to suspect that I was being led to the very top, though I still hadn't the foggiest as to why. If Ray had been behind all of this—if he had absconded to this building, if he'd been the one to leave tape strewn throughout it—then his reasons for doing it eluded me completely.

My suspicions were confirmed as I reached the end of the line. Racing thoughts and churning dread had made it difficult for me to keep an accurate count, but I wagered myself standing on the landing to the thirty-sixth floor when I noticed the tape along the rail had grown rather thick and the exit door had been marked by several lengths of it in an ominous X-pattern. Unless I'd been misled, this floor had been among those utilized by the news station as late as the mid-80s.

I yanked away the crude X and trampled the ribbons underfoot as I passed through the door. I was delivered into a large room reminiscent of a lobby, with at least three doorways leading into adjoining halls. There were no clues to be seen, no indication of which direction I ought to travel. I was back to probing the darkness in search of answers, and I turned my light to the first of three doorways, pushing my way into a cramped hall lined in doors.

Within a few steps my ultimate destination had entered into view.

As I have said, the passage was cramped, and something like a dozen doorways littered the expanse, the majority of which were open. There could be no telling what dwelt in the darkness that filled out eleven of those twelve-odd rooms; it was only the last one on the left that concerned me in the moment, for it was from that one that low, flickering light was actively emanating.

In a setting such as this one, where light is such a rare commodity, one may be forgiven for describing an unexpected glow as "ghostly". In this instance, the word was in fact a perfect fit, for the light issued forth in long, rolling waves, coating every surface in reach like a syrup. The frequency and duration of the waves varied, lending an illusion of deliberation—sentience. There was a not unpleasant warmth to this light, a warmth that reminded me of old televisions or computer monitors.

But standing in the passage one could not help becoming aware of something else in the scenery; a thing with no visual aspect, but which asserted itself just as clearly. I was assailed from every open doorway by malice. The fear—a nigh certainty—that I would be assailed from one of the open doorways to my right or left drove me to flee down the hall in the direction of the light. I charged through the passage, not daring to avert my gaze from the goal lest I spy something of the hateful presence that was crowding in on me.

I arrived at the source of light without incident but was dizzied for the strain. The hike up the stairs had already left me sore and winded, and this most recent sprint had sapped what little strength remained in my tired legs, leaving me to hug the wall till I'd caught my breath. I staggered toward the light, into the room on my left, and was faced with a strange sight.

The room was dark, save for the apparitional bluish glow of a dozen wall-mounted monitors. The glass screens—their curved surfaces dusty and staticky—flickered with various grainy scenes, and beneath, whirring violently, were stacks of tape machines. The rear of the room and the doorway leading to a yet unseen nook deeper in were clotted by a cache of unspooled tape, which wriggled across the floor as it was sucked up into the VCRs like spaghetti. The contents of each quivering strand were evidently being relayed onto the monitors. Once, thirty-odd years ago, this space might have been used by news media staff in recording each broadcast. It was a wonder the equipment still functioned after so many years; the monitors and tape decks appeared even older than the ones in Ray's room.

I sidled up to the wall of monitors and squinted at them, trying to take in the broadcast, and was more than a little shocked to find myself featured on one of those screens.

I was looking at myself on-screen; not the way I existed now, but the way I had looked as a ten or eleven year old. The footage currently playing showed me lounging on a bench outside an ice cream stand I remembered from back home, feasting on a cone. I could see nothing of the cameraman in frame and had no memory of any such visits ever having been videotaped, but was transfixed by the footage and spent a long moment soaking in the scene. The grass stains on my jeans, a scab on my right elbow from a bike accident, the smattering of freckles on my face that I would eventually outgrow—all of it took me to a distant place and time.

The cameraman spoke up, and his voice flowed sweetly from the cobwebbed speakers in the monitor with all the warmth and crackle of an old record. "*Want to go to Monarch's? I think they might have the new Spiderman by now.*"

The voice, I had zero doubt, belonged to a prepubescent Ray. The hairs along my neck stood at hearing that voice—a voice I had not heard in this particular form for many years. I squinted at the video, even reached out and touched the staticky monitor, wondering where this recording could have come from. Ray had never owned a video camera; the only video I was aware of that contained footage of us at this age would have been shot by our parents, during holidays or special occasions.

I had no recollection, either, of the scene on the next monitor being recorded by anyone. It was a recording set in the cafeteria of our elementary school, during lunch, and the noise of the student body strained the speakers. I was flipping through a pile of trading cards and eating a pack of fruit snacks, discussing the merits of a potential trade with some other kids—silent and faceless—seated nearby. "*Is it actually that rare?*" asked Ray from off-screen.

"Oh, yeah," I replied, looking up at the camera. "It's first edition!"

The taste of those fruit snacks, the slightly sticky surface of those old lunch tables, the dimness of the cafeteria—all of the details came racing back to me as I watched. I remembered that moment as though it had happened only a minute prior, though I couldn't for the life of me recall anyone recording it. This footage had been shot in the days before cell phones were common; anyone recording this event would have had to do so with a clunky camcorder.

I scanned one screen after another, coming face-to-face every time with another cherished memory. Here I was sitting in my own backyard, drinking juice boxes with Ray and catching bugs. My dad—mid-30's in this shot, with a full head of hair—was mowing the grass in the background. On the next screen, I saw myself riding a bike through the dark streets of our old neighborhood. As I watched, I remembered the shapes of the houses as they came into view, and long-dormant muscle memory saw my body stiffen at each of the bumps in the road.

On another monitor, a 90s pop song droned in the background as I knelt down in an aisle of the local video store, shuffling through the tapes on the bottom shelf. "How many should we rent?" I asked, looking up at the camera.

The camera was lowered as Ray knelt down beside me. I saw his arm enter the frame, slightly sunburnt for all the time we'd been spending outside. "*We should get at least three*," he replied.

"How are we going to watch three movies? We'll be up all night!"

"*Exactly! That's the point, man!*"

I knew that these conversations, these moments spent with Ray, had not been recorded by anyone. Our lives had not been catalogued by some hovering cameraman—no, I was seeing these events unfold from Ray's own perspective, as though the contents of his mind had been transcribed to a tape. I was further convinced of this by a clip playing on the lower monitors—a scene of us walking through the old neighborhood in the hours before dawn. I remembered that night; it had been a foggy one. And so it was on screen, the two of us shuffling down the mist-covered sidewalk, exhausted from hours of snacking and movies but unwilling to crash in the living room as planned.

"It's weird to think that we won't be able to do this again," I heard myself mutter through the speakers.

I heard Ray sigh from off-screen. "*Yeah, it's a drag. Everyone else is hyped to get out of here, to move into the dorms, but I wish we could just stick around here, like this. College just doesn't sound exciting anymore.*"

I remembered this very walk, this conversation, with a lump in my throat. The day before Ray had been set to go off to college a few states away, we'd hung out all night for old times' sake. The mood that day had been somber, and by nightfall we'd become restless, knowing that our lives were about to undergo violent transformations. Gone were the days of our cycling home from school together, our adventures in town. Most of our other friends had already gone, were attending distant universities. Now it was Ray's turn to leave, and the reality of it hit us like a load of bricks. That long night walk marked the end of an era for us—marked the start of a new life neither of us cared to embark on. It was the start, I think, of our obsessive pining for the past.

The two of us had been alone on that somber walk, and we'd never again spoken of it, much less recorded it for posterity. I knew then that I was witnessing something truly surreal—a private memory cast upon the screen from these mysterious ribbons of tape. I wasn't sure how it was possible; and for a moment, I didn't care. I was content enough to stand before the succession of monitors and to take it all in. I watched my childhood with Ray play out before my eyes in real time and could not help weeping; I wanted to see my friend again, to reach out to those boys on screen and advise them to savor every moment of their Arcadian youth.

"*It's strange to think that in a day everything will change,*" said Ray.

I nodded in agreement—both on-screen and as I stood watching.

A sound issued from elsewhere in the room, behind the screens and the monstrous web of writhing tape. I wiped at my eyes and stepped away from the glowing monitors, peering toward what looked like a doorway. It was from that direction that the mass of video tape was streaming, and where the noise—a gasping sob—had originated.

"W-Who's there?" I chanced. Taking a few steps toward the doorway, flashlight held low, I carefully moved the mess of tape aside. The ribbons passed between my fingers, gobbled up by the whirring VCRs to my back, and I found what seemed a never-ending tangle of them just beyond the threshold to this other room. It was as though a hundred—no, a thousand—VHS tapes had been gutted, their innards left in a heap.

I ventured further still, pushing the tangles aside as best I could. It was then that I heard the sobbing again—and traced it to the center of the mass. Within the pile of tape, I could make out a shape, slumped and scarcely moving. As the VCRs sucked up still more of the material and the space to my back was repeatedly lit up with scenes from my youth, I gradually came to realize what it was that dwelt within the sea of tape.

A man—shirtless and sobbing—was seated in a chair. His body hitched now and then as tape erupted from his ears, and I could tell, even though his back was turned to me, that unspooled tape was spilling out of his mouth and eyes as well.

"R-Ray!" I said, though my voice barely rose above the noise of the tape machines.

The figure in the chair did not react to the sound of my voice. Ribbons of tape poured from within him as he sat there, wracked by occasional sobs. There seemed no end to the stuff; I watched for what seemed like an age, the flow never once slackening.

"Ray, it's me!" I said, taking another step inside, the tape growing tangled around my shoes.

His head lolled back suddenly and he loosed another sob—though in that moment I was able to make out the lines of his face and was baffled by what I saw. His features were drawn into something like ecstasy; far from a trembling countenance, a sorrowful grimace, the tape sped out of open eyes and a mouth spread wide in a smile. The purging of this tape, of his very memories, had not reduced him to tortured sobs, but had instead raised him to tears of joy. His body shook as though his insides were being ravaged by the effort, and his hands clung to the armrests of the chair like claws, fingertips buried in the aged leather.

"Ray!" I shouted, shoving aside the torrent of film. I reached for the back of his chair, meant to pull him out of it, but spied something in my periphery that made me freeze. A shadow—neither my own nor Ray's—had come into focus mere feet away. Retreating back into the blizzard of black ribbons, I leveled my light at the new arrival and felt my stomach drop to the floor.

A withered human form dressed in a flowing black garment appeared against the far wall, and I knew from the very first that it was the woman Ray and I had seen on the tape. Her feet, clad in black leather shoes, did not touch the floor; instead she hovered there like a balloon without a string, face obscured by an opaque black veil. The levitating figure, hands limp at her sides, trembled softly at the light, then began to advance soundlessly across the room as if in answer to it. She drifted toward me slowly like a curious butterfly, veil clinging to the outlines of her skeletal visage. Ray did not react to her presence, didn't seem to notice even as her black garb tickled his bare arm. He was in another place then, buried deep within the world of memory.

I backed out of the room, tripping on knots of tape, and was forced to crawl through the shimmering mass in my escape. Everything leading up to that moment was expunged from my mind; I only knew that I must run, lest I meet the specter and end up like Ray. I gained my feet, snapping several sections of tape as I burst back into the room full of monitors, and watched as the veiled woman bobbed in the air after me, porcelain-colored hands outstretched.

I left behind the glow of the monitors and raced back into the endless darkness of the Keenan, jousting with the shadow in search of an exit. I floundered through the thirty-sixth floor, managed to find my way back to the stairwell, but suffered no few bumps as I ran down the first flight. My shoulder met the wall with a dense thud at one turn; at the next, I lost my hold on the flashlight and watched it ricochet off the handrail. I raced after it, the light guttering and glass tumbling from the barrel, and found that several of the LEDs had broken. I was left with a light that functioned only sporadically; I could, while shaking it, force a weak light to issue from the remaining bulbs. The remainder of my flight was spent largely in darkness.

I heard no trying of the stairwell door above me, but caught glimpses in my retreat of a form hovering just around the previous bend, homing in on me soundlessly. Rushing down the stairs half-blind, my chief success was in further injuring myself; I twisted my ankle in hopping down several steps at once and accumulated no shortage of bruises from run-ins with corners and other obstacles.

There was another thing which added still more difficulty and distraction to my chaotic escape. As I barreled down the stairs, I began to hear a voice. It issued from the darkness behind me, and no matter the pounding of my pulse, or the heaviness of my echoing tread, I could not help hearing it.

"If there was some way to go back to those old days, Silvio—a way to return to them, so that you could live in them forever and never leave... would you do it?"

Ray's voice filled the stairwell. Those words had been the last he'd spoken to me before disappearing, and yet this recitation did not square with my memory of the question. There was something about his tone—it wasn't dour like I remembered it, but possessed instead something of the amused, the *brazen*.

"If there was some way to go back to those old days, Silvio—a way to return to them, so that you could live in them forever and never leave... would you do it?"

The voice came again, and was this time tinged with laughter.

Whether the thing hovering down the stairs behind me was merely mimicking Ray's voice or properly channeling him, I was unsure, but to listen was to believe that Ray had left the apartment to find an answer to that question for himself; and that he had indeed found one.

His answer, evidently, had differed radically from my own.

"*If there was some way to go back to those old days, Silvio—*"

Eventually, I returned to the ground level. I groped and stumbled through the blackness, certain of my pursuit, and it was only by sighting the glowing panes of the southern doors that I ultimately made it out. I threw myself against the doors for all I was worth, pushing the chains on the outside to their limits and crawling through the opening like a madman. I flopped onto the concrete outside, tumbled down the steps and then rose, staggering toward the sidewalk.

The doors shut behind me, and in the moonlit panes I could make out a midnight-colored figure being reabsorbed into the building's inner darkness.

Despite my injuries I felt nothing of pain. It wasn't until I returned home, scarcely able to breathe and drenched in sweat, that the bumps and bruises began to ache. Upon arriving at the apartment, I put on every light available and sank to the floor before the balcony door. Tearing down the blinds, I looked out my window at the silent bulk of the Keenan building.

I began to scream.

The police, despite a reasonably concerted search, would go on to find no trace of my roommate in the Keenan Building. For that matter, their tour of the thirty-sixth floor and those adjacent yielded nothing of the unspooled tape or floating, shadowed figure that I had fled from. I was questioned thoroughly and was able to eventually file a missing person's report, though this, too, proved fruitless.

Years have passed. I have not seen Ray since that night.

For days and nights afterward, I tried to get to the bottom of things, sitting cross-legged on the fire escape and pleading with the impassive facade of the Keenan. The only conclusion I could draw was that Ray had been called by something in that building, something that had taken the repulsive shape of that veiled figure on the tape, and that it had granted him precisely the sort of escape into nostalgia that he'd always wished for. He had not merely disappeared; he had fled into the arms of a living nightmare—and he'd done it willingly.

I lived in that apartment another two months before breaking my lease and moving back home. I didn't leave because I couldn't afford the rent, but because I couldn't stand the thought of living there without Ray. His effects were still scattered about the apartment, and coupled with the shadow of the Keenan bearing down upon the building there were simply too many reminders of him for me to contend with. I couldn't go about my day without stealing countless glances at the skyscraper, and some nights, I could have sworn that someone was returning my gaze from one of those black, distant windows. On the verge of a nervous breakdown, I resolved to leave the city altogether.

I spent weeks packing my things, and I packed Ray's, too, for his parents, who were understandably distraught at their son's disappearance. When pressed for details, I could only offer them bland platitudes and vague hopes that, wherever he was, he was doing well.

I have since managed to live a reasonably normal life; as normal a life as one can hope to lead after having experienced oddities of this kind. I spent months at home with my folks and eventually, after securing a decent job in a different city, moved out on my own again. But now and then, when I see a large building looming in the distance, I can't help mistaking it for the Keenan; and some nights, when I hear kids playing on the school playground behind my new place, I peer out the window, half-expecting to see Ray and myself, as children, among them.

To this strange tale, I have only two further amendments.

One evening, as I was hauling things out to the dumpster and preparing for my move, I returned to the apartment only to find an unmarked VHS tape sitting on the welcome mat outside the front door. I froze at seeing it and lingered a long while in the hall, looking for the one who'd left it there but finding no trace of them. It must have been delivered swiftly, stealthily; I'd only been out of the building a moment or two, and had passed no one on my way in or out. At first, I left it there, stepping over it like a land mine and slamming my door. Curiosity, though, saw me retrieve it a few minutes later.

The tape was missing its recording tab. I couldn't say for certain what had been transferred onto it, but as I turned it round and round in my hands that night, finishing the last of Ray's whiskey, I felt I had some inkling as to its contents. I didn't play it; I stashed it with Ray's other things and did my best to forget about it.

Then, the night before I was set to clear out of the apartment, while dozing on the sofa, I awoke sometime before dawn. It had not been the watery moonlight streaming in from the balcony door that had awakened me, but rather a voice—a voice which seemed to call out from very far away.

"*Silvio.*"

I sat up, pawing the heaviness from my eyes, and listened more closely. I had nearly dismissed the voice as a dream when it sounded a second time.

"*Silvio.*"

The whispery call was coming from somewhere else in the apartment—from somewhere down the hall, I reckoned. I stood up and followed the third and fourth utterances of my name, tracing them back to Ray's room. Standing in his doorway, the moonlight pouring in from the little window, I scanned the space and was startled to find a bent form looming in the opposite corner.

I switched on the lights with a gasp and found only a teetering stack of boxes in said corner. The shadows had transformed them into something lifelike. I felt a pang of disappointment as I realized the room was, in fact, unoccupied. In the back of my mind, I had been hoping to find Ray there, sitting on the edge of the bed or reclining on the futon as I'd seen him do so many times before.

I put out the lights and turned back to the hall, only to hear my name whispered once more from somewhere within the room. "*Silvio.*"

This time, with only the moonlight to see by, I started slowly into Ray's old room, shuffling past the boxes of his belongings I'd left strewn about. Following the whispers, I soon found myself crawling across the floor, toward the box TV sitting against the wall. The voice had been coming from somewhere beneath it, though it had to register once more before I could track it to its source.

"*Silvio.*"

The voice—*Ray's voice*—was coming from within the VCR.

"R-Ray? Is that you?" I asked.

A minute passed with no reply.

Finally, I stuck a finger into the tape slot as though I might find him hiding within. Ray then spoke again, and I heard him more clearly than before. "*Silvio... Play the tape...*"

I knew at once what tape he was talking about. He wanted me to play the unmarked tape that had shown up at my door. I hesitated, but after a long silence I put on the TV and rifled through the boxes in its blue glow.

I have said that I never saw Ray again after that nightmarish episode in the Keenan, but that wasn't entirely true. That night, as I sat blearily before his television, I *did* see him again. I saw him, I think, in the way he most wanted me to remember him—as a happy kid and teenager.

I plopped down onto his futon and started the tape.

And I watched it the whole way through—made certain not to fast-forward through the middle parts.

DECATUR ROAD

There isn't much to see on Decatur Road. There aren't any strip malls out that way, nor any gas stations. But there *is* a house out there, and it's a real strange-looking thing for its lonesomeness. Squat and flanked by cornfields, it practically jumps out at you as you drive past. The house has a darkness about it, and its features are pinched and stern like those of a man in deep thought. It's the kind of place that'll make you turn your head, make you sit upright as you drive by and think, "*Hm.*"

I'd passed it half a million times on the school bus, on dreary, half-awake mornings of every season, and in the afternoons on the way home, too. And each time I looked at it from the bus window I'd sit there and wonder to myself, "What's it like inside?"

There would come a day when I no longer had to wonder.

Dwellers in small towns can't help but chase a good mystery. It's a bad itch, and the only thing waiting for you if you don't scratch it are reruns or aimless bike rides. So, you scratch. You scratch good and deep, and even when it hurts a little you hold out hope that you'll find something interesting—something that'll make it all worthwhile—underneath the skin.

I wish I hadn't scratched.

I got up one morning with some three months of summer still ahead of me and the idea that I was going to have a close-up look at that dark, old house. I couldn't tell you *why* I had to see it up-close. Decatur Road was on the fringe, far from my usual haunts. I suppose I fancied myself a modern-day Pizarro, and decided that place needed explored, documented. It was rightful Spanish clay.

I asked my father if he knew the place. Seeing as how he'd grown up in town himself, I expected him to be familiar with it. Imagine my surprise, then, when I learned that the house on Decatur Road didn't stir in him an equal fascination. The old man had never been the talkative kind, and that morning, as he was preparing to run errands, he'd given me one of his standard-issue shrugs. "It's probably full of tweakers."

After a late breakfast, I asked my mother if she knew the house. She didn't know a thing about it. In fact, the only thing she had to add was a stern warning not to venture that far from home. "That's a long way from here, so don't you even think about going. I don't want you loitering half-way across town, Simon."

My mother's warning just about derailed the whole thing, and I'll admit that I even second-guessed myself at that point. Why go all that way just to look at a crummy old house? What was the allure? My time would almost certainly be better spent at the arcade, the local pool, the movies...

And yet, as the hours passed, my mind kept on kicking at the notion of that house. It may have been a hornet's nest, but I wasn't afraid of getting stung. I just wanted to see with my own eyes what was inside.

I found myself at the local arcade, where I burned absent-mindedly through a pocketful of quarters over the course of an hour. When I finally gave up on the Soulcalibur machine, I spied a familiar face sitting at the food court, knocking back a large soda. It was Jack Hudson—a classmate of mine. He'd also ridden the same bus as me for the past two years. Ordinarily, I wouldn't have said a word to the kid. I didn't much like him. But that afternoon, I started into the food court and approached his table with the intention to strike up a conversation.

It occurred to me, since we'd been on the same bus, that he might know something about the house.

Jack Hudson was, well, a *big* kid. He was a whole head shorter than me, but substantially wider, and with a mop of grease-slick brown curls that quaked with his every step. He had a high, almost feminine voice on him, that one. Bordering on shrill, it was the kind of voice you couldn't bear to listen to for very long; but one of many reasons he didn't have any friends. I knew only a thing or two about him—his dad was locked up, and his mother was a hairdresser who packed him extra-big lunches, almost as if to try and make up for the lack of a father figure. On the bus, he'd always had headphones on, or his nose in a book.

We made some awkward small talk, exchanged the usual niceties about summer break, and then I came right out and said what was on my mind. "Say, Jack, you know that house on Decatur Road? We pass by it on the bus all the time. The one sitting in that cornfield? You know anything about it?"

He only had to think on it for an instant before he nodded. "Oh, yeah, I know it. I've been inside."

I gave him a dumb stare, like I'd just been slapped upside the head. "What, really?"

He nodded while his tongue went searching for the straw in his soda.

"I don't believe it," I said, cracking a grin.

He waggled his eyebrows as he slurped at his drink. "No, I mean it."

I couldn't wrap my head around this. Jack Hudson, of all people, had paid a visit to that old house that so fascinated me? The very thought all but robbed the property of intrigue. "Well, what for? Your granny live there or something?"

Setting his cup down daintily, he tugged on the hem of his polo and shook his head, the curls coming along for the ride. "Nah. It was awhile back. I went there once, with my dad. It was years ago, come to think of it."

"You went with your dad?"

"Yup."

"Why?"

He tossed his shoulders. "He had some work to do there. Something like that."

"So, what's it like inside?"

"I don't remember too well. I was only in there for a minute or two. And anyway, it was years ago, like I said." He smiled a tight smile that cut into his flabby cheeks. "Why, what about it?"

I chuckled. "I dunno. Just been a little bored. Want to see something new, you know? I figure that house must be abandoned or something." I blushed as I tried to articulate my interest in the place, and the more I talked, the more stupid I felt for wanting to go out there at all.

Jack furrowed his brow, and for a time he didn't say anything. I almost took that as my cue to leave, but he suddenly spoke up, his voice cracking a little. "Someone *does* live there, sorta."

"Oh?"

He nodded. "I, uh... I don't like to talk about it, really. It was a long time ago, and I only went there because my dad had to stop inside to do some business. This was before he went to jail, you know?"

"Uh-huh?" I prodded.

"Well, he left me in the car awhile, in the driveway. When I went into the house to find him, I saw him in one of the bedrooms and he was talking to..." Here, he paused, and his body seemed to fight back a shudder. "He was talking to a *snake-man*."

I waited a few seconds for him to break frame and start laughing, but when it became clear he wasn't kidding around, I burst out laughing instead. "A snake-man? Now what is *that* supposed to be?"

"Well," he explained with that pudgy smile and those pinched-up eyes, "it's exactly what it sounds like. He crawls like a snake." Here, he paused to give his rotund body a demonstrative shimmy. "And he kinda talks like a s-s-s-snake, too."

"So, he lives there? What's he do all day, eat mice?"

"I guess so." Jack's smile faded. "When I walked in there, I was real scared. My dad yelled at me, told me to get out. I did, and I ran back to the car. My dad came out a little while after that, and he wasn't talking much. I think he was scared, too. Not long after that, the police came and took him away." He cleared his throat. "You know, he's a good guy, my dad. He never did none of the stuff people accused him of."

"Huh," was all I could think to say.

Now, at fifteen, I was too old to believe this load, but also too young to dismiss it out of hand. When someone tells you about something bizarre they've seen in your hometown, even if it sounds unbelievable, you might be inclined to go along with it because you hope it's true.

"Thanks, Jack," I said. "I'll see you on the bus." I started out of the food court, already knowing how I planned to spend the remainder of my day.

I needed to pay the Snake Man of Decatur Road a visit.

—w/\/—w/\/—

I charged out of the mall parking lot on my Schwinn. I'd run through the ride in my head a few times and knew it would take me about an hour to get to Decatur Road. Once I got there, I'd take my time and explore. Then, an hour and a half's ride would get me home. Mom and Dad always expected me back by dark; the way things were going, I'd make curfew by the skin of my teeth.

Pausing only to grab a soda from the vending machine outside the grocery store, I rolled down Front Street, where the library and elementary school were. I then hung a left on Waterman, passing the video store, police station and health clinic. Further on, as I coasted onto Villiers Avenue, I left behind other familiar sights; the cathedral, the funeral home, the bookshop.

Finally, I hooked a right on Decatur and was surrounded on all sides by vast fields. Some were vacant, overgrown. Others, better manicured, boasted crops such as corn. Traffic proved almost non-existent out there, and as I charged down the shoulder, the only sound I could hear aside from the tinging of my spokes was the mumbling of insects.

The sky overhead went cloudy as I neared the house, offering me a welcome reprieve from the sun. Starting down a brief incline, I was careful not to slide into the drainage ditch to my right while scanning the distance.

Just as it had done from the bus, the house jumped into view suddenly.

My bike groaned as I wobbled to a halt. The house—the object of my obsession—stood silently before me, and this time I didn't pass it by at forty miles an hour. I was in a position now to take it all in, to compare the reality of the thing against the mental caricature I'd pieced together through my hundreds of seconds-long glances. Its three road-facing windows were intact and backed by dense darkness, and its roof sagged atop it like a well-worn beanie. The remnants of a gravel drive could be seen to one side, but the pebbles had been scattered by tall-growing weeds and the whole thing was overshadowed by dying cornstalks. I could tell no one had been here for a very long time.

I wheeled my bike up the drive and parked it as I studied the front door. It was the color of a walnut shell, and every bit as textured.

And it was ajar.

All signs pointed to abandonment. I could leisurely explore the entire property without getting into any trouble, it seemed.

Except, now that I was here, I wasn't sure I wanted to.

Part of that was the thought of putting an end to the mystery. We all need a little mystery in our lives, and I feared that going inside and seeing the place would bring mine to a close. But that was only a small part of my hesitance. The bulk of it was owed to a change in my perception of the house. Over the course of hundreds of bus rides the abode had cultivated a certain curiosity in me, but now that I stood before it, that curiosity had been silently and swiftly replaced by a palpable distrust.

It didn't look so friendly from up-close.

Jack Hudson had claimed to see a "snake-man" in this house, and as I gawked at it, I got the distinct feeling that it hadn't been such a ridiculous claim after all. If snake-men existed, then it stood to reason they'd live in a house like this one, far from the rabble.

Anxious, and yet curious about what awaited me within, I made my decision.

There was nothing to do but go inside.

I pushed open the door, and when it had finally stopped on its weatherbeaten hinges I waited in the doorway a long while, just getting a feel for the entryway. There appeared to be wood floors throughout, and nearby, a gaudy painting hung askew on the wall. *See? It's just a dirty old house. Nothing to get worked up over...* Sure now that the water was fine, I waded in a little deeper.

The door led directly into a large space I took for a living room, though there wasn't any furniture there to help me make that distinction. Whoever had lived here previously—whenever that'd been—had cleared everything out. The floors sagged and groaned as I gave the room a once-over. Grey light tumbled in sluggishly through the windows. The old glass looked a little warped, and it didn't treat the light at all like the newer panes at my house did. The effect was disorienting.

When my survey of that first room was complete, I went looking through the rest of the house. There was an adjacent room, somewhat smaller, that might have been a dining or TV room. A spacious closet sat between the kitchen and living room, but was lacking a door. The thing gaped there—black and empty—like a screaming mouth.

I inched into the kitchen, across a floor of yellowed, peeling linoleum. There were grooves in the stuff where hefty appliances had once sat, but that was the only trace of them that remained. The counters, where they still stood, were in a terrible state, and the cabinets buckled underneath them as though the slightest breeze might see them crumble.

I felt a lot of things as I meandered through that house. It was certainly exhilarating, finally getting a chance to explore, but after casing each room I shouldered less excitement and more melancholy. Houses were made to be lived in, and this poor old thing out here had been sitting empty for what seemed like ages. I felt pangs of disappointment and embarrassment, too—disappointment because I hadn't yet encountered the "snake-man" that allegedly dwelt there, and embarrassment because I'd been thick enough to hope for its existence in the first place.

The tour continued down a narrow hall. This portion of the house contained little of interest. A bathroom through the first hallway door showcased the same linoleum as the kitchen and nothing else. The sink, toilet and bathtub had been ripped away and the window boarded. Further on, I discovered bedrooms behind two other doors, but these, like every other part of the house, were empty.

Having reached the finish line, I paced about the anterior room and drew out a deep sigh. I'd come to the house on Decatur Road, seen all it had to offer, but the achievement felt utterly hollow. This room, with its partially boarded window, was darker than the rest. There was a closet built into the wall opposite, with an immovable sliding door that had fallen off its track, and a foul-looking water spot on the ceiling. This was what I'd biked across town for; this was what I'd pined to explore all those years.

When Jack Hudson had told me about his visit to the house—about the "snake-man"—I'd gotten my hopes up. I'd been dumb enough to believe that this out-of-the-way property might contain something sufficiently interesting to warrant the intrigue I'd heaped upon it over the years. It turned out to be nothing more than a shell, though—a hollowed-out husk of a house.

What had Jack and his father come to this house for, I wondered? Maybe they'd paid it a visit prior to its abandonment. Perhaps when the two of them had come, it'd still been inhabited and furnished. I knew next to nothing about Jack's dad, save that he was behind bars. There was no telling what might bring a disreputable guy like Mr. Hudson out here, but what *really* left me scratching my head was this supposed "snake-man". What had Jack seen that'd left him with that impression? Had he just been goofing around when he'd told me about it?

I went to glance at my watch, but startled as the silence broke. From the closet with the jammed door there came a sudden bout of rattling. Something weighty had shifted against the inside of the door, and with it came a mess of crinkling.

I learned that day that an empty room is never as empty as it seems.

The rattling continued, then transitioned into a steady thumping, as of something struggling to break free of the closet. I braced myself against the wall, heart thumping in my throat. Frightened though I was, I didn't run off immediately. I still possessed a touch of reason, and told myself that I was merely hearing some trapped animal trying to escape.

Superadded to the sounds of the struggle, though, was that crinkling noise. Echoing from the cramped space, it sounded rough—rough like a serpent's skin, perhaps. Now and then, a prolonged *hiss* not unlike that of a leaky tire would ring out, and from across the room I couldn't help imagining its maker boasting a forked tongue.

The Snake Man of Decatur Road, I thought. *It's real. It's actually real.*

I wanted to run, but my legs were numb with terror. I could hardly hold myself up, and had to rely on the wall to my back to keep from slumping to the floor.

The closet door began to bow outward as the pressure against it grew, and the bottom edge of the thing made an awful sound as it dragged against the floor, wood on wood. At some point, the energetic struggle behind it somehow loosened the stubborn door and it fell to one side with a crash.

I was not prepared for what I glimpsed on the other side.

No longer confined, something seized and rolled out of the closet. It tumbled to the floor with a wet smack, as though it'd been ejected. Covered in a semi-translucent skin, the thing immediately began to writhe upon the floor, and I saw in its filmy carapace vivid streaks of red. End to end it probably measured six feet long, and though I stared on in wide-eyed horror, I couldn't tell which end was its head. It had the appearance of a massive, glossy caterpillar, and as it thrashed and thumped against the floorboards, I half-wondered if it wasn't going to undergo a sudden metamorphosis.

But then other sounds began issuing from its crinkling body.

Between all the squelching and shuddering, I heard a monstrous hiss. Then a terrible gargling.

And then I began noticing other things about this creature—namely a human head deep within it, and a pair of bulging, blood-shot eyes staring out at me. What I'd taken for a crinkling, transparent skin was actually tightly wrapped plastic, and the bands of red that marred its length were streaks of blood dredged up by the feeble flailing of slashed limbs deep within the nest of material.

It was a man wrapped in layer after layer of plastic, and as he inched towards me like a worm, I saw him grit his teeth in a pained hiss, and watched as his throat—bright red and neatly cut—loosed a trickle of gore. Ragged breaths left the inside of the plastic foggy, and I noticed that the entire package had been tightly secured with what must have been a roll of clear packing tape.

I don't remember running. I don't remember getting onto my bike, either, but somehow I managed to ride several miles away. The next thing I can recall was wheeling into my front yard. Crashing to the ground, I was very slow in getting up, and when I did, I spent a solid five minutes heaving into the grass.

—wvʌ—wvʌ—

I didn't tell anyone what I saw.

Even at that age, I knew better. They wouldn't have believed me. All it would have earned me was a lengthy grounding for having disobeyed my mother. So, I kept it to myself, and really that was easier; I wasn't sure I could stand the thought of describing what I'd seen aloud anyhow.

When the nightmares finally stopped and I found myself wanting answers, I started poking around, asking questions. Naturally, I looked into the one who'd turned me on to it in the first place.

I'd never known why Jack Hudson's dad had been locked up. I'd assumed he was some kind of crook—maybe a drug peddler or a con-artist.

Wouldn't you know, it turned out he was serving a life sentence for murder.

Back in '84, after an illicit business deal had gone bad, Hudson had killed a man. The papers—which I managed to find at the library archive—didn't spell out everything, but gave me enough details to connect the dots.

The victim, a business partner of Hudson's, had lived in a house on Decatur Road. The two had had a spat, and after a heated altercation, Hudson had dispatched his associate with a knife. The body was then hidden within the house; Hudson went on to tell the authorities he'd left it in a closet. His plan had been to return to the house in the dead of night to dispose of it. He never got the chance, however.

The victim, with the last of his energies, had crawled from the closet, through the house, and made it nearly to the street before death took him. The body was discovered in the driveway by a passing motorist, and forensic evidence on the scene linked Hudson to the crime.

That had taken place over three years ago.

What the papers had left out was that little Jack Hudson had been there that day. He'd seen the dying man, had watched him squirm across the floor in his death throes—like a snake.

It turns out you can strip everything from a house, except for its memories. Sometimes, what happens between those walls gets stuck there and doesn't want to budge. The place can't help but showcase its wounds; the trauma plays on—sticks around like a busted lip you can't quit chewing at.

Those empty rooms are never as empty as they seem.

DREAMS IN BLACK STATIC

Neglect a memory long enough and it'll get soft around the edges. It'll start to dissolve till only the broadest strokes prevail. I believe that it's only because I can no longer recall the man's face with any real firmness—that the strange pull of his blank, staring eyes has, in these interstitial years, finally left me—that I can now speak about that night almost half a decade gone.

I'm speaking, of course, of that strange man I met on the street on an autumn night.

I am no stranger to the loiterers and buskers that wander the streets of this vast city at all hours, but on that particular evening, as I was leaving work, I found that the rain had largely chased these types away and I was left to wait alone in front of the Keenan Building in the accruing dusk for my taxi. Standing a few paces from the building's side entrance with an umbrella propped against my shoulder, I watched the cold rain fall. Fat drops struck the grimy pavement in a ceaseless cannonade; the cacophony of said drops was rivaled only by the roar of the curbside currents that gushed into the sewers.

As I said, I'd thought myself standing alone on that darkening stretch, but some minutes into my wait, I realized this was not the case. To my right—or was it my left?—I made out a frail silhouette through the pounding rain. Beneath a tattered awning there squatted a small, old man clothed in an oversized brown coat. Barely shielded from the rain, the lonesome figure was hunched against the stone facade of the Keenan and stared out from his huddled pose through narrow lids.

I hadn't been aware of his presence more than a minute before I wagered he was staring at *me*, rather than at some fixture in our waterlogged surroundings.

From the battered brown coat he presented a gnarled little hand; he waved, then drew up a small wooden box, which he shook feebly. The rattle of coinage sounded from within. I though him perhaps homeless, seeking charity, and having nothing to give was determined to keep my distance. I stared out at the street for a long while then, anxiously awaiting my cab.

The wizened man proved relentless in his beckoning, however. At regular intervals he gave that wooden box of his a shake, and when I chanced to look back at him, he dared another wave.

Against my better judgement, I took some few steps back and spared him a little smile. "Sorry," I said, "I don't have any change."

That should have been the end of our interaction, but for the noisy crash of the rain, or some willful inattention on his part, he outstretched his neck till his face had emerged past the furthest edge of the awning and leered at me. "I will tell you a story," he croaked, his arthritic paw patting the wooden box.

"I have no money," I reiterated. The taxi was still nowhere in sight; I considered then returning to the office and placing another call to the cab company; and in retrospect, I wish I had.

The old man didn't hear, or pretended not to hear, and licked at his lips. "For many years now, I have been blind," he began, and he turned his face up towards me, eyes wide, as if to offer proof. His eyes had about them a whitish, milky appearance; even so, one could not help feeling watched through their dead stare. "But when I lost my sight, I gained something more remarkable. In my dreams—yes, my dreams!—I am privy to incredible sights. The world of my dreams is a strange one, young man—very strange indeed—and night after night I glimpse things from that other world, bring them back with me. It's a strange sort of world, that one. A world where the darkness prevails and the sun never rises. Imagine seeing the world through a veil of black static and you'll know what I mean. It is a story of this untrodden country I now bring you..."

I should have retreated further down the sidewalk, should have left the Keenan and waited someplace far from the man, but instead, I stood and listened to him.

What follows, as best I can recall it, was the old man's story—his so-called "dream in black static".

I wish I'd never heard it.

"I dreamt of a less civilized age—an age where some still practiced the old ways. The dark ways... Do you understand? No, perhaps you don't. But I needn't tell you the whole of it; it is enough that you envision the turbidity of medievalism. Back then, men were sometimes put to death for dabbling in the old ways, and I tell you that I have had the opportunity to watch such a spectacle with my own eyes.

"The man accused was in the prime of his life; a fair and lithe thing whose recent workings in dark rites had earmarked him for execution. This youthful specimen was strung to a tall wooden pillar, and kindling was piled about his feet. A throng of villagers sought to burn him, and they flung their many torches into that tinder—spat at him, cursed him. The prisoner pleaded for his life, inhaled the smoke, struggled against his restraints... but in time, death took him—if only temporarily.

"I wish that I could relate to you the raw terror in the faces of those serfs when the body of the accused man did not burn. Yes, I tell it truthfully! Though the fire consumed the tinder, ate away at the ropes that held him, the youth's corpse remained untouched. And I can tell you why it was spared; it was because of all the many dabblers in forgotten rites, the devil loved this one *best.*

"Panic set in. Further attempts to damage the body proved fruitless. It was reported that his alabaster skin was tough as stone, and that those lungs which had so recently gasped their last now fluttered

with a new, diabolical life. When the fire had burned through the platform, the restraints, the corpse was set free, and as a marionette moves at the behest of a string, so too did the dead man stand and cast his empty gaze upon those gathered. The peasants fled. Meanwhile, the captive took flight on the devil's own wings and was gone.

"The nights were filled with a new terror as the dead man returned. He was seen from the fields as night reared its head—floating above the trees like a kite with no master. The townsfolk were forced to avoid their windows, lest they spy the revenant lingering thereabouts. It was said that the dead man's eyes were the color of smoke, and that to look into them was to invite it into one's home. In those domiciles where the revenant paid a visit, none survived. Those so struck down would appear to have been burnt, as if on a pyre, though nothing in their surroundings would have been charred.

"Some avoided this fate by wearing blindfolds after dark. When the figure drew near the village, they would hide and cover their eyes with something to avoid meeting its gaze. Even those who fled to other regions continued this tradition; I wager some keep to it still, for nothing good ever came of staring too long into the night, and that is an old truth.

"Many a town succumbed in this fashion. One supposes that the figure still remains, haunting distant hillsides, sustained on its ancient devilry..."

On the face of it, this strange tale was an obvious fabrication. Under any other circumstances I'd have had no trouble dismissing it out of hand. But I must confess that the seed was thus planted. It's easy for one to hear this account second-hand and laugh it off as nonsense, but for the man who stood in the crashing rain and listened—with increasing interest and unease, I hasten to add—to the old man's croaking voice, it left an immense impression and incited a creeping dread the likes of which I'd never experienced.

You will understand, then, that when my cab finally pulled up against the swollen curb some moments later, I lowered my umbrella and ran for it. I'd never been so happy to see a yellow taxi in all my life.

As I fled the Keenan Building, I heard the man shaking his coin box—demanding payment for that sordid little yarn of his, no doubt. He shook it repeatedly, and with increasing ferocity, as I rushed to my ride.

Would that I had nothing more to tell.

There was one last thing I noticed as I entered the cab. Panting, I told the driver my address, then chanced one more glance outside, into the rain-dappled scenery. I studied the building's exterior, meaning to catch one last glimpse of that strange little man, but found him absent. He had not struck me as particularly spry, and the fact that he'd vanished from sight completely in the space of a few moments left me puzzled and unnerved.

At the time, I was living on the top floor of an old apartment complex on the cusp of town. My unit's sole window looked out across a vast field. Whenever it rained, this patchy lot was transformed into a soupy morass, and on this sodden evening it had been so rendered.

I went about my routine in the hours after my return—ate something, took a shower—but at no point did I manage to fully overcome the unease that'd earlier taken root. Whenever it seemed on the verge of abating, I'd remember the leering old man, the grotesque lilt of his voice, and even the bizarre medieval landscape he'd described from his dream. As sleep approached and I failed to completely purge the details of that dream in black static from my mind, I sat on the edge of my bed, eyes closed, and fancied I could smell the burning tinder, could hear the footfalls of 15th century peasants in retreat.

It was nearly midnight when I finally set my sights on sleep, and I began putting out the lights. No sooner had I switched off the light in my bedroom did I hear something just outside the doorway however.

I stood in the darkness, completely still, and devoted everything I had towards listening.

I was sure that I was simply going insane. All the same, the noise I'd heard had sounded something like the ringing of coins in a wooden box.

Eager to debunk the sound as mere hallucination, I took a stroll through my dark apartment. Gliding silently from one room to another and assuring myself that it'd been the jangling of a dog's leash in the next unit, or the clanging of a loose pipe in the building, I had almost convinced myself that I'd misheard when it rang out again. This time, it was too clear to deny—and what's more, there could be no doubt that the sound had originated outside my door, from the communal hallway.

A queasy fear stirred to life in me. It wasn't until the rattle of coins sounded a third time that I found sufficient courage to sneak to the door and peer through the peephole. In doing so, I was frustrated to find the hallway empty—and more than that, dark, for one of the bulbs in the ceiling fixture had apparently just burned out.

Desperate to put the strange business behind me, I marched off to bed. The lights in my room were put out for the second time and I went to shut the blinds, too, to keep off the glare of the moon. As I fiddled with the cord however, I glanced out the window—across the soupy lot—and found something that robbed my legs of strength.

I nearly toppled over at the sight of something—no, it would be more accurate to say some*one*—hovering high in the air some distance away. My first thought had been that it was a kite, a large one, but the stark humanoid shape it cut against the turbulent sky suggested otherwise. The possibility that it was some large species of bird proved untenable as well; distant though it was, I could make out four limbs on the thing. In the glow of the moon, its flesh looked white as porcelain. Clouds of blowing mist wreathed its rigid body.

I backed away from the window, head spinning. Surely, I was dreaming? With a quivering hand, I steadied myself against the wall and leaned towards the window for another look. I sought anything I could find to keep me tethered to reality; something to keep me from spinning off into some mad, dark world, but on second glance the situation outside had only taken another step into nightmare country.

A wicked haze was rolling in from the distance—a harshly obscuring wave more of darkness than of mist. It was as though the rain had stopped falling, only to remain suspended in the air. And as the droplets hung cemented in the darkness, each of them fell somewhere onto a kaleidoscopic palette of pitch. I was looking out my window into what appeared to be a storm of black static.

And in the midst of that storm, having drawn nearer since my last look, shone the alabaster figure, still suspended in the air like a twisted, staring mannequin. The thing looked carved from marble, unmoving and yet somehow gaining ground.

The sound of rattling change pierced the silence as I cowered beside the window. This time, the noise had come from outside—from directly beneath my window, it seemed. However great my mounting terror, I had room enough then for a niggling rage. The old man from earlier—he'd found me, somehow. Now he'd come to my home, was still angling for the handout I'd neglected to give him during our last meeting. I'd evidently misjudged the old man; my current troubles were plainly owed to his deft linguistic talents—to some hypnotic suggestion he'd planted during that odd and winding tale of his.

I returned to the window, mildly invigorated by my anger and intending to curse at him, but the words were never realized. The scene had changed again, continuing its descent into abomination. The sky above and the moon that had hitherto been parked in it were no longer visible, nor was the field below. There existed now only the void of black static and the twisted white figure suspended within it.

That figure was close now—close enough to remove any doubt as to its general shape—yet it remained, mercifully, far enough away to spare me the full weight of its stare. At sighting the thing, the smell of moisture in the air was replaced with the smell of a raging wood fire. What should have been a cool autumn breeze, pregnant with icy mist, was instead a noxious smoke that filled my lungs and accosted my eyes. And with this smoke came heat. I felt a distinct and unnatural warmth all about me, like I was standing very close to an unseen pyre.

That entity—what a hideous thing it was. Though its body was as proportional and picturesque as a Grecian sculpture, the perpetual pose it struck was in keeping with the very architecture of the nightmarish. Its lengthy, muscled arms were wrapped around its midsection; its legs bowed outward somewhat, only to cross at the ankles. It was the pose of a body leashed to a pillar.

Once again, the rattling of the coin box sounded from the void. The coins clattered with great insistence, crashed like cymbals in the perfect silence. Having scrambled from the window, I backed deeper into my room, coming to a halt as I met the dresser with my back. Desperate to break the spell, I threw up an arm and knocked everything from the top of the dresser. My watch, wallet, and a small valet tray filled with spare change fell to the floor. At hearing the coins spill out all around me, I grabbed up as many of them as I could find and then crawled back to the window with fistfuls of quarters and dimes.

The window was home now to a very different sight.

Two stiff white legs hovered there—close enough that I might have reached out and touched them. The smell of fire waxed dominant; my lungs burned, eyes watered and an incredible heat washed over me in nigh-overwhelming waves.

Then, very slowly, the floating corpse began to sink. The tips of its feet fell out of view, and I followed the curves of its calves.

The tops of the legs, then a taut abdomen entered into sight; very soon now a chest would come into frame. It was lowering itself, inch-by-inch, and in no time at all would be looking in at me. It sought my eyes; wished to fix me with its dead stare.

At the moment I glimpsed a twisted white neck, I cast my fistfuls of change out the window and buried my face in the carpet. "Leave me alone!" I cried. Pulses of raw heat buffeted me; I felt the cold sweat on my skin bubbling—then evaporating.

Remaining huddled against the floor, I heard the coins raining down across the rain-soaked lot. There was a burst of furtive sloshing as some unseen gatherer set about plucking them up, and I heard each of them being noisily deposited into something like a wooden box shortly thereafter. *Clink. Clink. Clink. Clink.*

Finally, after seeming eons, the phantom warmth retreated and the sound of the rain reached my ears.

I can't tell you how long it took me to look at the window again. I was probably an hour in finally looking upward, and when I did, I saw that the rain had largely ebbed and the sill had grown very damp. Some time later, I summoned the courage to crawl to the window and look outside, but when I did I found only an empty lot. The rain quit soon thereafter, and the remainder of the night wore on in the expected fashion.

You may be telling yourself that this encounter of mine was the result of some temporary insanity or fever dream; that such things don't—and *can't*—happen in the real world. Believe what you will, but allow me to leave you with this...

Traumatized though I'd been by the whole experience, I found something of reason when the sun reared its head, and through sheer stubbornness I tried to convince myself of precisely that; that I'd suffered a nervous breakdown or had hallucinated the entire ordeal. I ventured out into that muddy lot outside in the minutes after sunrise, sure that no corroborating proofs existed.

Out in the field, I found two things, however.

First, I discovered that, despite my having tossed two handfuls of coins out my window, not a single dime remained in the field. It was entirely possible that someone had wandered by in the hours since my episode and picked them up; but how, in the darkness, had they managed to claim each and every one?

Well, this was a strange thing, but not so strange that it could not be chalked up to the commonplace.

The other thing I discovered in the field was harder to explain, and it is the chief reason why I no longer look out my windows at night, and why I make certain to carry spare change with me whenever I leave the house.

I discovered a series of small footprints in the mud, directly below my window. They were gnarled prints, the kind that might be left behind by ancient feet. I studied these prints for some time in the mounting dawn, and followed them a little ways—as far as was possible, anyhow.

From my window, the maker of these tracks had turned and gone back across the vast field. There was a lengthy series of prints in the fresh mud, and as I said, I followed them for quite some distance. But eventually, I reached a point where the trail ended without explanation. Beyond the last set of prints there existed only virginal mud, and a thorough exploration of the surrounding area turned up no recurrence of them elsewhere.

The trail simply ended in the middle of a field. It was as if the individual had ceased to walk—as if he'd taken to the skies on the devil's own wings.

DISTORTIONAL ADDICT

In the autumn of 1995, college friends Sibyl Marsh and Jason Darrow recorded a handful of dreamy pop songs on a 4-track and circulated them among acquaintances on a cassette entitled "*Gloworm*". The tunes consisted only of Marsh's breathy vocals, Darrow's crunchy, experimental guitar playing and a drum machine.

Owing to a warm reception, a further five-hundred copies of this independent tape were made, sold by the duo after shows as they began touring small Midwestern venues under the moniker Tandem Cuties. By the spring of 1996, all five-hundred copies had been sold and the pair had been joined by Detroit native Percy Stollsteimer on drums, whose jazz-inflected playing added a shoegazy sharpness to a sound that had previously been loose and atmospheric.

With this change in sound came a change in name; the trio retired the Tandem Cuties moniker and began performing as Silver Souls. The newly minted trio attracted the attention of Chicago producer Gerard Maxwell, whose Achille's Heel label had signed some of the most celebrated independent bands of the time, including Thee Ottoman Turks and The Starlite Walkers. Maxwell offered the band a contract and invited them to a small studio in Chicago to record what would become their debut album; 1997's *Shoot the Singer*.

The debut performed modestly, and the single "She Loves the Sun" saw heavy rotation on college radio. The reaction from the music press was unanimously positive; critics praised the album and ranked it highly on the year's best-of lists. Guy Laroche, writing for the Snapdragon Review, had this to say:

*In a crowded field of shoegazers, the Silver Souls have found a way to stand head and shoulders above the competition. The hype is warranted—*Shoot the Singer *is a new high water mark for the genre. Sybil Marsh lends these recordings a heart-warming earnestness; her vocals seem less breathy than painfully shy, but she manages a spectral sweetness in even her most warbling whispers. Darrow's guitar is a perfect melodic compliment, weaving in and out of each track without eclipsing the fragile vocals. Drumming is crisp; Stollsteimer's background in jazz shines through in the album's creative fills.* Shoot the Singer *is an instant classic whose only weakness will be the long shadow it casts upon the band's future endeavors.*

Bolstered by this early success, the band returned to Chicago in the summer of 1998 after months of touring to record a highly anticipated follow-up. Bassist Dean Mazarelli joined them in-studio as they began hashing out new material, but only five tracks were completed before disaster struck.

On July 20th, just after 11PM, all four musicians were involved in a fatal accident. Their tour van was struck head-on by a dozing trucker who'd crossed into oncoming traffic. The members of Silver Souls perished in an instant that night, leaving behind a cult following and an unfinished record.

Achille's Heel arranged for a limited CD release of Marsh and Darrow's indie tape, *Gloworm*, in the winter of 1999. A few thousand copies were produced and were promptly bought up by die-hards and music collectors. In early 2000, rumors circulated in the music press that the five finished tracks of the Silver Souls' incomplete sophomore effort would be released as an extended play, but the bankruptcy of Achille's Heel that spring left the recordings in limbo.

It is here that the story really begins, for sometime between January and April 2000, an anonymous Achille's Heel employee with access to the master recordings transferred the five completed tracks onto CD-Rs. These unauthorized discs were stealthily distributed amongst staff and well-known music collectors. An exact count of the copies produced is not known; estimates range from many dozens to many hundreds.

Some believed the smuggler had been a sound technician employed by the studio, someone who'd been a massive fan of Silver Souls and who'd released the tracks illicitly in an effort to honor the band's memory, which was already beginning to fade from the public consciousness. Others believed that the label owner, Gerard Maxwell, had been behind the leak. To this day the material has not seen an official release, and furthermore, there is some debate as to the whereabouts of the masters. It has been claimed that they were destroyed—a casualty of a well-publicized studio fire in the late aughts.

As can be expected, the CD containing these five tracks is quite the rarity and ordinarily commands a high price. Some have sold for incredible amounts in online auctions, while other copies have turned up in small music shops or second-hand stores, sold for a pittance by merchants unaware of the disc's notoriety and worth.

The CD—formally known as the *Poolside EP*—can be identified by a few common marks. Each copy of the disc that is known to exist has come in a white card-stock sleeve. A hand-written track listing appears on the reverse, giving the name of each song and its runtime. Collectors have been famously tight-lipped about the details of this track list, with only the title and runtime of the first song, "Poolside", being a certainty to those who don't own a copy. The top of each disc is also known to bear the scrawl "Here lie the Silver Souls" in permanent marker.

In this age where piracy and file-sharing are common, one might be surprised to learn that there are no known copies of the *Poolside EP* circulating on torrent sites or other media-sharing platforms. There is a belief amongst collectors that the EP should not be shared digitally; that it is a musical artifact worthy of respect and should only be listened to by those with a great devotion to the band.

This secretiveness has not kept music collectors from frequently discussing their opinions on the EP, however. Obscure web forums and fan sites are littered with reviews by those who've been fortunate enough to hear the thing, and its acclaim is universal. Without exception, every review of the disc is a glowing love letter. The recording has reached a pseudo-mythical status in the indie music community.

I first heard the music of the Silver Souls on a mixtape one of my college boyfriends made me. Though the relationship didn't last, the music *did*. I fell in love with their work and sought out everything of theirs I could get ahold of. I started with *Shoot the Singer* and was fortunate enough to snag a copy of *Gloworm* when it was re-released in '99. By connecting with other fans on the web, I've collected several live recordings of the band—spanning from early 1995 to the summer of '98, just days before the tragic wreck. I've sung along with the lilting chorus of "Necessary Evil" after a bad shift at work, and have had many a good cry listening to the three-minute instrumental outro of "Late Bloomer". I've considered getting the lyrics of "She Loves the Sun" as a tattoo.

The only thing missing, the only thing I hadn't been able to find, was a copy of the *Poolside EP.* I made a hobby of visiting record shops and second-hand stores in search of it, but for years I came up empty-handed.

One day, passing through the city on a lark, I happened to find it.

—wv\/\—wv\/\—

I was still staring at the menu behind the counter when the sound system overhead was commandeered by a familiar opening chord. I looked up to the distant ceiling, zeroing in on the speakers incredulously. After a few bars of crunchy strumming a galloping snare chimed in, and it took everything in me not to sing along as the vocalist began to coo. "She Loves the Sun" had come on unexpectedly as I idled in the cafe of the last chain bookstore in town.

"Miss?"

I snapped to attention.

"OK, so that was a large flat white and a chocolate croissant. Anything else?" asked the barista.

"No, that's all," I replied.

"And a name for the order?"

"Brigitte."

The barista wiped his hands on his apron and brought up the total. When I'd handed him a few bills and tucked away the change, he motioned to the nigh-empty seating area. "I'll call your name when it's ready."

I carried my bag of books to a corner table and stared out the window as the grey afternoon gave way to snow. "She Loves the Sun" continued as I dropped into one of the chairs, and I couldn't help tapping my foot to the chorus. I resented the roar of the coffee grinder as it eclipsed the bridge; I leered at passersby whose quiet conversations competed with Sibyl's singing. The barista called my name but I didn't leave my seat till the final note had faded and some other song had started up.

The morning had been spent in a slow crawl through the city's book and record shops in search of sales. At the Finder's on West Moreland I rifled through several shelves of secondhand CDs and came away with a handful of rare jazz discs. Next, I spent a few minutes paging through the stock of the used bookstore on Eleanor Avenue, where I picked up a pristine Murakami novel in hardback. From there, I'd taken the bus across town to the big bookstore to stock up on cozy mysteries and enjoy a coffee.

I'd been planning to head back home, but my hearing "She Loves the Sun" had suddenly set my mind on a different course. I thought about the *Poolside EP* for the first time in a long while. I had all but given up hope of ever owning it, and as I sat sipping my coffee I looked through the window at the frosty scenery and wondered if a single copy of the thing even existed in the whole of the city. I was quite familiar with all of the major local music shops, but I couldn't be certain that I'd exhausted *every* purveyor of used CDs in town. It was possible, if unlikely, that other shops in town still dealt in secondhand music, so I decided to do a web search for such retailers within the city, just to make sure I hadn't overlooked any hidden gems.

I scrolled through listings and noted the many familiar names. There was one result toward the end of the list that I *didn't* recognize, however—a place rather close to the bookstore I was currently sitting in. It was called Spectrum Video, and a public review posted by user "Mr. Ray" the year previous rated it a full five stars. "*Best place in town for VHS tapes, movies, CDs and vintage games,*" the user had written.

I had never heard of Spectrum Video, and if not for its proximity I wouldn't have bothered visiting. I doubted very much that they'd have what I was looking for, but since my day was clear and I couldn't stand the thought of leaving this stone unturned, I hurried through my croissant and coffee and took off through the chilly streets.

—w\/\—w\/\—

It was with some difficulty that I tracked down the entrance to Spectrum Video. The shop was nestled deep in an alley across from a dim arcade, making it very easy to miss when searching for it amidst the flood of shops along the main strip. I passed through the front door and was immediately greeted by a gentleman behind the counter. He wore a Hawaiian shirt with electric blue flowers on it and insisted on shaking my hand as I walked in. There was no one else in the store.

The place was not particularly uninviting, but in virtually every aspect it was spartan and threadbare. The posters sagging on the far wall were for movies some decades old, and almost everything in sight was coated in dust. The smell of the place—a perfume dominated by notes of urbanity and earthiness—made my nose twitch. The lights were very low, and in the near-silence their buzzing proved a bit distracting.

"What brings you in, miss?"

"I'm just looking for some CDs," I replied. "I hear you sell used ones?"

"That's right," said the man at the counter, who'd introduced himself as Hoon after a lingering handshake. "To the left of the DVDs. There must be a few hundred in stock at the moment, and we're always getting new material in. Just a dollar each, unless the sticker says different."

"Excellent, thank you!" I started across well-worn carpet, walked between tall metal shelves cluttered with movies, and approached a lengthy row of wire CD racks situated against the wall. To my dismay, I found that the "few hundred" CDs in stock were a completely unsorted mass. There were no divisions for genres or artists, just a well-loved copy of *The Very Best of The Doors* sharing shelf space with the *Grease 2* soundtrack and other jumbled pairings that triggered my OCD.

I worked from left to right, flipping through more than a hundred discs before I found anything that caught my eye. Many of the CDs in this collection came with brutalized jewel cases, and where liner notes could be found they were usually crumpled or torn. There could be little doubt that almost every disc present in this heap was scratched, perhaps beyond the point of playability, and my enthusiasm quickly evaporated.

One item saw me pause in my rummaging, though—a disc with familiar artwork and a slightly scuffed case that, relatively speaking, looked immaculate. It was a copy of *Shoot the Singer*. My copy at home looked very much like this one; the case a bit scratched by years of shelving and re-shelving, the seam of the liner notes a bit thin for countless references to the lyrics, and the black and white photos of the band marred by years of fingerprints. As I went to pick it up, a thin piece of cardboard clinging to the reverse of the case became unstuck and fell to the ground.

It seemed to me that a random piece of cardboard had gotten mixed in with this group of CDs, though as it landed at my feet it sounded heavier than I expected mere cardboard should sound. I knelt down to pick it up and found it was a white paper sleeve, the kind of temporary slipcase one might drop a burned CD into—and that there was, in fact, a disc within it. The case was threadbare and bore no outward sign of the disc's contents on the front, but when curiosity drove me to slip the CD from its sleeve, I froze.

The words "*Here lie the Silver Souls*" were written in a ring around the center hole.

Immediately I flipped it over and inspected the reverse of the disc. The play surface was pristine; not a scratch to be seen.

Easing it back into the case gingerly, I studied the back of the slipcover and found five hand-written song titles listed there, along with corresponding runtimes. It read as follows:

1. *Poolside—4:32*

2. *Coin Laundry Detergent—2:58*

3. *Is Life Delicious?—3:34*

4. *Tell Me You Love Me—4:01*

5. *Luminescence—9:49*

My heart skipped a beat as I read the track titles under my breath. I felt as though I'd stumbled across a precious relic from a lost civilization. My fingers passed over the hand-written characters one-by-one and my tongue stumbled over every syllable phonetically as though they belonged to some long-dead language.

This was it. For years I'd sought a copy of the *Poolside EP*, and finally, I'd found one here, in a pile of thrift store cast-offs. I placed the disc back onto the shelf, frightened that my shaking hands wouldn't be able to keep hold of it; then, imagining some other customer sneaking up behind me and making off with it, I snatched it back up with a shudder.

There was no price sticker on the thing. If the man up front was to be believed, this rare disc—which had gone for hundreds of dollars in online auctions—would cost me a mere buck. I couldn't believe my luck and even as I studied the disc and track list a second time, a third, a fourth, I doubted its authenticity. *It can't be the real thing. It must be a fake—a knockoff. There's no way that someone just sold it to this shop along with their other CDs.*

And yet, everything about the disc was on-point. The writing on the top, the presence of the track list on the back—headed by "Poolside", which I knew, based on my research, to run for four minutes and thirty-two seconds...

Everything was there.

I clutched the disc to my chest and returned to the front, setting it very carefully onto the counter. "Uh... sir, I'd like to buy this one, if possible."

He stood up and appraised the sleeved disc, removing his sunglasses and depositing them into his drooping breast pocket. "Er... where'd you find that?" he asked, gazing narrowly at it.

I felt my stomach drop as Hoon picked the disc up and inspected it. *Oh, no... he's going to tell me it's not for sale. Or else he's going to try and charge me hundreds of dollars for it.* "I, uh... I found it over there, mixed in with the other CDs," I explained while doing some mental math. *If he demands the going rate for it, I could put off paying the electric bill till next payday. I have a few hundred bucks in savings, too, that I could—*

"Sorry," he said, setting it back down, "I didn't know something like this wound up with the merchandise. It looks like a homemade CD of some kind. Usually, I throw that stuff out. Guess I missed one." Hoon chuckled, scratching at his greying hair. "I buy lots from all around town—garage sales, estate sales, you name it. Sometimes people accidentally include their junk. I can't in good conscience sell something like this to you—it's not worth anything. If you'd like, you can take it, though. I'll just toss it, otherwise."

Thrilled though I was, my conscience wouldn't allow me to take it without informing him of its true worth. "Sir, I don't think you understand. This disc *looks* like a homemade CD, but it's actually a rare bootleg recording. It routinely sells for a lot of money online. I couldn't just take it—not for free. I've actually been looking for it a long time and was amazed to find it." I must've sounded like a maniac, blathering at a higher and higher register as I went on. "Please, let me pay you something for it."

"Eh?" he replied, picking it up once more and inspecting it. "I don't understand... this is a recordable CD. What's on it, anyway?"

"It contains some rare recordings by the Silver Souls."

"Never heard of 'em," said Hoon, chuckling once more. He shook his head, evidently doubting my assessment of the disc. "Tell you what, I'm not too keen on holding onto something like this. It looks like a piece of junk to me, but if you really want it, go ahead and take it. No charge."

"I couldn't," I insisted. Reaching into my wallet, I pulled out a crisp twenty. "Please, let me at least give you *something* for it."

The man accepted the money reticently, opening the register and returning nineteen dollars in change, along with my receipt. "I told you each CD was a dollar, so I'll give it to you for a dollar. How's that sound?"

"A-Are you sure?"

"Of course," said Hoon, grinning widely. "Just remember me the next time you're looking for something new to watch or listen to!"

This time, I reached out and insisted on shaking *his* hand. "Thank you *so* much. I can't tell you how much I appreciate this." I tucked the disc into my purse very carefully and held it close as I left the store. I barreled out into the cold alley, cheeks flushed with excitement.

I'd found it. I'd *actually* found it.

Before taking a cab back to my apartment, I made a run to the nearest grocery store, buying a bottle of good wine and some appropriately lavish snacks. I was committed to making an event out of my first listening and hauled my sacks of books and goodies with me as I stepped into the cab.

"Any plans tonight?" the driver asked me as we passed through downtown and headed toward the suburbs.

I clutched at my purse, visualizing the disc within. "Yes, I'm getting together with some old friends," I said—and it wasn't a lie. In sitting down and listening to the *Poolside EP* I was set to connect with my favorite musicians in a way I'd never done before. I'd pined after this EP for years, and now that I finally had it I felt as though I were on my way to visit loved ones I hadn't seen in ages.

The cab ride brought us through the shop district, past the abandoned Keenan Building that looked out lonesomely across the city, and to the winding lanes of Kirkland Road, which we clung to till my apartment complex entered into view several miles later. I paid up the fare, adding a generous tip, and rushed inside.

Racing through the lobby, I began up the three flights to my apartment. The building, a rectangular six-story construction, contains five one-bedrooms per level, along with stairwells on both ends. It's an ordinarily cozy place, tenanted largely by graduate students and young professionals. Noise, even on the weekends, tends to be negligible. Though small, the place suits me perfectly. I live alone and rarely have guests over, so the lack of space doesn't bother me in the least. Its position on the cusp of the city, within a short drive of downtown, makes it an especially good fit for me.

No sooner had I slipped inside my door and turned the deadbolt did I immediately claw the disc out of my purse. Virtually everything else I'd picked up in my day of rummaging was tossed onto the bed, suddenly irrelevant. Upon dimming the lights, I kicked off my shoes and poured myself a glass of wine, settling onto my sofa and fumbling with the stereo remote. I eyed the small charcuterie board I'd picked up at the store but couldn't even think about eating as I prepared to slip the disc into the player.

I studied the contents of the track list. The names of the songs felt so evocative to me that I could almost imagine what they sounded like. I had longed for years after this disc, and in that time I had put forth no few guesses as to how it would sound. Finally, I'd be able to cease my wondering. With a steadying breath, I pulled the disc from its sleeve and loaded it into the player.

I waited till the noise of my pulse finally quietened before hitting play and returning to the sofa. It was hard to breathe as I perched upon the edge of my seat and watched my stereo mull over the new disc.

The glowing lines on the display converged into the words *TRACK 1 OF 5.*

Then, the *Poolside EP* began to play.

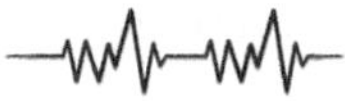

Once I'd heard it, I could no longer imagine a world without it.

The sound washed over me in warm, steady waves. The quiver of the speakers mirrored that of my own heart. I felt each pulse of the bass as though it were my pulse, felt every strum of the guitar as though it had come from my own fingertips. My throat ached, so great was my desire to sing along with these songs I didn't know yet. The EP lasted just under twenty-five minutes—both too short and exactly the right length. There were eternities in its echoing riffs. You could lose yourself in the heft of a single coda and feel it in the air even as the silence between tracks reigned.

The opener, "Poolside", began with a series of mutters. One of the male band members or studio staff could be heard moments before the brassy entrance chord, which led to a ragged, metallic strumming. Moving in very gradually from behind was a pulsing bass line, which emerged along with a distorted drum beat and grinding hi-hat. The whole of the sound, especially as Sybil began to sing roughly forty seconds in, was like a roar—incredibly raw and possessed of a depth that made it seem as though the song had been recorded in a deep cavern. Probably, these five tracks had not been fully mixed or mastered; they were, at best, polished studio demos. But the coarseness of the audio did not detract from its aesthetic quality in the least; rather, it only added to the charm and mystique of the songs.

I could go on, waxing poetical about the mournful melodies of "Coin Laundry Detergent", whose main accompaniment was a slightly out-of-tune Hammond organ, or about the tear-jerking crescendo of "Luminescence", whose almost-ten-minute length draws to a close with a lone, slightly sinister, bass riff. Suffice it to say, I was transfixed from the first note to the last and spent the bulk of my first listen curled up on the floor before the speakers. When the final track had ended, the stereo reverted automatically to the first, and when the EP began to play a second time I dared not move a finger to stop it.

There was something utterly disarming about the music on this disc. Sound waves have no physical form to speak of, and yet the rhythms were so heavy I almost felt as though I could nestle up within them, bodily. The vibrations passing through the floor and carpet entered my skin and set my bones quivering. I could feel the album in my teeth as I sat listening; the gentle strum of the bridge on "Tell Me You Love Me" resonated so deeply I imagined Jason Darrow's fingers running across my spine as though it were a fretboard.

I could scarcely think as the EP played—there was only room enough in my mind for the sound. The melodies and ghostly vocals rebuffed the stresses of everyday life, sent my every concern into retreat. By the third repetition, I was splayed out on the carpet, staring dazedly at the ceiling. The opening notes of "Poolside" returned, ushering me deeper into aural bliss. The sound was like a steady stream of Lidocaine; it was administered via the ears so as to better soak the brain and render it numb.

Such was my enjoyment and immersion in the music that, with each passing minute, I felt less and less tethered to my physical self. The songs seemed to carry my mind out of my body altogether, till I lay slack-jawed and panting on the carpet. The room around me faded into a beige blur as my involvement with the music deepened. I felt I had been transported through time and space back to the little studio where these tracks had been recorded—that Sybil Marsh and the others were gathered, just out of view, and performing these songs for me personally. I could not see them, but as the sound of their performance filled me I very much *felt* their presence.

Minutes passed into hours. I felt a thread of drool roll down my chin, sensed my cheeks grow damp with tears—but it was a change in the rumbling of the floors that ultimately returned me to awareness. The vibrations of the music had been coursing through the carpet all the while, but superadded to these familiar tremors were stirrings of a different sort, as of someone walking across the room toward me. My heart, hitherto paused, was suddenly jumpstarted, and I felt it climb into my throat. I blinked, possibly for the first time in several minutes, and succeeded in turning my bleary eyes to the right, towards the front door.

From across the living room, I found someone staring back at me.

A withered figure crouched near the door. Rooted to the carpet by a bundle of spidery grey limbs, the visitor glared from enormous eyes fixed in a drooping, waxen face. These eyes, large and white as cue balls, rotated furiously in their softened sockets as they met my own, and the thing's rubbery lips were bunched into a trembling frown. The nostrils of its sagging nose, which itself had the appearance of a stubby, half-melted candle, flared as they sampled the air. The whole of the terrible face was half-buried in a mane of black, wiry hair whose coarseness resembled the fur of a wild animal.

I watched, still incapacitated, as the thing began creeping toward me. Its skeletal back arched like a cat's, the figure stole carefully across the room on hands and feet, stilted limbs straining beneath its bare, wilted torso. For fingers and toes it possessed only blackened nubs, and as they dragged across the carpet I became cognizant of a faint rustling I'd previously attributed to the music.

The album, only moments ago so arresting, was forced into the background by the toil of my sickly heart, and as I began to writhe I could once again feel the floor beneath me. Shifting against the carpet, I fought to regain control of myself, to roll over or stand, but the disconnect between my mind and body seemed an unbridgeable gulf. I felt a scream charging through me but lacked the wherewithal to release it; it burned behind my lips and set my chest alight as I struggled.

The rustling drew very near, and a shadow passed over me as the figure arrived at my side. It lowered itself, studying my face with such great intensity that one of its bulging white eyes began drooping from its socket and inching down its cheek. My thrashing had reached a fever pitch; I dug my heels into the floor, flailing wildly in an effort to evade the thing.

Suddenly, the music stopped and a long, sharp whimper stole past my lips. The figure had disappeared, too, and I found myself outstretched across the living room floor, the carpet beneath me damp with sweat. Something hard asserted itself against my left elbow; it was the stereo remote, which I'd accidentally rolled over in my writhing. Without meaning to, I'd mashed several of the buttons and ejected the disc.

The apartment was utterly still and silent as I sat upright. I felt as though I'd just awakened from a fever dream and crawled very slowly toward the sofa, where I found my phone. I was stunned to find that almost seven hours had passed since I'd first put on the *Poolside EP*—it was now past midnight.

For several minutes, I leaned against the sofa cushions, shivering. It seemed I'd fallen asleep while listening to the CD and had suffered a terrible nightmare. That was the only explanation I could think of for the haunting episode—though as I sat there I certainly didn't feel as though I'd been asleep for several hours. I kneaded my achy brow and finally rose, claiming the disc from the stereo. I returned it to its sleeve and powered the whole thing down, marching off to the shower.

Strange though it was, I could hardly remember how any of the songs went despite having listened to them all evening. I could recall certain details—instruments, pieces of riffs, the overall mood of each piece—but my entire listening experience felt incredibly hazy.

Sleep came in increments of thirty to forty minutes, and between them I found myself sitting up in bed, listening. I listened for unexpected noises in my apartment—noises that would confirm the continued persistence of my earlier nightmare—but found only deafening silence. Tossing and turning till dawn, I staggered out of bed at first light and started the coffee maker.

As a journalist for a local magazine, I find myself working from home more often than not. A strict adherence to routine, along with a concerted effort to avoid distractions, is the key to meeting my deadlines and remaining productive. I've earned a reasonable income and a string of accolades for my writing over the years—not to mention a good bit of workplace freedom—and this modest success is owed to no little daily discipline.

But where I could routinely ignore the specters of social media and entertainment till my articles were written, I could *not* resist the uncanny pull of the *Poolside EP*. I don't mean to say that I put it on that morning as I attempted to get to work, but that its mere presence in the apartment was enough to stifle me creatively. I often listened to music while drafting, even dipped into the works of the Silver Souls on occasion, but something told me that this newest acquisition would prove far too distracting, and so I stationed myself at my desk and fired up my laptop in silence.

Even doing my best to ignore it, I could scarcely think of anything else, though.

I found myself trying to hum the chorus of "Poolside" as I culled my inbox, but despite having listened to it many times the night prior the melody eluded me. I longed to give the album another spin, to lose myself in the music the way I'd done the night before, but with deadlines fast-approaching I couldn't risk that level of distraction. Instead, I put on one of the jazz discs I'd bought the previous day—a famous bebop record—and looked over my calendar while fixing my coffee.

I didn't even make it through the first piece before I shut off the stereo. The album was a strong one, critically acclaimed, but every note sounded sour to me—and I knew why. It was because the jazz record paled in comparison to the Silver Souls EP I'd become so obsessed with, failed to lift me to the same transcendent heights. The *Poolside EP* had been like a drug for me; I was jonesing for another hit.

When I'd completed some banal correspondence, I swung by *Midnight Music,* a Silver Souls fan site I frequently post on, and scrolled through the handful of new threads its web forum offered. As usual, petty arguments and discussions of live recordings dominated the main feed. I chimed in just long enough to announce to the other users that I'd recently acquired our long-sought-after white whale, but even this short forum post filled me with an almost irresistible desire to listen to it and I had to close out of my browser completely and pivot back to my work to keep from doing so.

Promising myself that I would listen to the EP during my lunch break, I managed to eke out a brief, dull piece about a string of local charity functions, and to start a second—this one about invasive insects turning up in local metro parks. A call to my editor ate up another thirty minutes, and when she'd quit gushing about her toddler and let me off the phone, I wandered to the fridge and began throwing together a makeshift lunch. I wasn't really hungry—hadn't been all morning—but I couldn't bear to put off the *Poolside EP* any longer.

I settled on the sofa with half a sandwich, a handful of nuts, some yogurt and the stereo remote. When this lunch break was over, I felt confident that I would be able to return to work; that, having gotten the urge to listen to the disc out of my system, I'd be able to settle into a productive afternoon.

Instead, as the music began seeping from the speakers, I found myself utterly absorbed.

The air trembled with the opening notes of "Poolside" and I was overcome by a torrent of emotion. As though a switch had been flipped in my brain, I recalled now—with great firmness—the many moving parts to the title track. I could feel Sybil's voice in my ear as though she were seated on the sofa beside me, and heading into the chorus I felt driven to hum along. I had taken a bite of my sandwich just before the song had begun and had chewed it thoroughly, but as I listened my every fiber seemed fixed on the music and I couldn't marshal my throat to swallow it down. I spat the bite of food onto my plate instead, reclining on the sofa and staring dazedly about the room as if waiting for the music to manifest physically.

Track one faded into track two; track two into track three. Twenty-five minutes elapsed and I found the disc on the verge of repeating. My intention had been to sit and listen to it *once* while enjoying my lunch, but I entered into a second helping of the album without the least resistance. I couldn't think of a good reason to turn it off; work seemed so distant just then and the swell of the opener's chorus seized me by the scruff of the neck. I melted into the sofa, felt it become a part of me as I closed my eyes.

The music filled my body; it flooded in through my ears, rushed into every hollow space, till I contained more of it than I did anything else. Its pleasing vibrations jarred my cells apart, dissolved me atom by atom. Soon, I would disintegrate. My very essence would be subjected to the wax and wane of the music and I would become one with these precious melodies.

The songs only grew sweeter with each successive listen; just when I was sure that no greater song had ever been penned than "Is Life Delicious?", "Tell Me You Love Me" would start and I would declare without hesitation that I'd never heard anything so beautiful. The effect of the record grew headier with every repetition, and when it started into its third play-through that afternoon I slipped onto the floor, laughing till I cried, unable to believe that such perfect music could exist but simultaneously reveling in it.

It was a masterpiece with no ceiling—so good, I felt certain, that it would ultimately exhaust me, overload my brain. Though the stereo remote was within arm's reach, I would have rather died in that moment than turn it off.

And I likely would have if not for what happened next.

Through the haze of my ecstasy, I became aware of another presence. To my right, at the mouth of the hallway leading back to my bedroom, the very air began to darken. From this nebulous expanse where the glow of the sun could not reach, four spindly limbs the color of soot were birthed, joined to a cratered, rawboned carcass. The head that crowned the cadaverous thing was smothered by shocks of wiry black hair and dressed in pasty, drooping flesh that seemed poised to slough off the misshapen skull beneath at any moment. Bulbous eyes like white button mushrooms widened in sockets scarcely large enough to house them.

As the abomination began to shamble from the corridor on feet that were little more than necrotic black stumps, the music was backed by a not unfamiliar rustling. I was summoned from my bliss to a state of wild—though petrified—alarm. When its eyes met my own and I understood that it intended to approach, my agitation and panic were doubled, though I proved helpless to react physically. I trembled on the floor, unable to feel the sofa behind me. Whatever strength had existed in me prior to putting on the EP was gone now, seemingly pillaged by the music. Joints quaked and muscles tightened but coordinated movement was an impossibility.

The figure stepped closer. If the CD was still playing I could not hear it; the odious rustling was all I could make out. When I had first glimpsed the thing the night before, my ears had rung with the hammer of my pulse, but now my heart was still, hesitant. All the warmth that had swept over me at listening to the album had been traded for a bone-chilling cold. I felt as though I had lost the spark of life; that I had entered into my death throes.

The hateful figure loomed nearer.

My quivering against the sofa evolved into a fit of tremors; mind struggled toward union with body, life rallied in an effort to ward off death. Head lolling backward in a fit of desperation, I managed only to knock the stereo remote to the floor from the cushion behind me. At sight of it resting against my trembling thigh, I remembered the nightmarish episode of the night before, and how it had come to an abrupt end when I'd accidentally mashed the buttons on it, ejecting the disc. Was that the answer? Was this dreadful visitor somehow tied to the music? I now threw everything I had into repeating the act, straining with numb hands for the remote.

Never before was a reach of some few inches more difficult. My right arm struck out toward the black rectangle, but my digits were curled tightly into a fist—unresponsive. The EJECT button on the upper right was in clear view, but the notion of extending a single finger to push the thing was alien to my body, and the best I could do was to strike the remote with quaking knuckles, like an animal bashing open the shell of a wild nut with a stone.

My senseless blows rained down upon the buttons. I pressed several of them at once, pushing the whole of my dead weight against them, and kept on striking the remote till I fell to my side and the batteries had sprung out the back.

The rustling and the sinister shadow of the lurker were retracted at once.

Face-down on the carpet, I drew in several gasps and felt my limbs reawaken one after another. Dripping with sweat, I clutched the edge of the sofa and forced myself up with a pained grunt, casting my starry eyes about the living room.

I was alone there and the stereo had been turned off completely.

What's more, I had utterly lost track of time. The room was buried in shadow and the nearest window was clotted with the hues of night.

—w\/\/—w\/\/—

In all the reading I'd done about the *Poolside EP* I had never once encountered tell of something like *this*. The disc was touted as a musical triumph within our circles, declared a transcendent masterpiece by all who heard it, but absent from reviews had been any mention of the otherworldly menace that the playing of *my* copy seemed to invite. And while hyperbolic reviewers had frequently claimed to have "out-of-body" events while listening to it, I knew that my own experiences—the steady loss of vitality in exchange for unparalleled auditory pleasure—were not the norm.

The only conclusion that I could draw was that my copy of the EP was different from the rest, that it was tethered to something—something supernatural and truly dangerous—and that continuing to play it was to court certain death. Somehow, after all I'd been through, this seemingly insane conclusion was the only thing that made any sense to me.

And yet, I didn't destroy the disc or rid myself of it.

In fact, despite the gut-wrenching terror I'd faced after my second listening session, I found myself *more* drawn to the disc than ever before. My every waking moment was filled with desire for it and the completion of even the simplest tasks became a Herculean effort in the face of the temptation it posed. Risk of terror, of bodily harm or even death could not deter me.

But it was clear enough that any further involvement with the disc would require some degree of caution on my part. Like the addict of any other drug, I sought to limit my dose of the thing—to maximize the pleasure derived from it while minimizing its side-effects. I began by allowing myself to listen to it only one day a week—an immensely difficult undertaking which frequently strained my willpower, but which helped me to carry out my daily affairs without the risk of upending my life and work.

Furthermore, drawing upon previous experience, I made a rule of only listening to it once per session. To this end, I fiddled with the settings on my stereo, making it so that, upon reaching the conclusion of the final track on any given disc, it would automatically cease playback. The hideous specter had only ever shown up after several successive listens; I hoped that this limited approach would allow me to enjoy the album's fruits without allowing the ghoul to manifest.

For close to eighteen months, I kept to this routine. My entire life came to revolve around Saturday nights spent listening to the *Poolside EP* and maintaining the aforementioned controls. Every time, I felt compelled to listen on, to give it "just one more" spin, but memories of the terrible figure stayed my hand. The music on the disc never lost its effect. With every listen, the tunes only became sweeter to my ears, more irresistible, though they retained their transience, too, and no matter how many times I listened to the album I could never fully recall the words or melodies of the songs when it finished.

There were some instances where, enraptured by the music and held prisoner by it for twenty-five minutes, I did get the sense that I wasn't alone in the apartment—that someone was standing just around the corner, out of sight. Had I strayed from my plan, something would certainly have emerged, and it was only this that kept me from playing the album on repeat and marching willingly to my death.

Some months ago, everything changed, however.

One Saturday afternoon, upon returning home from the grocery store, I found my apartment had been broken into. The lock on the door had been forced and thieves had made off with various of my possessions. My Television, jewelry and tablet were among the stolen items, but none of these mattered to me one iota when

I realized my stereo—containing the *Poolside EP*—had also been taken. In the mess the burglars had left, I found only the paper sleeve the disc had come in. The CD, my most prized possession, had been unknowingly carried off along with the stereo.

I grieved after the loss of that disc as though I'd lost a child. My efforts in reclaiming the stolen stereo—which involved the filing of a police report and a neurotic weekly tour of every pawnshop in town—could be described as nothing short of heroic, but in the end they yielded nothing. Even as I searched for weeks on end in seedy secondhand stores for my stereo and the precious disc that had been left in it, I laughed in spite of myself. For years, my free time had been spent combing stores for that rare album; now, it was spent trying to get it back.

More recently, there has been a stir on *Midnight Music*, the Silver Souls fan site of which I am a member. An anonymous user recently got ahold of a copy of the *Poolside EP* and, despite immense resistance from the community, leaked the song files. For years, there had been an embargo on sharing the album digitally among fans and music collectors, but in the space of a night, thousands of eager listeners the world over downloaded them. The *Poolside EP* has subsequently spread to every corner of the internet. It can now be pirated as readily as any album on the Top 40, and music journalists are hailing the leak as long overdue.

I was among those who downloaded the tracks. I wanted more than anything to feel the bliss of the *Poolside EP* once again and, abandoning my scruples, hastily pirated the album. No sooner had the tracks finished downloading did I realize something was wrong, however.

With the exception of "Poolside", the five tracks I downloaded had unfamiliar titles. None among the five were called "Tell Me You Love Me" or "Is Life Delicious?"—no, the tracks had *different* names. The track list of the leaked EP, corroborated by various outraged collectors in the music press as authentic, is as follows:

1. *Poolside—4:32*

2. *San Francisco—3:59*

3. *1000 Tambourines—4:52*

4. *Cream Soda—3:32*

5. *Calm Evening's Blues—4:04*

Incredulous, I sat and listened to these five songs *dozens* of times.

And I felt nothing. There was no warmth, no bliss. Just unpolished 90s shoegaze.

I don't mean to dismiss the tracks as worthless; compared to the rest of the Silver Souls' work, the songs on the EP were decent, if a little rough. But these five songs were so far beneath the ones I'd obsessed over that no comparisons could be made. The disc that had been stolen from me and the one that was now being spread across the web were clearly two *very* different things.

Even so, the tracks circulating digitally have been confirmed by notable owners of the physical disc to be legitimate, which leaves me with a troubling question:

If the disc I'd become obsessed with wasn't actually the *Poolside EP*, then what was it? That is, if it didn't contain the last five tracks recorded by the Silver Souls... then what, exactly, *did* it contain?

I plan to spend my weekend combing the secondhand stores and pawnshops in the area for my stereo, and if ever I'm reunited with that incredible disc, perhaps I'll arrive nearer an answer to that question.

TRIM

No matter how many times she washed her hands between clients, Ingrid always came home with other people's hair beneath her fingernails. She stood at the bathroom sink, taking her digits to task beneath a stream of hot water till the shear callouses on her fingers softened.

As expected, a few slivers of hair—black, brown and blonde—remained lodged beneath her nails as she glanced them over.

She started for the laundry room, collecting her apron on the way and preparing it for the wash. From the large pockets on the front she dug out her cell phone and name tag—though around the latter there clung a thick lock of smooth, black hair. She startled at seeing it, but as she disentangled the hairs and carried them to the garbage can, she hesitated to throw them away. She remembered who this hair belonged to and, strange though it was, felt compelled to keep it. In her five years at the salon, she'd never once kept locks of a customer's hair.

This hair had fallen into her apron pocket during her last trim of the day. As the washing machine started up, Ingrid once again admired the perfect, glossy strands in her palm.

Her day at the salon had been uncommonly stressful. All but the last thirty minutes of her ten-hour shift had flown by, the stream of walk-ins so steady that she'd skipped her lunch and managed only a hasty restroom break between dye jobs. After Mollie's shift had ended at two and Kate had tapped out around four, complaining of stomach upset, Ingrid had been left running the entire show till eight—closing time.

Five clients had come in during the final four hours; two of them had required only simple cuts, but one among them had opted for a brow waxing *and* a full style, which had been a time consuming combination. Another client, a middle-aged gentleman, had requested a cut and beard trim, though he'd had precious little hair on his head to work with, and the sparse clusters of frizzy wire on his cheeks could not have been called a proper beard. After clipping a few stray hairs, Ingrid had sent him on his way looking virtually unchanged.

These long, beautiful hairs left in her apron pocket had come from the fifth and final client.

—W\/\/—W\/\/—

While restocking the shampoo and conditioner in the entry display, she turned to the front windows and peered out into the evening. The sun had almost completely dropped out of the sky and heavy clouds rolled in from the east. The signs of most nearby businesses—the restaurants, boutiques and bars along the downtown strip—had started coming on, clashing against the dusk. In the hopes of beating the rain, she doubled her efforts to get the salon squared away.

With the clock winding down, Ingrid managed to give the floors a quick sweep and to balance the register. She'd begun another pass with the broom, catching stray hairs of every color in the dustpan as she went, and had made it almost half-way across the room when the door was heard to open. Someone shuffled inside, bringing with them the scent of brewing rain.

At only ten or fifteen minutes till close, Ingrid wasn't keen on the idea of fitting in another client. She turned around to meet the visitor, intending to say as much, but as her eyes met those of the newcomer, she froze. Standing at the entrance, in a pretty floral dress and staring back with eyes of icy blue, was a beautiful young woman. She couldn't have been a day over twenty, and was possessed of the most delicate features imaginable.

More striking than the woman's gorgeous eyes or rosy cheeks, more attention-grabbing than her pouting smile or comely button of a nose, was her elbow-length black hair. Despite working with hair on a daily basis, Ingrid had never seen such perfectly maintained locks as these—except, perhaps, in magazines. The voluminous hair had an incredible luster, and Ingrid was overcome by a desire to run her fingers through it. She cleared her throat and spared the customer a sheepish smile. "How can I help you?"

The young woman, approaching the counter and holding a small leather purse in both hands, returned the smile with perfect teeth. "I'm sorry to be dropping by so late. I see that you close at eight. I'd been hoping to get a trim, but if it's too much trouble..." she said in a dulcet voice.

Only moments ago, Ingrid wouldn't have dreamt of taking another client ten minutes before close; but now, as this lovely specimen stood before her, offering her a chance to play with that pristine hair, she couldn't steer her into a chair fast enough. "Oh, it's no trouble at all. Please, sign in and pick any chair you like," she replied, motioning to the sign-in sheet at the counter.

The young woman, combing a lock of that fine hair behind her ear, leaned down and jotted her name on one of the blank lines before starting into the salon proper and settling into the first chair on the right. Ingrid swung by the counter and took a close look at that paper, curious to know what name the owner of this flawless hair might go by. The name written had been "Corrine".

"All right, Corrine," the stylist began, draping a nylon cape around the girl. "You're in for a trim? How much are we taking off today?" At that moment, as she situated the chair and planted it at the correct height, her willpower failed her and her hands dove at once into the sumptuous ink-colored locks. She ran her fingers through the entire length, hardly able to contain her surprise. "You have such *beautiful* hair," she gushed. "It's gorgeous." Studying the ends, she found them pristine—not frayed in the least. To cut this hair in any significant way felt like a crime, and Ingrid couldn't help saying so as she continued to tease the girl's locks. "It looks lovely just as it is. I can tell you take great care of it—not a single split end. Are you sure you want to cut it?"

Something distant entered into the girl's eyes—something sad, perhaps. "Yes," she replied softly. "In fact, I'd like you to chop a good bit off." She unearthed one of her dainty ears and tugged on the lobe. "Can you bring it up to about here?"

Ingrid nearly gasped. "Y-You want me to cut *that much* off?" She blinked at the customer in the mirror, astonished at the request. "You want it cut into a bob?"

Corrine nodded.

The stylist's first thought was to ask "why?", though Ingrid was not much in the habit of interrogating her clients. When someone came in and asked for a particular cut, she did her best to give them what they asked for. Arguments with customers in the past had shown her the futility in asserting her own opinions. And yet, in this case, something precious seemed at risk of loss. It was just hair, yes—but *what* hair it was! She ran her hands through it again and wondered if, in complying, she wouldn't rob the girl of her breathtaking charm—if she wouldn't play the part of Delilah to this beautiful Samson.

"I've been looking for something different," continued Corrine. "I want to turn a new page, you know?"

It was the type of bland sentiment that Ingrid heard on the daily, though this time it smacked of earnestness—and what's more, there was a hint of melancholy in the admission, too. Over the years, Ingrid had been party to many trims of this kind. Clients, most often female, would seek to shake things up after getting out of a long-term relationship, choosing cuts that were drastically different than whatever they'd come in with. Hacking away what once was and leaving the salon with something new allowed them to cast off whatever negative associations had gotten tangled up in their former styles. Perhaps the long hair reminded this girl of a bad boyfriend, a toxic workplace or home life.

"You're sure?" said Ingrid—and though she tried her best not to make it seem so, it sounded like a warning.

The girl nodded, if a little reticently, and the process began.

Several inches of that perfect hair hit the floor. Mounds of inky locks accumulated about Ingrid's feet, and as she reverently trimmed still more away, she took special care not to tread on them. The whole operation only took twenty minutes, and at the end, using a mirror to show Corrine the back, she felt a knot form in her stomach.

The girl was happy enough with the end result, and technically speaking Ingrid's work had been textbook. One could not have asked for a finer bob than this. And yet, knowing what had dwelt on that head prior—having seen those incredible locks only minutes before, but still consenting to and actively participating in their destruction—left the stylist feeling ill.

It was precisely as Ingrid had feared, though she dared not breathe a word of her feelings to the girl. Whatever beauty or charm Corrine had possessed upon entering the building was gone now, buried somewhere in that pile of hair on the floor. The stylist would have felt guilty thinking such a thing if the transformation hadn't been so plain, so absolute. The girl had walked in an Aphrodite; she would leave little more than dowdy.

The client settled her bill and tacked on a nice tip. She thanked Ingrid for her work before starting out into the misty evening, and her thanks seemed genuine enough. Even her walk seemed to have changed as she left the salon, however—there was something childish, timid in her gait now, where before she had commanded herself with the pride of a fully grown woman. The dress and heels she wore, which had earlier struck Ingrid as pretty and stylish, seemed cartoonish now, as if Corrine were merely a girl playing dress-up with her mother's clothes.

Alone in the salon, Ingrid locked the front door to fend off any other late-comers and then stared down at the heap of lush hair scattered about the floor—the same hair that, unbeknownst to her, had accidentally found its way into her apron pocket. She had the mess swept up in minutes, but the act of dumping Corrine's leavings into the waste bin proved almost painful.

Now, staring down at the lock of hair in her palm, Ingrid couldn't even be certain that its appearance in her apron pocket had been truly "accidental". Though she couldn't recall doing it with any clarity, a hint of self-doubt bubbled up within her, and she wondered if she hadn't grabbed up a lock of the stuff for herself while cleaning up; if she hadn't kept some of the girl's hair in a misguided attempt to preserve something truly beautiful.

"So, how was work?" asked her husband from the sofa.

The walls of the living room crawled with flashes of white and blue cast by the TV. A noisy game show was on and her husband was slumped over one of the sofa armrests, beer in hand.

"It was all right," she replied, still tightly clasping the lock of hair. "Busy."

Mason grunted. "I was thinking, it's been awhile since we've had pizza. You know that place on West Moreland—the one that does the deep dish? I've had a hankering for it. Sound good to you?"

"Green peppers and onions," she said.

He sat up, stretching. "You read my mind. I'll place an order real quick."

"I need to change," replied Ingrid, starting toward the hall. "Grab a beer for me, will you?" With that, she walked back to the bedroom and put on the light. She needed to find a place to stash the lock of hair.

The last thing she wanted was for Mason to find it and tease her. To be sure, her keeping a lock of a random customer's hair was bizarre; she knew it was a strange thing to do, and that anyone stumbling upon it would be understandably weirded out. Nonetheless, she couldn't bear to throw it away. She felt like a dog burying a bone in the backyard. There was no rhyme or reason that she could articulate for this act of hoarding; she was merely driven by instinct.

Walking a circuit around the room, she looked for a good place to put it and discovered her jewelry box on the dresser. The little varnished box seemed as good a place as any, and she slipped Corrine's hair into the lower chamber, closing it carefully.

Ingrid chuckled as she changed her clothes. *Why are you so hung up on this hair? Why are you keeping it? It's kind of creepy...*

But try as she might, she couldn't rid her fingers of the pleasing sensation that'd come from playing with that hair—couldn't chase the memory of that lovely young girl from her mind. She was wracked with guilt, too, for having lopped so much of it off and wondered if she shouldn't have tried harder to talk the girl out of it. By chopping away those precious locks, Ingrid felt like she'd ruined a fine piece of art—spat on the Mona Lisa.

What's done is done, she told herself. *She liked her new haircut. And anyway, it'll grow back eventually.*

With the hair safely deposited in her jewelry box, she felt an odd sense of relief. She knew where it was and could return to it whenever she liked. The strange impulse thus indulged, she put out the light and wandered back to the living room, joining her husband on the sofa to wait for the pizza.

—w/\/—w/\/—

The combination of beer and pizza had never much agreed with her.

It was just past two in the morning when Ingrid awoke to raging heartburn and was forced to roll out of bed in search of antacids. While Mason snored away contentedly, she crept down the hall, feeling her way to the kitchen cupboard where she kept the bottle of chalky tablets. She shook a couple into her hand and munched on them in the darkness with a swig of lukewarm tap for a chaser.

Owing to the waves of acid inching up her throat her sleep had been very poor—though not so poor that she had been unable to dream. As she leaned against the counter in the darkness, tonguing the powdery antacid residue from her molars, she thought back to the moment of her awakening, tried to recall what those dreams had been like. She retrieved nothing concrete; she could only be sure that the scenes playing through her sleeping mind had been as sharp and unpleasant as her reflux.

The night proved intensely dark; the moon had nestled deeply into the clouds, rendering every window in sight with only the barest blush of moon-glow. Ingrid massaged her throat and began a sluggish return to bed, but made it only half-way across the living room before coming to a distracted halt. Something in that rich darkness warranted a closer look.

Just barely visible at the end of the hall was a shadow—thin, vague, but undoubtedly humanoid. She knew at a glance it wasn't her husband; she hadn't heard him get out of bed, and what's more, the form was too slight—too *feminine*—to be Mason's. It appeared a wan thing, head low, with hair reaching well past the shoulders. She shook her head, wiped at her eyes with the back of her arm, curious what fixture in the house could possibly cast so strange and lively a shadow as this.

She was fast convinced that this was no mere shadow, however. Blinking into the darkness and feeling weak in the knees, she saw that it was a woman, or a thing *like* a woman, with a piercing stare and a pale blur of a face.

Before Ingrid could react, before she could stagger back or rally her voice to call out to the figure, another shape entered into view, throwing her heart into a fit. This new shape barreled out of the bedroom doorway, through the hall and disappeared into the bathroom.

She allowed herself a guarded sigh. It was Mason. The subsequent flash of the vanity light proved blinding as he flipped it on and prepared to relieve himself. At the same time, the hallway, too, was suddenly wiped clean of staring shadows. Gawking dazedly from the mouth of the hall, Ingrid saw there was no one there after all—no long-haired silhouette, no silent watcher. Whatever optic effect had been responsible for the hazy apparition had been interrupted by the soft white light flowing out of the bathroom doorway.

Ingrid placed a hand to her breast, kneaded her rollicking heart. *You just about gave yourself a heart attack.* The sounds of Mason's presence in the bathroom helped plant her back in reality, reeled her in from the edge of nightmare country. Having all but forgotten the reflux that'd drawn her out of bed in the first place, she started through the hall.

She crept to the bedroom, leering from the doorway for a beat before finally easing herself inside. All was as she'd left it. Sure now that she'd been seeing things—that her tired eyes had conspired with the shadows—she returned to bed with a sheepish half-smile. The toilet flushed and the light in the bathroom went out; moments later, her husband's sloppy steps and groggy yawns drew nearer. She felt him flop back into bed beside her, where he tumbled into peaceful sleep with impressive ease.

In her heartburn-driven haste, she'd managed to kick her blankets to the floor, and finding the night somewhat chilly, Ingrid rolled to her side and reached for them. She made a sweep of the bedside, hand trawling blindly against the valance, only to encounter something unexpected. Her fingers became entangled—not in the bedspread she'd been seeking, but in something finer, softer.

She stole in a sharp gasp as she realized her fingers had become tangled in long, smooth strands of hair.

Pulling her hand free with a yelp, Ingrid sat bolt upright and frenziedly batted at the bedside lamp. The thing blinked on, illuminating her corner of the room. The lamp brought to light the fallen bedclothes, the nightstand beside her and Mason's slumbering bulk.

But as she peered tremblingly over the side of the bed, she saw no sign of the long hairs her fingers had just been trapped in, nor of the head they'd been attached to. The room was still and empty as it ever was.

Mason grumbled. "What's up?" he muttered on the back end of a yawn.

Ingrid took one last look around the room and promptly clawed up her blankets before shutting off the lamp. "Never mind, it's nothing," she said.

* * *

The next day's shift didn't start till two, which gave Ingrid time enough to sleep in and luxuriate over a large breakfast. She packed a lunch, kissed her husband goodbye and set off into the city. At the salon, she took over for Mollie and handled a smattering of walk-ins. The flow of customers was reasonably slow, and those that came in proved good tippers in high spirits.

With her shift running smoothly, Ingrid took her break around five-thirty, absconding to the office in the rear of the salon. She plucked her lunch bag from the staff fridge and leafed through a copy of the local paper someone had left on the table. Between bites of apple and sips of seltzer, she scanned the day's headlines. The front page was largely concerned with a gaffe made by a city official during a presser; page two contained a story about a long-time local grocer that was shutting its doors and a snippet about a celebrity's recent appearance at a charity golf event. The third page offered various shorter items—talk of humane society fundraisers, new art installations at the museum, and a tragic accident downtown.

Ingrid lingered on this last without quite knowing why, her gaze drawn to the grainy photo of the victim. And then, recognizing the eyes that stared back at her from that black and white picture, she nearly inhaled her apple.

The evening previous, sometime after 8:15 PM, a local resident by the name of Corrine Ellis had been struck and killed by a vehicle just outside the Keenan Building. Rushed to St. Anne's Hospital, Ellis, 19, had been pronounced dead on arrival. The perpetrator had not been caught and there were no known witnesses, though law enforcement agencies were working with nearby businesses to get ahold of surveillance footage. The photo—a senior picture, featuring the poor girl in a varsity jacket—showcased a brilliant smile set in a delicate face, both sides of which were framed in smooth curtains of jet black hair.

The stylist felt her throat tighten, her grip on the apple fail as she stared at the girl's picture. Ten, perhaps twenty minutes before the girl's death, Ingrid had played with the hair in this photo—had butchered it.

And a lock of this same hair was presently sitting in her jewelry box at home.

There was no way to be sure, but it was possible—likely, even—that Ingrid had been the last person to speak to Corrine, the last to interact with her before the accident.

Her mind was addled by shock. She skimmed the article several times as if the words—and subsequently the girl's outcome—might change, and with every pass the sickness welling in her gut threatened a mutiny. Up until that moment, she'd looked back happily upon her interactions with Corrine. Those memories were tainted now by morbidity, though, and the knowledge that she'd gone out of her way to keep a lock of the dead girl's hair made her skin crawl.

What had been behind the perverse urge to hoard some of Corrine's hair? What had incited her to do such a strange thing? Despite having worked with hundreds, perhaps thousands of clients over the years, Ingrid had never thought to do such a thing until the night before. She could not help believing her desire had been owed to some kind of foreknowledge; that, subconsciously knowing the girl was soon to die, she'd been driven to keep a lock of her hair so as to preserve her memory more concretely.

None of it mattered now. She regarded her actions of the prior evening with only horror and shame, and resolved to dispose of the hair the moment she got home. Wadding up the newspaper and tossing it into the garbage with the remainder of her lunch to keep from obsessing over it further, Ingrid paced around the office till her stomach settled and then returned to the floor. The final two hours of her shift seemed an eternity of false smiles and empty conversation.

As she trimmed and colored hair, all she could think of was Corrine.

Before she even thought to lock the front door behind her, before taking off her shoes, dropping her keys or purse on the entryway table, or changing her hair-flecked clothes, Ingrid rushed through the house, entered the bedroom and seized her jewelry box. Mason was in the shower, getting ready for work, his uniform already spread out on the bed. A night-shift security guard at a local hospital, he was set to work 11 to 7.

Sitting on the edge of the bed, Ingrid carefully opened the lid of the lacquered box and removed the upper chamber and all its contents. She then rifled through the items in the lower chamber, searching for the collection of glossy black hairs she'd deposited there the night previous.

Though she removed every last item and upended the box, she found no trace of the girl's hair inside.

One by one she examined the earrings and bracelets taken from the box. Not a single strand of hair clung to any of them. Once more she scoped out the four corners of the vessel; save for a bit of dust, it was utterly empty. The hair was nowhere to be found.

Bewildered and not a little panicked at its absence, Ingrid tried to puzzle out its whereabouts. Since placing the cluster of hairs into the box, she hadn't removed them. It stood to reason that someone else may have done so, though the only possible culprit was Mason, and in all their years of marriage she'd never known him to look at her jewelry box, much less open it.

A noxious thought occurred to her as she carefully returned her belongings to the box, and it brought with it a shrill, nervy laugh. *Maybe* she *took them. Maybe she came back for her hair.*

She struggled to remember the events of the previous evening. While her memory of finding the hair in her apron and of placing it in the box seemed firm, she couldn't help wondering if she'd misremembered the episode. Not so much as a single strand of the stuff remained in the vessel, which seemed incredible to her. *Even if someone took the hair out of here, surely they would have missed one? One or two stray hairs would have remained tangled up with my jewelry, right?* And yet, there was no sign of Corrine's hair in the box, nor any sign that it had ever been there.

Had she, in fact, brought home any of the girl's hair? Or had she imagined the whole thing? She'd been in such an odd mood the night before, pacing around her bedroom as if in a trance, seeking to hide what she'd found in her pocket. Her stomach began to churn. Something didn't seem right.

Mason ambled out of the bathroom, tugging on his undershirt. "Oh, hey, you're home. How was work?"

"Work was fine." She rose from the bed, still holding onto the jewelry box. "Hey, just out of curiosity... have you messed around with my jewelry lately?"

"Huh?" He arched a brow. "No, why? Something wrong?"

Ingrid would have liked to explain the situation to him, but such an explanation would have required her to admit she'd kept a lock of a dead client's hair. She sighed, returning the box to its perch on the dresser. "No, never mind."

Mason worked three overnight shifts a week, eight hours each, and on those nights Ingrid struggled with her solitude. She looked forward to the day—hopefully soon—that he would be able to transfer to the afternoon shift, but at present had little choice but to spend his working nights alone.

On such evenings, it was all Ingrid could do to keep busy. She'd share a late dinner with him and then tackle the dishes as he set out to work. On her own, she'd work through her Netflix queue or read a book while attempting to ignore the total stillness of the house and the deposits of shadow that deepened in every corner as midnight approached.

She knew there was nothing much to fear. They lived in a good neighborhood and always kept their doors and windows locked. The house—however large it seemed as she cowered on the sofa—was small enough that no unexpected activity in any of the rooms could escape her notice. The frights that plagued her on these nights, the creaks and odd shadows, could be explained away easily enough, or were otherwise products of her overactive imagination. She'd done this song and dance long enough to know it was so.

But this night, something was different. She'd entered into the darkness and solitude with an already unsettled mind. Recent weather patterns prevailed, leaving the night sky cluttered with clouds and their small property odiously dark. She found herself turning up the volume on the TV to almost unpleasant highs in order to shield her ears from the house's settling noises.

She'd chosen a comedy, an old favorite, and forced herself to laugh along with the gags. The chocolate-covered pretzels she'd grabbed as a snack were tasteless and hard to swallow, but in the interest of normalcy she consumed a steady stream of them. By the fifteen-minute mark, her gaze had begun to drift from the screen toward the curtained living room window. Her eyes had been drawn there by a subtle suggestion of movement just beyond the starlit pane.

The light brown curtains fluttered in the draft, and between them she caught a glimpse of something—*someone?*—outside the window. She stiffened on the edge of the sofa, tracking the folds of the drapes and holding her breath. *You're seeing things,* she thought—though she carried sufficient doubt to get up and check. With her phone locked in her fist, she rose and crossed the room, taking a narrow look from up-close. She was hardly able to part the curtains for the shaking of her hand.

For half a minute she stood at the window, peering out at the dark front yard. No survey of the hedge, no inspection of the driveway or fence, yielded anything like what she'd been expecting. The dim night had drawn a number of tiny, translucent insects to the glass, but nothing else stood out to her. Ingrid retreated from the window with a sigh. *See? You're going to pieces over nothing!*

She returned to the movie, to her munching. Gradually, the film proved absorbing enough to push her dark surroundings out of focus and she even began to chuckle in earnest at the jokes. Taking refuge beneath a blanket, she stretched out on the sofa and temporarily lost herself in the world on-screen. She ate a few more pretzels, funneled them into her mouth as she watched, finally savoring their crunch after so many indifferent helpings. The salted pretzels were coated in a generous layer of milk chocolate, and—

Ingrid paused in her chewing. Beyond the crunch her mouth registered an alien texture that made her salivate for all the wrong reasons. This latest bite had contained something extra—something that tickled the back of her throat and asserted itself unyieldingly against her teeth. She sat upright, tongue working through the mass of un-swallowed food, and quickly determined what it was.

She'd unwittingly begun munching on a strand of thick hair. Rushing to the kitchen sink, she spat out her food, only to find that the hair remained anchored around one of her molars. Retching awfully, she reached into her mouth and clawed at her teeth, struggling to grasp the slippery strand. She finally extracted it, pulling it free from between her teeth like a piece of floss.

Ingrid continued spitting into the sink for a long while, stomach roiling, and inspected the hair in the light. Nausea gave way to dread as she studied it; the strand was jet black and, to her watery eyes, *familiar*.

That this was Corrine's hair, of course, was impossible. Till she'd sat down to start her movie, the bag of pretzels had been sealed. This hair had undoubtedly come from some negligent pretzel factory worker who hadn't worn a hairnet. And yet, the shade and thickness of the hair fit her dead client's to a T. When she was sure she wouldn't vomit, Ingrid washed her hands and rinsed out her mouth. Her subsequent search of the pretzel bag yielded no other hairs, but they were dumped into the trash all the same.

Movie night was over. She was tired of pretending to enjoy herself, tired of the paranoia. Nothing much appealed to her save the blissful oblivion of a solid night's sleep, and so she began putting off the lights and marched off to bed. If she could only drift off quickly, without fixating on the day's events, she would awaken to the light of morning with her husband by her side.

Ingrid burrowed under the covers and closed her eyes, but her mind remained altogether too active to let sleep take root. Thoughts of the missing lock of hair, of Corrine's smiling face, threatened to break the surface whenever she lowered her guard and sought to relax. She couldn't help imagining the missing hairs as sentient; she pictured the mass of gorgeous strands inching out of her jewelry box and crawling up onto her bed. She pictured, too, the beautiful young client as she'd appeared in the salon, and then couldn't help wondering what she must have looked like after she'd met her end, struck dead on the street. The harder she fought to oust these morbid thoughts, the more insistent they became. Ingrid rolled this way and that, burying her face in the pillow, and hoped that her husband would come home early. It didn't happen often, but sometimes, when things were slow, his supervisors would send him home before the end of his shift.

Just forget about it. What happened to that girl is really sad, but it's none of your business. Forget about her—forget about the hair. You're making yourself anxious over nothing.

She kept to bland dismissals of this kind till she succeeded in chasing out her darker thoughts. Gradually, her mind powered down and she was allowed a brief respite.

It was still dark when Ingrid's eyes snapped open. She awoke with a start—surprised that she'd managed to drift off at all—and rolled onto her side. It had been the sound of footsteps in the hall that'd roused her, and stealing a glance at the alarm clock she saw it was nearly five in the morning.

She sank back into bed with a sigh of relief. It seemed Mason had been sent home early after all. She listened to his slow steps through the dark house, waited to hear him drop his uniform into the laundry hamper.

Her husband was always very careful not to make a ruckus upon returning home, not wanting to disturb his wife's slumber, though this morning he proved especially quiet—his steps were almost *too* slow, *too* light.

She cleared her throat and turned to the doorway, pulling down the bedclothes so as to make room for him. "Things were slow, huh?" Her eyes struggled to parse the darkness, and as she listened to the faint steps grow nearer, receiving no answer, she was plagued by a vague unease. "Mason?" she chanced, calling out more loudly.

The steps in the hall ceased at the sound of her voice, but still there was no audible reply. Sleep fled her once-heavy eyes, and with them she was better able to search the dark, finding traces now of a shadow lingering to one side of the doorway. It proved neither tall enough nor broad enough to fit her husband's profile, however. The moment she realized herself looking at a stranger across the room she very nearly fell out of bed. But then, her trembling study of the thing by the door gradually revealed itself to be anything *but* unfamiliar.

A woman was standing outside the door of her bedroom—a woman with long, black hair. From behind the impressive mane there stared ice blue eyes. Little else of the figure's face could be deduced for the profusion of ebony hair, but that she was clad in a tattered floral print dress and wearing a single kitten heel became apparent as Ingrid watched in horror. The figure was possessed of a rigid and unnatural posture, neck forward and head hinging to the right, and held her arms at her sides—though in this latter case one hung conspicuously lower than the other. This silent woman in the hall had the look of one seriously injured—of something bent badly out of shape.

Ingrid held the intruder's gaze, scarcely able to breathe, and blindly reached behind her, toward the bedside lamp. "W-What do you want?" she stammered, determined to put on the light as soon as she could locate the button.

From behind the wall of hair, those blue eyes widened and a growling voice emerged. *"I want it back."*

"What?" Ingrid's trembling hand teased the lampshade, the alarm clock.

"*I want it back,*" uttered the figure, cocking its head to a still sharper angle. "*I want it back...*"

"Are you... are you..." Before Ingrid could say the name hovering on her tongue, she located the button on the lamp and gave it such a forceful click that it fell onto its side. A jarring flash of light stole across the room, forcing the shadows into retreat and crowding her field of vision with stars. She blinked hard, gaze remaining fixed to the doorway as her eyes grappled with the brightness.

"What the—" When her vision finally stabilized, Ingrid found no sign of the figure.

She panned about the room in search of the leering phantom. Her gaze darted from corner to corner, skirted the far edge of the bed, but ultimately turned up nothing.

Still, she remained on high alert, certain that the spectral visitor loitered just out of view. "H-Hello?" she said, daring to step slowly out of the bed. Remaining very close to the lamp, she plumbed the nearest edge of the hall, looking for the long-haired silhouette.

When a minute of this surveillance brought nothing to light, she started across the room.

By small degrees, she crept to the door and dared a proper search of the hallway, finding it empty. The air along the corridor felt unnaturally chilly as she continued shuffling toward the living room, putting on the lights, almost as though the elusive figure had emanated an unearthly cold. The living room and kitchen, the laundry room and foyer, once inspected, showed no trace of the intruder, but rather than bolstering Ingrid's nerve, this absence only served to intensify her discomfort.

She was *certain* there had been someone standing outside her room, *certain* that she'd heard a faint, droning voice in the night. "*I want it back*," the figure had said.

It'd been the dead girl—Corrine—and she'd come looking for something. Something that Ingrid had taken without permission. "The hair," she muttered, kneading her brow in the kitchen. Her dead client had come looking for the lock of hair she'd accidentally brought home from the salon. There could be no other explanation, no other way to translate the specter's demand.

Just then, as she paced back into the living room, she was arrested by a furtive rustling from down the hall—a sound, it seemed to her, like a brush passing through long hair. She stiffened at the noise, had to place a hand to the wall to keep herself upright. It was issuing from the bathroom.

The slow passes of the brush continued unabated for thirty, forty seconds. Probably, if Ingrid hadn't set off down the hall to investigate, the sound might've gone on for hours, but she began a slow creep down the corridor and paused outside the bathroom door, nudging it open with a cautious tap of the foot. At the threshold, she glanced in narrowly, the brushing noise remaining an eerie constant, like a fearful metronome.

Just as her earlier glance into the hall from her bedroom had been fruitless, the bathroom proved empty, too. She hit the light switch and took in the space's narrow dimensions, finding nothing much out of place—nothing, that is, save for her own hairbrush sitting on the edge of the sink. Its presence there was strange, since she ordinarily kept it in the vanity drawer, but it was at reaching for it that she became most unsettled, for the handle was warm to the touch, as though it'd recently been clasped firmly in someone's hand. Worse still, there were several long strands of black hair—far darker than her own light brown—wound around the bristles.

She cast the brush into the waste bin in disgust and backed out of the bathroom. "Leave me alone... Please, leave me alone..." Ingrid peered up and down the hall, looking for the eerie figure but only startling herself with her own shadow. Finally, leaving all of the lights on, she retreated to the sofa and spent the remainder of the night curled up on it. It was nearly eight in the morning when Mason returned home form his shift—perhaps the longest two-and-a-half hour stretch she'd ever lived through.

Upon entering the house, Mason kicked off his shoes and began quietly into the living room, baffled to find his wife camping out with every light in the house glowing. "Hey... what's up?" He gave a weak smile. "Trouble sleeping, er... ?"

She wanted badly to tell him everything, but once again could not bring herself to admit she was seeing things, that she was haunted by visions of a young client and, perhaps most of all, that she'd been compelled to keep a lock of the girl's hair. She stumbled through a number of excuses and joined him in bed, managing a few hours of sleep at his side.

Even after she awoke in the afternoon however, she could not help feeling someone else was in the house with them. She took her corners slowly in moving from room-to-room, and kept her head on a swivel even as she showered or brushed her teeth.

Mason, inadvertently spooking her on his way out of bed, poked fun. "You're awfully jumpy. Sure everything's OK? Got a guilty conscience?"

She wished she could have told him the half of it.

—w^v—w^v—

It had been nearly a month since Ingrid and her husband had gone out for a night on the town, so when Mason suggested they dress up and grab a table at a nice restaurant, Ingrid didn't argue. Far and above the pricy cocktails and entrees, what'd really appealed to her was the prospect of fleeing the house, however briefly. Its usual coziness had been replaced by a marked inhospitality; she couldn't dwell in any corner of the place without feeling herself shadowed by an ominous presence.

Mason opted for a shirt, tie and quick shave, and was ready to go long before Ingrid had even chosen what to wear. Seeking comfort more than anything, she picked her favorite black dress and spent awhile rifling through her closet for a comfortable pair of shoes to go with it. While she would have loved to wear sneakers, she settled on a cute pair of black flats—though not before discovering something else in her small collection of shoes that gave her pause.

Mixed in with her footwear was a single shoe—a touch smaller than the rest and not immediately familiar to her. She picked it up and looked it over. It was a light brown kitten heel, a size too small for her.

Then, inhaling sharply, she dropped it.

Recently—*very* recently indeed—she'd seen this shoe.

The disheveled, shadowed thing lingering outside her bedroom the night before had worn a shoe just like this one—and only one of them, as the other had evidently been lost.

Now Ingrid knew where it had gone.

As though she were handling something truly disgusting, she picked the shoe up by its slender strap and tossed it with a grimace into the closet. *H-How did this get in here?* She truly felt she was losing her mind, and for some minutes she remained seated on the floor, rocking back and forth and gnawing on her thumbnail.

The lock of Corrine's hair had gone missing. Long, black hair had turned up in her bag of pretzels, and she'd glimpsed the specter of the dead girl outside her room in the hours before sunrise. That same apparition had left several black hairs tangled in Ingrid's own hairbrush, and had now deposited this heel in her closet.

She stood, pacing about the room. *Why is this happening? All I did was take some of her hair! Why is she following me?*

"You almost ready, babe?" asked Mason from the living room.

She snapped to attention, eyeing the black dress she'd left spread out on the bed. "Y-Yeah, just a second..." Ingrid carefully brought her flats out of the closet without even looking at the dead girl's shoe and hurriedly dressed. After nervously fussing with her hair for ten minutes—and constantly glancing at the corners of the bathroom mirror as she did so—she emerged with a serviceable bun and grabbed her purse.

You need to get out of the house. Breathe the outside air. Maybe, later, you'll be able to find the hair and put a stop to all of this—but not if you're too scared to think straight.

The couple set out to the restaurant, and she was hopeful that this dinner would provide her some much-needed relaxation.

A lovely young hostess showed them to their table—a booth beside a window, which allowed them a prime view of the bright downtown lights and of the slow flow of pedestrians milling about the streets. The drinks were generous and well-mixed, and the appetizers handsomely plated. When time came for them to order entrees, Ingrid found her steak very nicely prepared—but she was at no moment during the dinner able to enjoy herself.

Her unease had tagged along, stifling her appetite. Conversations with Mason about every topic, save the one that most needled her, left her feeling agitated, and where usually Ingrid enjoyed the ambiance of this particular restaurant, she could not help focusing on the din of the kitchen staff, or on the scraping of silverware against the plates of neighboring diners.

There was one other stressor—chief among her anxieties—which drew her attention repeatedly from the meal and conversation at hand.

All told, Ingrid and her husband sat at the table for about an hour and a half; and in that time, she witnessed a particular pedestrian walking by the window no less than a dozen times. It had been the look of this individual that'd captivated her and served a tremendous fright—for the woman, wearing her long, black hair draped over one shoulder, was garbed in a darling floral print dress and heeled in shoes whose like Ingrid had very recently found in her own closet.

The first time this individual had walked past the window at a brisk clip, she'd visibly startled, but had subsequently composed herself, certain that the resemblance to Corrine must have been merely coincidental. *Long hair isn't exactly uncommon, and I'm sure that dress probably came from some local store. There are probably many girls wearing it around town.*

Further sightings of the woman through the window eroded all doubt, however.

The raven-haired woman seemed to be walking circuits around the restaurant—always turning up when Ingrid least expected it and going by so quickly that her face remained conveniently out of sight.

She's followed me even here... thought Ingrid, wringing out her cloth napkin under the table.

Halfway into the meal, when the perennial pedestrian had made no fewer than five appearances by their window, she thought to ask Mason if he, too, had noticed her. "Have you noticed, there's some woman that keeps walking by?" She pointed through the glass, trying to single out the woman's form as it retreated into the distance. "She's come by this very window several times now. The one with long hair and a flowery dress. It's creeping me out. Did you see her?"

Mason studied the sidewalks for a time but was unfazed. "Weird. Could be that she's waiting for someone."

No, she wanted to tell him, *it's not just weird. I know who that is. She died days ago and I've been seeing her around the house every night! She won't leave me alone because I held onto a lock of her hair. I want her to go away but I have no idea what to do. The hair's missing! She said she wanted it back but I have nothing to give her! Help me think of some way to put a stop to this, please!* Instead, she remained silent, shifting uncomfortably every time the floral blur popped up in her periphery.

Sensing that Ingrid wasn't much in the mood to stick around, Mason settled the bill and the pair left the restaurant. She did so very sheepishly, standing at the entrance awhile and looking both ways to ensure she wouldn't run into Corrine. They hurried back to the parking lot and Mason held open the passenger side door for her. After she'd climbed in, he lingered outside for a bit, frowning as he studied the front fender.

"Can you believe it? Someone smacked the car."

"Huh?" she asked.

Mason climbed in and started the engine. "The fender—up there on the right side. There's a pretty big dent there. I didn't notice it when we were leaving the house. I think someone ran into the car and drove off. Didn't even leave a note!" He uttered a string of curses. "Gonna have to call the insurance company. I don't see any surveillance cameras posted out here, do you?"

She took a cursory glance of the lot and shook her head feebly. She had much more to worry about than a minor ding. Mason pulled out of the lot and sped most of the way home, complaining about the looming deductible, and she half-listened to him.

Most of the ride back was spent combing the scenery for that black-haired figure, though.

—w/\—w/\—

There was no trace of it in the dresser, the bedside table, the closet or any other nook of the bedroom. Desperate, Ingrid rummaged around in the bathroom waste bin, retrieving the tainted hairbrush she'd tossed the night before, but found only her own brown hairs clinging to it. Mason had changed out of his dress clothes and passed out on the sofa not long after they'd returned home, which was the only reason he didn't find her slumping against the toilet with her head in her hands.

The lock of hair was gone. Simply put, it had vanished. Once again, she doubted it had ever been in the jewelry box in the first place; doubted her own memory. How could she be expected to return something she'd lost herself? Why, for that matter, did Corrine insist on remaining in the world of the living over something so trivial as a lock of hair?

Ingrid mulled this over while pacing through the house. She made her way to the kitchen and yanked a bottle of rum from the cabinet, preparing to mix herself a stiff drink, puzzling all the while after the girl's persistence. Ingrid hadn't asked Corrine why she'd wanted to cut away so much of her beautiful hair; she'd merely supposed that the old hairstyle had carried with it some sort of negative association. Like so many of her previous clients, she'd assumed Corrine had asked for a drastic trim in the hopes of distancing herself from the old look and all its baggage.

Now, the girl was dead; the victim of a tragic hit-and-run. Only the hair—with its nebulous baggage—remained. Perhaps that was it. Perhaps, in keeping some of that cast-off hair, Ingrid had inherited the girl's troubles, had preserved whatever negativity Corrine had sought to free herself from. This was as good a theory as she could formulate without speaking to the apparition. But then, if the girl had come to hate her long hair in life, had opted to cleave it away, why would she come looking for it after death? It made no sense.

She pulled a glass from the cupboard and dumped a few ice cubes into it, followed by a glug of Coke and a still more generous glug of rum. As she screwed the cap back onto the bottle of booze and prepared to return it to the cabinet, a harsh squeal sounded to her back—the sound of a well-worn hinge. Realizing she hadn't fully shut one of the cabinets, she turned, only to discover that one of the lower cabinets had swung open and that a crouching figure stared at her intensely from within.

Ingrid froze as her eyes met the occupant's. From within the compartment, the figure's mane of black hair shifted to reveal a scowling maw from whence came a single demand. "*I want it back.*"

She hadn't yet sipped at her drink and already she felt herself woozy. Ingrid staggered back a few paces, meeting the counter. "I—I don't have it..." she muttered, licking her lips nervously. "I'm sorry, but I... I don't..."

"*I want it back,*" repeated the specter, extending a bone-white hand and dragging its flower-garbed body out of the cabinet. With no little effort, Corrine gained her feet and shambled across the room with wide, staring eyes and snarling lips half-obscured by the sway of her hair. "*Give it back!*" she screamed, breaking into a sudden run through the kitchen with her thin arms outstretched.

Ingrid jerked violently, shielding herself from the apparition and simultaneously losing her grip on the bottle of rum, which loudly crashed to the floor. "Leave me alone!" she begged, dropping onto her haunches and cowering by the sink. She covered her head with her arms, socks growing damp with spilt rum. The bottom of her right foot began to sting as she inadvertently stamped on a shard of the broken bottle and then stepped into the puddle of high-proof alcohol.

There she remained till Mason rushed confusedly into the kitchen. "Whoa," he said, catching sight of his wife huddled up on the floor. "You OK?" He approached her carefully, stepping past the mess, and helped her to her feet. When she winced at the effort, he lifted her gently onto the lip of the sink. "Oh, no, you stepped in it?"

She nodded, but all the while her teary eyes were scanning the kitchen in search of the ghoulish thing that had just rushed toward her.

Mason peeled off her sock and inspected the sole of her wounded foot, frowning. "OK, hold on. I don't think there's any glass in there, but lemme grab the first aid kit. Sit tight." He wandered off down the hall, tossing down a few kitchen towels on the mess as he left. When he returned shortly thereafter, inspecting the wound more closely and dressing it, he helped her down from the counter and to the bedroom. "Here, relax a minute," he said, guiding her to the edge of the bed. "I'll clean up in there."

"T-Thanks," she managed, though as he departed she felt a wave of despair crash against her heart. She didn't want to be left alone. Teetering on the edge of the bed, pawing at her bandaged sole, she felt sure the spirit was still nearby, biding its time.

She wiped the tears from her eyes and the sweat from her brow, trying to catch her breath and quiet her pulse. "Please, leave me alone," she mumbled, in case Corrine was still within earshot. "I don't know where your hair has gone. I don't have it anymore. I'm begging you—leave me be! I'm sorry I took it. I'm sorry. But I... please..."

Something lurched *beneath* her, brushing against the underside of the mattress.

Then, from the edge of bed skirt, there emerged a porcelain-colored hand studded in cerulean veins. With icy firmness the hand was locked around her ankle.

Ingrid threw herself off the bed and scampered across the floor, kicking her leg to free herself of the specter's grasp. Sobbing now, she clawed her way through the room, pressing her back to the closet door as the apparition continued emerging slowly from under the bed. The headful of gorgeous black hair burst out from behind the valance, and the crooked, disheveled body it was attached to scraped its way over the carpet, blue eyes cast hatefully upon Ingrid all the while. The tatters of Corrine's floral-print dress stained in crimson, she began to scurry like a roach toward the cowering hairstylist.

Ingrid shrank back, dug her fingers into the carpet while the specter arrived within inches of her.

"*I want it back,*" said Corrine, the ends of her long hair teasing one of Ingrid's forearms.

"I… I don't have it…" replied Ingrid, shaking. "I don't have your hair…"

"*I want it back.*"

"I told you! I don't have it!" pleaded Ingrid. With a savage cry, she reached up and took a fistful of her own hair, ripping it free from her scalp and holding it out to the spirit. "Take some of mine if you want. Just… just leave me alone!"

At this, the apparition straightened a little, raising a jagged hand and motioning to the closet door. "*I want it back,*" she repeated.

With no little confusion, Ingrid pivoted to her right, struggling with the knob and throwing open the closet door. "Y-You want something in there? Sure, b-be my guest…" she spat, curling into herself.

But Corrine did not enter the closet. Instead, she merely kept pointing into it.

It was clear that Ingrid was intended to enter the closet and seek out the spirit's desire, and she had only to turn her bleary eyes to the pile of shoes therein to deduce what Corrine was after.

Very slowly, so as not to provoke the apparition, Ingrid shifted toward the open closet and reached for something atop that heap of shoes. Just as slowly, she lifted it out—the light brown kitten heel she'd found earlier while getting dressed. "Is... is *this* what you want?" she chanced.

As Ingrid turned to offer Corrine the shoe, she was startled.

The figure before her was no longer the sinister, leering thing it had been only moments ago. Instead, Corrine—as young and beautiful as she'd been upon first entering the salon—stood before her, smiling widely. The comely specter made no move to receive the shoe, but merely said, "*Now, do you remember?*"

"Remember?" echoed Ingrid, still shaking. "Remember what?"

Corrine pointed at the heel in Ingrid's grasp. "*You took that. Do you remember?*"

Ingrid looked down at the shoe, let her trembling fingers run across the thin strap. Her fingers remembered that strap—recalled the satisfying *pop* of the buckle when removing it from someone's foot.

Studying the shoe more closely, she began to remember other things, too.

That night, after trimming Corrine's hair, she'd locked up the salon and hurried to the car, eager to beat the rain. She'd failed on that count, though, with the showers already having begun while she'd been finishing that final trim. Still wanting to get home before the weather worsened, she'd sped up along the side roads, cutting toward the Keenan Building in the hopes of bypassing downtown traffic.

She couldn't recall if she'd been toying with the radio or answering a text from Mason when she'd heard—and *felt*—it.

Ka-THUNK.

Ingrid had stomped on the brakes, nearly head butting the steering wheel. She thought she'd veered onto the sidewalk, perhaps striking a street sign or fire hydrant. Her scan of the surrounding road had showed no such damages, however—only a dark shape huddled in the street ahead.

Her heart had quaked at sighting the unmoving heap in her headlights. Hardly able to feel her legs, she'd stepped out of the car and wandered toward the body—yes, it had indeed been a body—and had been filled with a greater horror at recognizing the flower-print dress and heels it wore.

"Oh... oh, no... C-Corrine?"

The victim's cute bob had been her own handiwork. The lips that had made that charming, perfect smile were drawn back now in a silent scream. The blue of the girl's eyes had been overcome by a certain glassiness—which had only made their stare all the more piercing. The body had been terribly contorted, and oozing scrapes had been many for her rough slide across the asphalt.

"Corrine?" Ingrid had whispered, reaching out to nudge the girl's twisted leg. "Corrine... please, talk to me. Are you OK? Can you... hear me?"

There'd been no response from the girl, and that hadn't come as a surprise. From the moment she'd set eyes on the body through the windshield, Ingrid had known her dead.

Still, she'd persisted in attempting to rouse the girl, taking hold of one of her feet and giving it a little shake. "Corrine! Can you hear me?" When this, too, had failed to produce any response, Ingrid had tried again. And again. On her third try, more furious than the last, the heel had popped off the girl's foot. Stunned, and knowing Corrine beyond help, Ingrid had fallen back on her rear, still clutching the shoe. Panic had seized her.

She'd looked up and down the dark side-street, ears combing the distance for the sounds of oncoming traffic. The particular stretch she'd found herself in had proved rather quiet, however—and, what's more, as she'd studied the other buildings near the Keenan, she'd found most of them unlit and empty.

Probably, she wagered, no one had seen this terrible accident occur.

And it was just barely possible, she'd thought, that she would be able to leave the scene without attracting undue attention—but only if her exit from the narrow side-road was a fast one.

The decision had been hastily made, driven by pure self-interest.

It was an accident, she'd told herself as she'd stumbled back to the car. *I didn't mean to do it. It was an accident.* Unbeknownst to her, she'd brought the heel into the car with her. Not wishing to leave behind anything that could link her back to the scene, Ingrid had stuffed it into her apron pocket. Checking her mirrors and reversing, she'd raced down the street, turned the corner and continued on her way back home, merging into the line of downtown traffic.

Upon returning to the house, it hadn't been a lock of hair she'd admired in the laundry room, but the girl's shoe.

In a panicked frenzy, she'd gone looking for some place to hide it. *What better place to hide a tree than in the forest?* Corrine's shoe had been stashed in the one place least likely to attract attention—among her own.

That night, while changing her clothes, she hadn't been able to exorcise the sensation of the girl's hair against her fingers. She'd become obsessed with it, had been unable to think of anything else. For several minutes she had scrubbed at her nail beds in the bathroom sink, wishing to remove every last trace of Corrine from her own body. She'd made certain to wash all of her work clothes, to rinse off her shoes, lest that black hair turn up somewhere.

And then, staring at herself in the vanity mirror, she had resolved to forget the entire incident.

If only it had been that easy; if only she'd been able to forget the girl's beautiful hair. She had not, in fact, brought any of it home with her, but she had become entangled in the girl's locks all the same.

Ingrid was summoned from her thoughts by a loud banging. She startled, finding herself alone in the bedroom, seated on the floor. She still held the girl's shoe, but Corrine had disappeared from view, no longer standing before her as she had been only an instant prior. There came another bout of loud banging from deeper in the house, and at this she finally stood, shuffling out of the room and into the hall.

The walls of the living room were lit in flashing blues and reds for some kaleidoscopic display just outside the house. Mason was standing at the front door, speaking to what appeared to be several men on the porch. "B-Babe," he managed, clearing his throat and turning back to face her. "The, uh... the police are here. They want to talk to you about something... ?"

Ingrid looked down at the shoe in her hand.

Then, approaching the door, she put on an artful smile and held it firmly behind her back.

SUBTERRANE DREAM

I never much cared for the taste of tea till after the heart transplant.

The call came late one evening in early summer. My dad picked up the phone, muttering about the string of bogus robocalls he'd received earlier that day. "They keep saying my vehicle's warranty is about to expire but they can't even tell me what kind of car I drive!" He plucked the phone out of the dock and answered gruffly, "Reinhardt residence."

This, as it turned out, was no robocall. A nurse working under Dr. Patel in the surgery ward was calling with urgent news.

After more than four months of waiting, a donor had been found.

There was a lengthy pause as my father attempted to process this information. He gripped the edge of the kitchen table where only moments ago he'd been seated, playing solitaire with an old deck of cards. "You... you found him a heart?" he replied incredulously.

The nurse assured him that a suitable donor heart had indeed been found, and furthermore, that time was of the essence. "Every minute counts. The doctor wants John here right away." We needed to drop whatever it was we were doing and report to the hospital within the hour.

Wild-eyed, my dad chased me out to the garage in his sweats and slippers, and after the single most aggressive car ride I've ever taken, he got us to the valet within twenty minutes.

They rushed us to pre-op the minute we set foot in the lobby. My dad handled most of the paperwork while I was wheeled into the prep room and briefed by the doctor. "A gentleman in town, not much older than you, passed away this evening. He was listed as an organ donor and his heart seems a perfect fit. You're very fortunate, John," he told me from behind a surgical mask.

They had me sign a few things as they brought me into the suite. The ink hadn't even dried before the anesthetist introduced herself and I started feeling loopy. It all happened so fast.

When next I opened my eyes, six hours had passed and the surgery had been completed.

I awoke from it with a scar running from my sternum to my navel and someone else's ticker plugging away in my chest.

After my days in the ICU were up, I was transferred to the medical-surgical ward for a few more days of monitoring. I remember that my father had come to visit one afternoon. He was sitting in one of the uncomfortable folding chairs for visitors placed across from my bed and sipping at a bottle of iced tea he'd picked up in the hospital cafeteria.

"Hey, dad," I asked, staring at his tea with uncharacteristic intensity. "Can I have a sip of that?"

"Oh, this?" He chuckled. "You won't like it. It's tea—unsweetened. If you're thirsty I can run downstairs and grab you whatever you like. What sounds good?"

I sat up in bed, licking my lips. It was true; I'd always hated tea. Green or black, sweetened or unsweetened, I'd never cared for the stuff. Since coming to after my surgery I'd been plagued with cravings for a certain something I hadn't been able to put my finger on, though. Eyeing the bottle in my father's hand, I suddenly realized what it was I'd had a hankering for. "I'd *really* like some tea, dad."

He was visibly confused, but handed me the bottle all the same.

I drank down the entire thing in just a few gulps—guzzled it so quickly that my throat ached.

My dad laughed, throwing out the bottle when I was through with it. "That's funny, you've always hated tea." He motioned to my chest, to the edge of the scar peeking out from behind the seam of my gown. "Maybe the fella who owned that heart before you was a big tea drinker!"

I laughed along with him, unable to explain my sudden affinity for the beverage.

It was the first time, too, that it occurred to me I might've inherited something more than the donor's heart during the transplant.

At twenty-one years old, I never expected to have a heart attack—much less three of them.

But that's precisely what happened. Halfway into my third year of college, I started having strange symptoms; shortness of breath, excessive fatigue, swelling in the legs and a lingering cough. Visits to the campus health center resulted in diagnoses of dehydration and asthma, but the treatments for those ailments brought me no relief. I began to suffer from dizziness, even chest pain on some occasions, and finally collapsed in my dorm room one night while studying. My roommate dialed 9-1-1 and I was admitted to the university hospital where a cardiologist delivered some shocking news.

Despite having enjoyed twenty-one years of reasonably good health, it turned out I'd been born with a heart defect—previously undiagnosed—which had caused certain parts of the organ to atrophy over time. Had it been discovered earlier in life, a simple catheterization procedure would have patched it up nicely, but the window for that had passed and my already atrophied heart had been weakened by a series of minor heart attacks. "You have heart failure. Your heart is only working at twenty percent capacity," he told me. "At this rate—unless we manage to get you a transplant—your life expectancy is in the range of nine to twelve months."

Having received this death sentence, I was put on a number of medications meant to slow the inevitable and left school, moving back in with my dad in the suburbs. I was also placed on a transplant waiting list, but due to the length of said list and the difficulty in securing a healthy heart from a compatible donor, I was politely advised not to get my hopes up.

I have no other siblings, and my mother is some years deceased. It was just my father and I, then, sharing the three-bedroom house I'd grown up in. My dad, a former lawyer, had been enjoying his first year of retirement when his dying son had been forced back into his care. For his part, he welcomed me home warmly, doted on me with uncharacteristic enthusiasm, but I could tell that the whole episode was a massive strain on him. During the day, he would take me where I wanted to go, would spend time paling around with me as though I were a young boy again. But at night, when he thought I was asleep or otherwise occupied, the mask would slip.

I walked in on my father crying no fewer than a dozen times in those months after I returned home. Late in the night, I would sometimes glimpse him sitting on the edge of his bed, rocking back and forth as if in a trance and muttering to himself. He'd greet me in the mornings with a bright smile, fix me breakfast, but his red eyes would betray his grief and sleeplessness.

After the transplant, things got better for awhile. My father and I were both incredibly grateful and the operation had gone about as smoothly as Dr. Patel could have hoped. Thanks to recent breakthroughs, it was possible—with compliance on my part—that the transplant would continue to function for many years. Before receiving that call from the hospital, I'd been at death's door, just waiting for my time to run out. Now, with a new heart thumping in my chest, I'd been given a fresh lease on life.

My new heart didn't *feel* so different from my old one. It was hard to believe that the organ toiling away beneath the sizable scar had once belonged to someone else. I wondered where my new heart had come from, what its previous owner had been like.

And then, over the course of weeks, I began to form some idea.

I have mentioned my suddenly developing a taste for tea after my operation, and my desire for the stuff, hot and iced alike, did not abate after I returned home. I began drinking it on the regular, to the exclusion of the sodas and juices I'd once preferred. This change in palate proved quite entertaining to both my father and I, though the other changes I began to notice in myself were somewhat less amusing.

Prior to the transplant, those acquainted with me would have been inclined to describe my personality in the blandest terms. "Quiet", "Pleasant", "Non-confrontational" or "Shy" could have summed up my usual demeanor, but after the surgery something changed. Most of the time, my mood and personality remained very much in the realm of good-natured timidity, but would on occasion veer violently off-course into something alien to me. Now and then, for seemingly no reason, I would be given over to bouts of incredible anger. My humor, ordinarily tame, would become crass and sardonic. I, who had never once uttered an unkind word toward my father, found myself at times chewing him out without the least inkling as to why. Dad was kind enough to take it in stride, but these uncharitable outbursts invariably left me shaken, as though my brain had been hijacked by some outside force.

Another change, somewhat harder to explain or quantify, had to do with my dreams and memories. Before the operation, I had never known my dreams to be particularly vivid, but *after* it I was host to dreams of almost unbelievable depth and color on a nightly basis. These dreams had a way of lingering in my head long after my awakening, and roused in me what seemed like long-buried memories.

Certain dream-borne sights and sounds would trigger grainy snippets of memory, would remind me of events I could not remember having lived through but nevertheless retained knowledge of. Forced to suppose a cause for these foreign imaginings, I decided that the stranger's heart I now bore was behind it; that its cells retained something of the donor's life and memories, and that these stored fragments could not but seem unique and incredible when loosed upon my own staid consciousness.

The dreams were always centered around the same scenery. Dense woods painted in the colors of night served as my backdrop. Through the close-knit trunks I would catch shafts of moonlight, and in them would be highlighted the gnarled planks of an ancient, tottering cabin nestled between rocky hills. The cabin's lone window would sometimes flutter with shadows as something within stirred subtly. I felt quite sure I had never seen this place in waking life; yet, as I dreamt of it, I was always convinced that, in fact, I knew it *very* well—knew it with the intimacy of someone who'd been there in-person.

The weeks after the surgery were spent in reading, and I happened upon anecdotal accounts which seemed to hint at the manifestation of such symptoms in other transplant patients. Here, a kidney recipient and long-time vegetarian found herself craving the award-winning smoked brisket that her donor, a Southern restauranteur, was known for. In another case, a man with a newly transplanted liver found himself a virtuoso pianist where before his operation he had never once touched a piano. He was later amazed to discover that his donor had been a promising young music student.

All of this drove me to wonder whose heart I now possessed. Were these odd mood swings, these dreams and memories in my head, someone else's? Had I inherited someone's taste for iced tea or merely changed my mind about the long-maligned beverage?

I decided, during my first post-operative exam, to ask Dr. Patel where my heart had come from, and after sitting in the lobby with my father for ages, I was called back to the examination room, where I was weighed and assessed by the nurse. The doctor dropped in some ten minutes later, shaking my hand and getting right to it. He listened to my heart, studied my scar, and was thorough in his questions.

Finally, having run through most of the routine, Dr. Patel draped the stethoscope around his neck and took a few notes. "Looking excellent," he said, grinning. "How are you feeling these days, John?"

"Fine," I replied. "The incision was sore for a bit there but it's finally healed."

The doctor had me lift up my shirt and took another glance at his handiwork, nodding firmly. "Yes, it's looking very nice. Give it another month or two. The color will fade slightly." He referenced his notes and rose from his stool. "Blood pressure is normal, pulse is fine. Everything looks and sounds good. Any questions? Concerns? I don't suppose you've had any shortness of breath or fainting spells, have you?"

"No, I'm all good on that front," I said. "Honestly, except for the scar and the meds every morning, I don't feel so different. It's strange to think that someone else's heart is beating away in there." I chuckled, then raised the question that had been on my mind for some time. "Doctor, I was wondering... is there any possibility of my finding out who this heart belonged to? Who the donor was?"

Dr. Patel glanced up from his paperwork, tucking his pen back into the breast pocket of his lab coat. "You want to know who the donor was?"

I nodded.

"I'm not sure I'll be able to give you that information," he admitted with a pained smile. "I don't know where the organs come from, I just install 'em! And anyway, that sort of thing is almost always kept under wraps. There are systems in place to connect you with your donor's family—but, as you can rightly imagine, this sort of thing is sensitive. That family had to suffer a great loss in order for you to receive this heart, so the organizations in charge of harvesting donor organs prefer to protect the privacy of those involved. It's possible that the donor's family opted not to remain anonymous, in which case you may well be able to reach out. I can put you in touch with the organization, if you'd like."

I was more than a little disappointed to hear about all this red tape. "I had no idea," I said. "I'd been hoping you'd be able to tell me more about the donor—what they were like, what they enjoyed." I chuckled again, more to allay my discomfort than anything, and added, "You know, since the transplant, I've noticed something weird."

"Weird?" asked the doctor, arching a brow.

"I've had, uh... some strange cravings. Before the transplant, I hated the taste of tea, but now it's all I want to drink. My dad joked that maybe the donor was a tea fanatic and I inherited his love of tea along with his heart."

Dr. Patel cut me off with a laugh. "Is that right? Well, don't overdo the tea! I don't want you wearing out this ticker with all of that caffeine!"

He made a few more notes, and as I sat there, I couldn't help rambling on. "Is that... is that possible, doctor? To have someone else's likes and dislikes transfer over to you after a transplant? Or what about their memories? I've read some things online, stories of people getting transplants and finding themselves with skills they didn't have before, stuff like that."

At this, the doctor shook his head. "Many people have written about things of that kind—the transference of cellular memory, etcetera. I don't buy it. No serious study has ever shown evidence that such a phenomenon exists." He continued, leaning against the examination table, "Your newfound taste for tea could have everything to do with your age. As you get older, your taste buds change. You acquire new tastes for things and sometimes swear off flavors you once enjoyed. A few years ago that happened with me and soda. I loved it as a kid, but I can't drink the stuff anymore—too sweet."

I was sent on my way with a clean bill of health. Dr. Patel planned to see me again at the three-month mark and advised me to ask the secretary outside for the donor organization's number, which I did on my way out. Upon returning home, I immediately placed a call and was connected to a clerk willing to take down my information and dig into my case.

To my surprise and delight, my heart donor's family had not opted for anonymity. "Sometimes, when a family wants to reach out to the recipients of their loved ones' organs, they'll do this," the clerk explained. "I can give you the donor's name, hometown and the phone number provided by their family. Any conversations or face-to-face meetings would have to be mediated between you and the bereaved, of course."

I learned then that my heart had belonged to one Lucien Grappeli, twenty-seven years old. He hadn't lived too far from me—only about thirty miles away, in a rural area near the mountains. I was given a phone number—his mother's, I was told—and a cause of death.

I was not prepared for the unease I would experience at being given this latter piece of information, however. "Cause of death is listed as suicide," the clerk told me with practiced apathy.

"I see. T-Thank you," I replied, and I hastily jotted down the details. Any further connection with my donor's family was up to me now, and I first turned to the web, wondering if Lucien hadn't left behind social media profiles or other digital relics I might mine for additional info. I was intensely interested in who he'd been, what he'd been like, but once again I was unprepared for what I found when I typed his name into a search engine.

The first hit—the only one I really needed—was a news article from a State paper, and what it reported was so incredible to me that I doubted the search results. I felt certain I must have mistyped his name and even went back to double check. Surely the heart in my chest hadn't belonged to the infamous character described in this article? The more I read however, the surer I became that no such mixup had occurred; the man named in the story and the one who'd provided me with a working heart were one and the same, and as this fact dawned on me I was overcome with nausea.

The day of my transplant—less than eight hours before it, in fact—twenty-seven-year-old Lucien Grapelli had committed suicide. Surrounded by police, who sought to apprehend him in connection with a kidnapping case, Lucien had shot himself in the head with a pistol. In what had surely been a freak occurrence, the bullet had passed through his brain but had somehow missed the most vital areas, resulting in critical injury but *not* immediate death. In fact, he was rushed to the same hospital where I had been an inpatient and put on life support. With no hopes of resuscitation, Lucien, an organ donor, had been kept alive till his organs could be harvested.

His heart, mere hours after the incident, had been placed in *my* chest.

I had to step away from my computer while attempting to process this new information. My emotions ran the gamut as I paced nervously around the room, bile rising in my throat. Most uncomfortable was the way the perpetrator's heart quickened in my chest as I read this account of its former owner's demise. Someone in need of a life-saving transplant as I had been could not exactly be picky about where their new organs came from, and yet I could not help but loathe the foreign tissue thumping behind my sternum, could not but associate it with the evils perpetrated by the one who'd kept it warm for me these past twenty-seven years.

Reading on, I found that Lucien had been suspected of kidnapping a local child, a six-year-old boy, and that he still hadn't been found. There was mention of Lucien's alleged association with a strange group—a regional cult, it was written—implicated in the disappearances of children throughout the area going back several generations. The mountainous county where the cult was thought to reside had seen an unnatural amount of missing children year after year. Cases of vanished children were more far more numerous in this rural area than in any of the more densely populated settlements adjacent. The article ended with a plea for anyone with information about the missing child, Elliot Davies, to reach out to authorities.

All desire to learn more about my donor faded away just then. I no longer wished to reach out to his family, to find out more about his likes and dislikes. I powered down the computer, making certain to scrub my search history first, and didn't breathe a word about my findings to my father.

Although I had gotten my fill of Mr. Lucien Grapelli, it seemed *he* had not yet finished with *me.*

No matter its presumed association with my infamous donor, I continued to enjoy tea on a daily basis, and my moods would at times veer toward the vicious and chaotic—shifts I could not help but attribute to vestiges of criminality still present in my new organ. I did my best to put everything I'd learned about the man out of mind and to focus strictly on the good. It was true that Lucien had been a seedy character, but his loss had been my gain. As heir to his heart, I would use it as long as I could to live out a just and righteous life.

However effective this selective focus may have proven in waking life, I was at the donor's mercy when I slept. My dreams only grew more vivid, the scenery better-defined, and I felt drawn to the dark, forested set pieces that haunted my sleeping mind, and to the ramshackle cabin couched between stony hills. Each night, I would pass soundlessly through these settings, drinking in the detail, and would awaken at the moment the cabin's solitary window would begin to flutter with a mass of shadow.

Those shadows, I became gradually convinced, were cast by a fretful occupant—someone straining to remain out of view.

And I began to feel I knew precisely who it was.

Though Dr. Patel had dismissed all talk of cellular transference where memories were concerned, my own experiences left me doubting his professional opinion. He was a kind and learned man, but even his years of schooling could not clue him in to *all* of life's mysteries, and my limited reading online about similar phenomena brought to light other physicians—with admittedly questionable credentials—whose arguments in favor of such inheritances were not a little persuasive.

Taking into account the strange changes to my palate and demeanor, along with the insistent scenery of my dreams, I began to entertain the possibility that Lucien Grapelli—through whatever remained of his consciousness in my second-hand heart—was attempting to influence me. I could not say with certainty to what end this influence was aimed, but the odd dreams, in particular, with their recurrent alpine settings and visual motifs, gave me the impression that he intended to clue me into something—to share knowledge he had not publicly divulged in life.

One night, at the tail-end of my dream, when I stood outside the window of the cabin, disembodied, and peered inside, the shifting shadows yielded what looked to be the form of a cowering boy some six or seven years of age.

I awoke, certain that my donor was attempting to tell me where Elliot—the boy he'd been suspected of kidnapping—was kept.

It was no small feat to leave the house without my father. When I expressed a desire to go out, citing a nebulous intention to "run errands", he insisted on tagging along. Through gentle refusals, I ultimately dissuaded him. It had been more than a month since the operation and the doctor, while advising me to take things easy, had not forbidden me from going out. "You took your meds, right? Have your phone? And don't you go for a run or anything stupid! If you overdo it you could really hurt yourself," he nagged. I plucked the keys from the kitchen counter and assured him I'd be careful.

I set out for rural Logan County, the mountain-peppered region where Lucien had lived, in the hopes of meeting his mother, Constance. I had used the phone number given me by the transplant organization not to arrange a meeting with her, but to suss out her full name and address. A web search of the phone number, coupled with the surname "Grapelli" had produced that name, along with the street and house number in Logan County I presently sought.

I was sure that the lonely cabin glimpsed in my dreams was a real place. Many degraded ruins of that kind were likely to exist in the remotest corners of Logan County's densely forested borders, but only one of them might contain the missing boy I hoped to rescue. It stood to reason that this twilit scene in the hills persisted in memory at Lucien's insistence, and that certain others, most probably those close to him, would be familiar with it as well. Authorities had combed the area surrounding Lucien's home but had found no trace of young Elliot, and the locals thereabouts, a close-knit and tight-lipped group, had offered no assistance. I felt somehow sure that the boy, if he still lived, was stuck inside that crumbling cabin. I could not be completely certain, of course, but until I had seen and explored the ruin myself I would not be able to quiet the urgings of my conscience—urgings, I felt strongly, which were informed by my donor's inside knowledge on the matter.

I wanted to ask Constance about her late son—to learn of his likes and dislikes, his temperament—and to describe to her the persistent dream scenery I had routinely begun inhabiting in my sleep since inheriting Lucien's heart. It was possible this visit of mine was ill-advised; that I was being naive, for there was no telling what this woman might be like. Whether she would react kindly to my unannounced presence on her doorstep, or whether she herself shared her son's associations with the infamous sect known to operate in the region, remained to be seen.

My drive through that mountainous country took closer to fifty minutes than it did thirty, but after some wrong turns down winding mountain roads I did eventually run across the slender dead-end avenue which brought me to the residence of Constance Grapelli. It was a quaint if rundown little house some miles from its closest neighbor and stationed within a copse of pines. I slowed as I approached it, finding no driveway to speak of, and was forced to park on the side of the road—the terminal end of which had been reduced to rubble. Two narrow windows parked to the left and right extremities of the facade were hung in tightly drawn off-white curtains, giving them the look of heavy-lidded eyes, and from the one on the left I sensed a hint of movement. At the sound of my car door slamming shut a small, pale face emerged from between the curtains, leering out at me from within the gloom-soaked panes.

I was struck at the density of the silence that reigned. I had been a fool to think that I could ever sneak up on a house as remote as this one—a house so removed from the city and all its noise. The hum of an engine, the closing of a door, were rare and aberrant sounds in this place and would not escape the ears of any dwellers in the house. I dared a sheepish wave at the figure in the window and was startled as it promptly departed, leaving the curtains aflutter. By the time I had started up the gravel walkway leading to the front door, the pale occupant was already on her way out to meet me.

A silver-haired woman in a black dress crept soundlessly out the front door and approached with a wide, knowing smile and outstretched arms before I could even muster an introduction. She seized me, frail hands taking hold of my shoulders and yellowish eyes boring into mine with what I could only describe as familiarity. I couldn't help breaking away from her and stepped back, unnerved. Then, rummaging up a polite smile, I asked, "Is this the Grapelli residence?"

I knew the answer to that question before the woman even nodded, before her diabolical grin widened, before she reached out and took my hands in hers, and said, "I was wondering when you might turn up." She had a very rich and pleasing voice; there was something youthful about it that did not mesh nicely with her apparent age. "Come," she said, urging me closer, and at the pull of her thin arms I acquiesced, till she stood on tip-toe, with her left ear gingerly pressed to my chest. There, for almost a minute, she stood and listened to the beating of my heart—*her son's heart*—and at odd intervals she would chuckle as though it were telling her jokes.

This forwardness had taken me completely off-guard, and I admit that I stood there awkwardly until she had gotten her fill of the sound. The woman's seeming possessiveness over my heart was not so difficult to understand, seeing as she herself had birthed its donor, and I tolerated her till finally she drew away and motioned to the door of the little house. "I'm sorry I didn't call first," I began as I fell into step behind her.

My arriving unannounced was apparently not inconvenient for her, as she ignored my words completely and instead led me past the screen door and into a grimy, cluttered kitchen some little ways into the abode. I was then steered into a chair at her table. "I just made some fresh tea," she announced, and she poured me a tall, frosty glass without invitation. It appeared she already knew who I was—understood, to some degree, the purpose of my visit. Still, I introduced myself formally, offered my condolences on the passing of her son, and mentioned, too, my intense gratitude for the transplant. She accepted my words with a mischievous, preoccupied look that left me doubting whether she'd heard them at all.

The offered beverage was not offensive; in fact, despite the grunginess of the glass in which it had been given me, I found it delicious after a tentative first sip. A wedge of lemon had been buried beneath the heap of ice in my glass, lending it a pleasant tartness. As I sucked down a generous mouthful, Constance was quick to top me off. I thanked her for her hospitality, adding, "It's funny, before the transplant I never cared for tea. Was your son a big tea drinker?"

The woman did not reply, as though the answer to that was plain. Instead, she buried an elbow against the table and propped up her small chin in the palm of her hand, staring into my eyes. She laughed to herself, apparently amused by what she'd found there, and then asked me a question of her own. "What has he told you?"

"Excuse me?" I asked—not certain that I'd understood her correctly.

She extended a vein-ridden hand, nudged my sternum playfully. "What has he told you?" she asked again with an unsettling twinkle in her jaundiced eyes.

It was a strange question to ask—and it proved all the stranger because I had been drawn to this out-of-the-way home precisely because Lucien had been communicating with me. The fact that she already seemed aware of this raised a tremendous red flag. I chose to play the fool, shaking my head. "I'm sorry, I don't understand. What has *who* told me?"

For the first time, Constance stopped smiling. Her expression contorted into something hateful and ragged, and her voice—pleasing to the ear only moments ago—followed suit. "Hasn't he spoken to you yet?" She sat upright, locked eyes with me again and attempted a strange sort of interrogation. What followed was a series of words—their meanings then unclear to me—obviously intended to provoke some unknown reaction. "The debt to the *Depth-Walker* must be paid. *He Who Dwells in the Hollows*"—and here, she made a very odd sign with her left hand—"hungers still. The pact must be honored, and this season the duty is yours. Would you betray *him*? Betray *us*? No—you will pay the debt, I know it, just as soon as the boy is recovered." At this last, I betrayed myself by a not inconspicuous widening of the eyes, and the woman—practically climbing onto the table and taking my hands in hers—pleaded. "Where is he? Tell me—where is he?"

I knew then who she was referring to—and that my visit to this house had been a grave error.

"I'm sorry," I said, pulling away from her, "I'm afraid I don't follow. Who is it you're looking for?" Though I knew full well that she was talking about young Elliot, I dared not discuss my theories on his whereabouts. Constance had revealed herself as a cog in the cult's machinery, same as her son had been, and I could not bear the thought of giving her even the slightest clue as to the boy's potential location. The language she'd used in her curious soliloquy had filled me with dread. The missing boy had been abducted for a dark purpose, was the intended payment for some sinister debt.

Constance settled back down into her chair, cutting into me with hostile eyes. Once, twice she appeared on the verge of speaking, of continuing her questions, but my feigned ignorance apparently had the desired effect and she disengaged, rising from the table and disappearing into the depths of the dim house.

I took this as my cue to leave. No good would come from my lingering. Every moment spent here would only increase the likelihood of my mentioning something about the dream scenery and potentially betraying poor Elliot's whereabouts to someone bent on snatching him up. I made my way quickly out of the house, jogging to the car despite my father's warnings not to tax my heart, and once behind the wheel made a tight turn, gunning it toward the highway.

Lucien had died without divulging Elliot's location. His reasons for kidnapping the child remained murky, but that he'd done the deed with a nefarious end in mind had never been in doubt. The knowledge that the cult was still seeking the boy told me I had precious little time to secure him. And to think I'd nearly hand-delivered him to the villains myself!

I pledged to find the setting of my recurring dreams as soon as possible, and hoped to recover the boy before harm came upon him. I still had no leads to go off of, however. The one person I could have relied on to identify the rickety cabin I'd glimpsed in the throes of sleep was not to be trusted, lest the boy wind up as some token in a dark transaction.

Constance had mentioned someone in her ramblings, referring to them only as "*He Who Dwells in the Hollows.*" Subsequent reflections on this epithet kickstarted my heart without fail; though it meant nothing to *me*, it seemed almost as though that title had held no little significance to my donor.

—wʌ—wʌ—

The dreams did not cease; in fact, that very night after my return from the country, they assailed my sleeping mind with an almost unbearable intensity.

The vividness of my dreams was such that I could smell the pine-scented air of the scene, could feel the gritty trunks of the trees. The experience was so immersive that when I awoke, covered in a cold sweat, I expected my surroundings to match the dream's contents, and was subsequently confused to find myself in bed. Waking as I did with the smells and sensations of the brush upon me, I would have labeled the experience as anything but a mere dream.

I went about my day nervously, unsure of how best to proceed. The boy, if he still lived, was being actively pursued by the cult, and the odds of them stumbling upon him before law enforcement did seemed likelier with every passing day. Reaching out to the authorities and informing them of my dream-borne suspicions did occur to me, though I knew the odds of such notions being accepted were low, and that I stood only to be mocked, considered delusional, by coming forward.

The job of seeking out young Elliot was mine and mine alone. I needed only a straightforward lead, some thread that would tether the scenery of my hyper-detailed dreams to reality.

That thread finally appeared on the following night.

Nursing tumultuous thoughts, I sank into bed just after sundown the next evening, feeling utterly drained and hopeless. No sooner had I slipped into the arms of Morpheus was I cajoled back into the nighted forest scenery, the dense pine wood, and faced with the facade of the lonesome cabin. But there was, in this instance, a new development—a new feature superadded to these now familiar surroundings which I clung to and committed to memory.

I was made aware of a meandering footpath leading away from the cabin. It wound through the woods, between the sparser growths, and its sandy soil seemed almost to glisten in the light of the moon. My sleeping mind probed the length of this starlit path, strolling through hills and past ravines, till it terminated upon the shoulder of a two-lane highway. In the instant before I awoke, I looked across the empty lanes, followed the yellow lines a little ways, and glanced at the green mile marker planted some ten or twenty yards from the edge of the forest path.

The marker read "29".

I awoke with a terrible jerk, covered once again in a cold sweat that left my clothing matted to my body. "Twenty-nine," I muttered before even wakefulness had fully stolen over me. "Twenty-nine." I rose from my bed, staggered across the room, and in searching my desk for a pen managed to topple a stack of books I'd left atop it. Unable to find a slip of paper, I clumsily removed the cap of a permanent marker and scrawled "Mile 29" in large, nigh-illegible characters directly onto the wooden tabletop.

Still clutching the marker and panting, I fully awoke some moments later and hurriedly switched on my work lamp, re-reading the scrawl and chasing the retreating details of my dream with all the effort I could muster.

I had, on my way to the Grapelli house, driven past this mile marker. I could not be certain, but I believed that the path I'd glimpsed in my dream was located some ten or fifteen miles from Lucien's home—effectively in the middle of nowhere, in an area where the forest growth and the gradient of the surrounding land began to increase.

The only way to know for certain whether this path existed—whether it would lead me to the mysterious cabin and, subsequently, to the boy—was to go there and seek it out. I glanced at my phone; it was just past two in the morning. This was an ideal time, where the reality would align perfectly with the starlit scenery of my dream.

I quickly changed my clothes and snuck out of my room, careful not to awaken my father. Quietly taking the car keys, I slipped out of the house and made my way to the car.

Both hands on the wheel, I sped through the empty streets toward the highway entrance ramp.

I was thirty-odd minutes in finding mile marker 29.

Racing down the highway at a clip far removed from the posted limit, I nearly missed the little green marker planted just feet from the gravel shoulder. Upon sighting it, I hit the brakes and pulled off the road, leaving the car half-sitting in the grass. In my speedy approach I hadn't seen any sign of the footpath, but wandering a little ways from the car I noticed a meager break in the trees, and—when the clouds shifted sufficiently to expose the moon—the narrow stretch of sandy soil meandering through the pines became evident.

It was real; the path existed. I shuddered violently at its discovery. I had long suspected my dreams to possess something of truth, but to see with open eyes the exact scenery I had—just an hour prior—known only from dreams, chilled me to my core.

I wasted no time in alighting down the path. In my haste to leave the house undetected, I'd brought nothing with me but my keys and cell phone. Thankfully, the moon was bright enough to light the way, and I was able to see the trail without much difficulty even as I left the highway behind and was surrounded by dense forest. Actually walking the path was another matter, however, for the rise and fall of the trail in keeping with the swell of the terrain taxed me awfully. I tried to control my breathing, to slow down when my heart rate grew too rapid, but the strain was not negligible, and by the time I'd passed into the denser regions of the woods and snaked between several rocky outcroppings, I felt dazed.

I am no seasoned hiker, little used to exploring the great outdoors, but the dearth of animal noise as I trudged down the path was profoundly unsettling to me. Owls and other nocturnal birds, if they existed in this area at all, made no sounds whatsoever. I heard neither the howls of distant coyotes nor the buzzing of mosquitos. There was only taut silence here, punctuated by the sounds of my lagging effort.

My surroundings in that hour of rough hiking were so indistinguishable from the dreamscape I had earlier occupied that I doubted myself fully awake. The trunks of certain trees, the crisp, rural air, called to mind visions I had experienced on a nightly basis since the transplant, and I found this setting a perfect facsimile of those memories my donor had thrust upon me. That Lucien had walked this path many times, that he had been intimately familiar with the area, was a certainty.

And then came the moment I had been waiting for; the moment when, panting, dizzy and dripping with perspiration, I reached the end of the path and happened upon the leaning borders of that crumbling cabin so often glimpsed beyond the border of sleep. It was—as it had been in my dreams—couched between two stony hills, and in such a state of decrepitude it was no small wonder it remained standing. The sagging of its ancient roof, the disintegration of its warped exterior, was shocking to behold—and yet it persisted with an almost charming stubbornness.

I began for the little structure slowly, giving my heart a much-needed break and sucking down great lungfuls of the cool night air. As I had done so many times in my dreams, I approached the cabin's lone window—open and glassless—and peered inside. With the help of the bright moon overhead, I was able to see much.

In large part the floorboards had been scattered pell-mell throughout the structure, exposing the sub-flooring of packed earth beneath. In one spot where the flooring remained in place, I spied a crouching, silent form very near the wall opposite the window. Squatting beside an impressive mound of snack wrappers and assorted bones was a child of approximately seven years, with tousled blonde hair and ruddy cheeks. He was dressed in filthy rags and watched me with wide eyes as I came toward the window.

I didn't even have a chance to call out to him before he stood and walked to the window to meet me. "Is it time?" asked young Elliot, face gaunt and limbs stick-thin.

The boy was not afraid of me. For that matter, he did not seem particularly happy to see me, either. By his tone and manner, I could not help but get the impression he'd been expecting me—that my presence here had been long-foreseen. Somehow, he had survived over a month in this remote cabin, feeding on convenience foods and whatever animals he'd been able to trap. This was quite the marvel; but perhaps more incredible was the way he seemed in no rush to leave, the way he had seemingly chosen to remain here despite the existence of a conspicuous path mere feet from the cabin. A boy of his years surely had the capacity to keep to a trail of that kind, to seek rescue, but he had not done so, choosing instead to stay.

"My name is John," I told him. "I'm here to help."

The boy exited the cabin, but as he looked up at me in the moonlight there was something strange in his gaze. He appeared confused. "It's not time yet?"

"Time for *what?*" I chanced.

Elliot said nothing more. When I offered my hand, he took it without protest and I began leading him toward the path. "You've been out here for a long time now. Are you feeling OK?"

He only nodded.

I took out my phone and tried placing a 9-1-1 call, but couldn't get a signal. As we walked, I continued to press him, trying to figure out why Lucien had abducted him in the first place, but I was only more and more unnerved at his sedateness. "About a month ago, a man brought you out here, didn't he? Did he tell you why he was doing it?"

Elliot didn't respond at once, but instead looked up at the night sky through the breaks in the trees. Finally, he said, "He planned to take me for a walk in the woods. But he kept saying the time wasn't right yet—so he brought me food to eat and told me to wait. So, I did." There was something airy and distant about the boy's tone as he spoke. He sounded as though he was dreaming.

"He was going to take you for a walk in the woods?"

"Yes, but the last time he came, he said it wasn't time for that," he added.

The boy seemed too calm, too composed for someone who'd been abducted and forced to survive in the wilderness for a month. I wondered if he hadn't been drugged or hypnotized, or if the stress of the situation had broken him.

"So, he brought you here and told you to stay put in that cabin?" I asked.

He nodded again.

"And you didn't try to leave? You... you listened to him? People have been worried about you, Elliot. They've been searching for you everywhere."

The boy considered this briefly, then said, "The man said it was important."

"What did he plan to do with you in the woods?" I chanced, looking down at my phone again. This time, I managed a slight reception. I held the phone aloft, hoping the signal might improve, and then made my call.

Elliot tailed me by a few feet as we neared the highway. "He was going to take me to meet someone very special," he said—but he did not elaborate.

I explained the situation to the dispatcher. "Mile marker 29," I repeated. "He was in an old, tiny cabin about an hour's walk from the highway."

By the time we emerged from the woods, I could hear the sirens.

My involvement with the boy ended there. He was returned to his parents after a stint in the hospital and, to the best of my knowledge, suffered no lasting physical problems on account of his time in the woods. Whether his aberrant mental state ever cleared, or why he did not attempt the short hike to the highway on his own and seek rescue, I have not been told.

I was celebrated for finding the boy. I was interviewed by the local media, thanked by the governor and Elliot's family. If you search my name on the internet you will find me now among those famous transplant patients who, like the liver-recipient-turned-concert-pianist, retained something of their donor's memories or sensibilities. I have little doubt that my recovering the boy, driven solely by the memories that'd hitched a ride in Lucien's heart, will soon become the stuff of urban legends.

Would that my story ended there—that I had nothing more to tell.

But in the days and weeks after the rescue, I found myself still a slave to alien dreams, an explorer of remote and terrifying scenery. My dreams were no longer concerned with the cabin, but with other, more sinister things.

It could not have been more than a week or so after my recovery of the boy when I suffered the most hideous and convincing nightmare I had ever experienced in my twenty-one years. The general scenery was not unlike those recurrent dreams I have earlier described, which led me to the cabin and its kidnapped tenant. I was surrounded in this dream by towering pines which sprang to such great heights they seemed to rake the misty clouds from the sky. There was moonlight, but a good deal less of it than I should have liked, so that all my travels through this dream-land were mediated by touch more than any other sense.

As though blindfolded I staggered through the wilds, cognizant only of my own rustlings through the brush, all other sound eclipsed by the timpani-like thumping of my racing heart. I climbed great hills and descended into low stone-choked valleys whose depths had been carved out by the progress of glaciers when the continent was still young. The cold disagreed with my air-thirsty lungs, making it harder for me to regain my breath for the relentless exertion.

It is said that dreams are, in waking reality, very brief things—neurological impulses lasting only some few seconds—but my wanderings through the wooded hills felt to me an entire season, a succession of cold, lonely and silent nights with no days inserted between. This long trek brought me finally to what the moonlight revealed as a yawning crevasse in the stony ground—an aperture of enormous dimensions whose rim was clotted over with detritus and ringed in natural formations of rock. I have since learned the proper name for such an opening; geologists call them "cenotes".

Staring down into this abyss and scanning its furthest reaches with the aid of the waxing moon, I found it floored in what, at first glance, appeared to be smooth stones. Further study in the pale light brought forth a marked yellowing in a great many of them, and I then understood that the floor of the pit was filled not with rocks, but with bones. *Human bones.*

No sooner had I made this discovery did I become aware of movement from within the pit. Some enormous thing—bigger than any man I have ever seen—lumbered out from one of the dark recesses and turned to face me with burning red eyes. Its body was black, seemed coated in coarse fur or ragged plumage—or *both*. My view of its face was mercifully limited, but as best I could tell it had no proper face to speak of—merely a bare skull. From twenty, perhaps thirty feet down, it set its eyes on me, and I could feel them boring into mine as though they were hot coals. A commanding voice oozed from the abomination's calcified maw—a voice so profoundly deep that I felt it more than heard it.

I had come all this way, covered all this ground, only to hear the monstrosity utter this:

"*The debt... must be paid. Bring me... another...*"

Here, the dream ended.

At least, for *that* night.

Visions of this untamed land, of this miserable horror dwelling in the shadowed depths, became a nightly occurrence—and with each passing night its burning gaze became more horrible to behold, and I was forced to look upon still more of its terrible countenance. Its face was indeed a mask of pure bone, though not entirely in keeping with the shape of a human skull, and it wore for a crown several antlers and wing segments. Fur and feathers coated its dense body and its feet were cloven hooves.

Night after night, I awoke in tears, hardly able to rein in the thundering of my heart. When I had suffered these visions for ten days straight, I broke down and begged to see Dr. Patel, who upon hearing of my troubles referred me to a psychologist colleague of his. The specialist listened to me recount my dreams with patience, but his evaluation was ultimately dismissive. I was given a prescription for a powerful sleep aid, his theory being that my mind was not properly cycling through every phase of sleep. This diagnosis was questionable at best, but in my desperation I picked up the pills at the pharmacy and followed the directions on the bottle.

The dreams did not stop—were not interrupted in the least—but the usage of the medication did provoke new, more troubling symptoms. I began, while on the sleep aid, to wander out of bed in the night. I had never been a sleepwalker, nor a particularly graceful person, but while on the medication I proved both, on three occasions slipping out of the house undetected and wandering the streets till morning. In each instance I awoke with no knowledge of what I'd been up to all night, further and further from my home, and was forced every time to call my father to pick me up. The psychologist, concerned by this development, put me on a lower dosage, but had no other recommendations.

The monstrous thing sought to enlist me. "*The debt must be paid.*" That was what it told me every night, and I realized I had heard those very words in my brief visit with Constance. She, a member of the nefarious sect that had tried to abscond with young Elliot, had said exactly that—though at the time I had not quite understood what she'd meant. I was barely able to function in the day, so ragged was I for my nightly terrors and wanderings. When my patience with the situation had reached its limit, I decided one afternoon to call her—begging her to reveal to me precisely what this Faustian bargain with the thing in the pit entailed. It urged me nightly to bring it "another"... But why, I wondered, was it necessary that *I* should bring it anything?

Constance answered the phone. We spoke only two or three minutes, but she revealed enough before hanging up on me to elucidate things.

"What did you mean, 'the debt must be paid'?" I asked without even saying hello. "When I visited you, you told me that a debt needed fulfilled. You wanted to know where the boy was. What's the meaning of this?"

The woman sighed, speaking quietly into the phone. "My son made a promise. He was going to offer that boy. You set him free. The debt must be paid. Bring him another and the matter will be settled."

"But I'm not your son!" I cried out.

"No," replied Constance, "but he still lives in you."

"He still lives in me—?" I felt my pulse quicken and immediately placed a hand to my heart. The organ toiling away in my breast was not my own. It had come from the maker of this diabolical pact, and so long as it continued pumping, it did not matter whose chest it was in. "But I... I didn't make any kind of promise. I don't... I don't even know what this thing is! It has nothing to do with me!"

"It has everything to do with you, *now*," she replied before hanging up the phone. "My son tried to help you—told you where the boy was kept. You chose to set him free instead of repaying the debt. Now, you must find another. Until you do, he will call on you every night—draw you to him."

The line went dead.

—w/\—w/\—

My situation deteriorated further and faster than I could have possibly imagined.

One afternoon, I went out with my father for milkshakes. The weather that day was pleasant enough, and my dad had thought me in need of some fresh air. We took our drinks with us to the small park across the ice cream shop and stationed ourselves at a picnic bench across from the playground. We sat there a little while, enjoying our drinks, but the noise of children playing kept interfering with my thoughts, and before long I found myself completely ignoring my father and focusing instead on the children.

There was one little girl with pigtails, running circles around the swings. She seemed a happy kid, very energetic, with cherubic cheeks and an adorable pink jumper. Dangling from the monkey bars I found another fine specimen—a boy of ten or eleven wearing a football jersey and grass-stained jeans. I watched him hang there awhile, admiring his hearty laugh as he teased some playmate. These and others I observed from my spot on the bench, and I found myself wondering—not altogether consciously—whether the offering of any of these children might satisfy the nightmarish debt I was being called to pay.

When I realized what I had been thinking, I nearly spat out my milkshake. My stomach soured and I had to turn away from those happy children, tossing out the remainder of my drink to keep from vomiting. I was disgusted with myself, but there could be no denying that the nightly shakedowns were having an effect. White-faced and ill, I contemplated my future. Would I suffer these nightmares forever? Would the beastly thing in the pit break me, or would I die before giving in to its demonic whim?

The sleeping pills offered no relief. Therapy sessions left me no saner and the doctor could only propose new and more powerful sedatives. I went so far as to install a lock on the inside of my bedroom door to hamper my nocturnal wanderings, and my life devolved into a haze of constant fear. My father, only weeks ago suggesting that I resume college classes during the upcoming semester, now thought me too haggard, too unwell, to continue my education.

Then, one night, everything came to a head.

I was in the thick of it when I woke up. The dense pine wood, the sparse moonlight, the rocky hills—all of it precisely as I'd seen it so many nights before.

But when I opened my eyes, curiously, the scenery was unchanged.

I blinked—actively opened and shut my eyes—and took in the very same tableau I had just cast off in sleep. I reached out and touched the trunk of a tree, finding it solid, textured. I felt the wind on my face, squinted up at the pale moon. I felt, too, an ache in my feet, and that was when I came to realize what had actually happened.

I looked down at my bare feet and found their soles slashed to ribbons. I had evidently been walking in my sleep for some time without shoes on. I still held my car keys in one hand, though there was no telling where I'd abandoned my father's car, and I had no memory whatsoever of getting behind the wheel.

I had, in almost trance-like fashion, gotten out of my bed, unlocked my door, driven from the house and wound up in the middle of the wilderness. I had not bothered to put on shoes before leaving, which had led me to tear up the soles of my feet on this ragged terrain. It had probably been that pain that had ultimately roused me, and I shuddered to think of what may have become of me had I not regained consciousness.

For that matter, I still shuddered, because I knew I had wandered to that shadowed corner of the woods where my recent dreams had been set, and because I knew what dwelt there. I had been—just as Constance had suggested—*drawn* to the place, lured there to speak with the owner of my alleged debt.

I had awakened just short of the big reveal, and knew myself close to the cenote where the abomination dwelt. Precisely how close I was just then I could not say, though as I resumed my trek—awake this time, and awfully distracted by the sores on my feet—I wanted only to exit those woods and return to civilization.

I was altogether too near the pit to avoid it altogether, however, and not ten minutes from my awakening I happened upon its rock-strewn borders with a barely checked gasp. I had arrived to the spot, been drawn to it as surely as though I'd been dragged on an invisible leash. Standing now some feet from the lip of the aperture, I felt my tired legs weaken and my heart leap in a fit of panic.

The woods were as silent in waking life as they ever were in my dreams, but as I stood there, dumbstruck and woozy, I heard a noise riding in on the breeze that sent me into tremors.

It was the sound of laughter—*children's laughter*.

And it seemed to be coming from the pit.

I can't say what possessed me to take those initial steps; neither curiosity nor noble intention could have driven me to take them alone, but perhaps together they'd provided sufficient inspiration to get my stubborn legs to move, and to dare a glance into the hollows.

Words fall short of what I found there. I felt the blood drain from my limbs as I peered into the moonlit cenote, lost control of myself and fell ill in the grass. I have earlier described the contents of this sinkhole, as well as its most loathsome tenant, but somehow, those things had been transformed by my waking eyes into terrors far greater than those glimpsed in dreams.

Where in my dreams the floor of the pit had been cluttered with bones, I found now only a sea of wriggling, blue limbs. The sounds of children laughing—it must have been many hundreds of them—erupted from the depths of the hollow as though it were a giant mouth. Disembodied arms jutted from the rocky floor, from the walls of the aperture, waving frantically as if to summon me thence, and from deeper in, treading upon this roiling ocean of waggling digits, came the immense black thing—that fiend whose name Constance would obscure through strange epithets. This was "*He Who Dwells in the Hollows*", "*The Depth-Walker*", "*The Wanderer in Darkness*".

And where my previous descriptions of the thing conveyed—to the best of my ability—its hideousness and innate malignity, I would be hard-pressed with even ten-thousand words to describe here the full extent of its evil as I gazed upon it in waking life.

It retained the bleached skull of a face and the fiery eyes with which I was familiar, but elsewhere it had radically changed appearance. The body and limbs earlier attributed to the thing were but a small part of its overall bulk; the cloven hooves mere fore-legs for an odious whole that spanned tens of feet behind, winding through the interior darkness of the aperture. It boasted a segmented carapace of enormous length, like a centipede, which was coated in dense black hair reminiscent of the fur on a tarantula's thorax. Flanking both sides of this succession of grotesque, unending segments, were myriad chittering legs forged of bone. The massive creature unfurled its impressive lengths and sped with insectival fury up the edge of the chasm, lobbing its gaze of glowing red toward me. I now saw that those eyes, like two burning rubies, strained far beyond the reaches of the hollow sockets on a pair of fleshy stalks.

I ran, blubbering and insane, away from the cenote. I dashed my arms on trees as I fled, soaked the forest floor with the leakage of my rent soles. The woods, ordinarily stock still and silent, came alive with the sounds of a thousand clacking legs. The Depth-Walker's hundreds of limbs sought purchase on everything within reach, and it propelled itself through the trees with impossible speed. The roar of childish laughter from the pit had ceased, leaving only the thrum of bony limbs as they struck the ground. The night hid much, and the black beast blended in nicely with the shadow despite its titanic girth, but I had only to turn around to find those blood-red eyes glowing in the murk, and each and every time I did I found them locked upon me.

At some point in my maniac flight, the strain became too much for my heart. The donor organ palpitated, seizing so tightly in my chest that I nearly collapsed. It was this, I think, that ultimately saved me.

The fiend had forged a pact with Lucien, my donor, and so long as his heart was still beating, the link between the two of them would remain. The sudden onset of cardiac troubles as I attempted to barrel out of the woods served, I suspect, to muddy that connection—to temporarily throw the abomination off my trail. I staggered through the brush, clutching at my chest, and was surprised to find the eyes further off than before, and seeming to scan the woods with confusion. When I slowed and my pulse regained its proper rhythm, the thing resumed its chase, zeroing in on me with uncanny precision. A second bout of palpitations once more interrupted its ability to track me however, and this latter incident coincided with my discovering a break in the woods.

I burst through the treeline, hardly able to breathe, and found myself standing on the edge of the familiar two-lane highway. At the moment I'd hobbled into the road, a motorist in an SUV had been cruising past at nearly sixty miles per hour, and slowed to a halt when I subsequently fell to my knees between the lanes. Unable to explain my troubles to the driver when he exited his vehicle, I merely clutched at my chest and uttered, "*My heart...*" This was all he needed to hear, and he helped me into the passenger seat, quickly whisking me off to the nearest hospital.

Having a chance to rest, my heart stabilized a short while into the drive. I thanked the driver, told him that I'd gotten lost in the woods, and he was kind enough to help me into the ER lobby before setting off.

On the drive there, however, I never once looked out the window and into the woods for fear that I would find red, burning eyes staring back at me.

—wv\|\—wv\|\—

I spent only two days in the hospital. My surgeon, Dr. Patel, lambasted me for my carelessness but reported no lasting injury to my heart. The wounds on my feet were dressed and I was given a round of antibiotics.

But while the physical wounds are mending, my situation continues to deteriorate even now.

I am plagued every night with the same dream—a dream of that black sinkhole and the serpentine horror that dwells in it—and I am drawn to him by forces outside of myself even as I sleep. It was only due to the supervision of nursing staff and the efforts of hospital security that I did not flee my hospital room during the nights of my admission to seek out that abomination in the woods. Furthermore, I am driven to the limits of my will by the constant temptation to deliver unto that arch-villain the very thing my donor had promised.

I wish that I could give this heart back to Lucien Grapelli, that I could live without it. The transplant that was supposed to give me a second chance at life has instead proven a crueler end than slow death by heart failure. I am forced now to sleep under restraint and have been prescribed potent sedatives that render me partially paralyzed for hours each night. I hope that I will not develop a tolerance to them, as these interventions are the only thing keeping me in my room after sunrise.

I am sitting now on the front porch, taking in the sun as my father prepares dinner. It's a fine day, but I cannot enjoy it. I spend my time cowering in anticipation of the coming night and the vivid dream it will bring. In the yard across the street, several children are playing. Their sweet laughter fills the air.

One of them, a young boy, kicks a soccer ball into the street. It rolls over the curb, a little distance into my yard.

I think I'll pick it up, hand it back to the lad.

Yes, yes—I think I'll introduce myself.

ORCHARD

In the months since their son had died Samantha had grown distant, numb. Henry hadn't expected things to remain the same, of course. The loss of a one-year-old son to unexpected illness was enough to drive even the hardiest couples into a permanent depression. He couldn't blame her for these changes; these new silences were merely her way of coping. Even so, he longed for a return to the smiles and pleasantries of days passed.

She was not visibly sad, did not weep, did not express anything, save for a dull sort of trance. Even that fateful night they'd spent sleeplessly in the hospital hadn't seen the remotest trace of sorrow flash across her even features. And that was fine. She was entitled to her reaction, as all are entitled to grieve in their own fashion. What really stuck in Henry's craw, though, was the lack of discussion between them. Samantha never mentioned their son; seemed to regard his name as a taboo. When she had—with almost callous determination—cleared out the nursery not a week after the incident, neatly arranging the deceased child's effects on the curb so as to lessen the burden of the trash men, Henry had been devastated. And yet, he'd held his tongue, unable to remark or protest lest he break the unspoken rule.

It felt as though their child had been reduced to a series of stored photographs, scarcely glanced, and a lonely grave plot. A story seldom told. A barbed memory.

Henry had begun to truly worry about his wife. Even as he struggled to cope with the pain of loss one year out, he feared that Samantha, an ordinarily sentimental woman, was bottling up her own anguish, distilling it, hiding it away for his benefit. She went about her daily life with a marked stiffness superadded to her motions. Where grace once dwelt she was now a creature bereft of it, a hollow machine to whom the actions of living were but another directive. Replies to even simple questions were stilted; she rationed every syllable.

Desperate to rouse her from this state, Henry began to formulate a plan.

An artist of some local renown, Henry survived primarily through the painting of murals. Local businesses and citizens of means often contracted him to paint large works on the exteriors of buildings or tasteful scenes upon the walls of expansive dining rooms. In the previous year however he'd busied himself largely with other work; work that served as catharsis for him in his time of mourning. Without a wife to commiserate with, Henry had dedicated himself to painting.

Night after night he poured his heart out in his cramped basement studio, setting upon the canvass scenes so wretched and dismal that Goya might have quivered for them. It was the only release he knew for the feelings of grief and desperation that surged through him. The paintings, a dozen in all, fell into a collection he titled *Ode to Misery*, and in a moment of seeming madness, he'd put them on display at the city's downtown art show.

To his surprise and eventual dismay, the ghastly paintings had been enormously received, and in short order he'd been presented with offers for his cathartic paintings—great sums he'd been unable to refuse.

And so it was that the townspeople bought off little pieces of his grief, hanging them in their houses as bleak curiosities without knowing the extent of the anguish that had seen them thrust into existence on those dark nights while he'd wept over his easel. It was a terrible realization that his suffering was eminently profitable, capable of being commodified. But it was in these sales that Henry had now found his chance. He could afford to take time off from his commissions, could schedule a trip with his wife and, perhaps, resume a normal life. A trip to some new locale, to a setting far from the familiar, might serve to shake Samantha from her stupor. At least, that was his hope.

Loss had made Henry nostalgic. He could not but indulge in memories of past, joyful experience, and chief among them had been the yearly vacations he'd taken with his own parents to Michigan's Upper Peninsula. Those times were distant now, staggeringly so; he could scarcely believe any such place still existed in the world. The passage of time had eroded so many things, had robbed from him so many happinesses. That the beaches and woods of his youth remained intact, unscathed by that same stretch of years that had treated him with such cruelty, seemed unthinkable. Nevertheless, he dared to hope and longed to revisit them.

He brought up the idea of a trip meekly, half-expecting Samantha to veto it. It was a late night and the two of them had just climbed the stairs to bed. They stretched out uncomfortably on their respective halves of the mattress, a psychical partition wedged between them. "I've been thinking," uttered Henry, "it might be fun to take a trip. Go somewhere new, you know? It's been years since I've been up to Michigan. What do you think?"

To his surprise, Samantha was agreeable to the idea—more agreeable than she'd been toward anything in a long while. "All right," she replied, her voice weighed down by dreaminess. To anyone else, a response like that one might have seemed unenthusiastic or uncaring, but in Henry's position anything but a firm "no" was grounds for celebration.

He was not long in making the arrangements. The area in question, the Arcadia of his youth, was nearly two days away by car. He'd never driven there himself, but recalled with no little fondness the way his parents had quibbled over the massive paper atlas that'd crowded the front seats of their family van. For the purpose of their trip, he picked up an affordable GPS unit, did research into lakeside cabins and boat rentals. Detail by detail he took to the task of recreating the trips of his childhood. There would be fishing, campfires and cabins at the mouth of a great wilderness.

All of it fell together neatly, easily, and after a few days' worth of packing, the two of them set off.

Upon departing from their small, two-bedroom home, it had begun to rain. From the onset their trip had been marked in a thin film of mist, as if to herald the dreariness yet to come. Henry had launched into some pleasantries at the trip's start, but by the time he'd handed off a bit of cash to the man at the turnpike booth, he'd known Samantha to be uninterested in reciprocating. She'd reclined in her seat and closed her eyes, as passive a passenger in the SUV as the bags they'd packed.

Samantha was a beautiful woman by all accounts, and her lack of spirit hadn't much diminished that. Long, brown hair of a woodsy shade hung down over the shoulders of her thin, grey sweater. She'd actually bothered to dig into her wardrobe for the occasion, opting for something other than the T-shirts and sweats she usually wore. Into this he'd chosen to read only good things, hoping that it indicated some willingness on her part to make the best of the outing.

It had been in glimpsing the tops of her sandaled feet that Henry first noted her paleness. She'd had perfect, olive-colored skin, once. Now she was closer to porcelain, a result of her having spent many months indoors. She hadn't gone out much in recent months and had spent her time reading, watching television or sleeping. Often, one of those pastimes would blend seamlessly into another, leaving her days a sloppy blur.

They'd been married for three years. How quickly that time had passed, and how tremendously their dynamic had shifted during that brief window. Falling for one another in college, they'd dated only half a year before eloping. Their families had thought them fools initially, but upon further appraisal couldn't but rave about their happiness and compatibility. They'd seemed made for one another in those early days, the very image of wedded bliss. With each passing moment their bond had only deepened, culminating in the conception of a son. They'd named him Samuel.

Samuel had been an easy-going infant, eating and napping regularly. With his mother's pleasant temperament and her same brown hair and fetching hazel eyes, he'd melted the hearts of all he'd met. Extended family had doted over him, strangers had remarked on his warm, toothless smiles. Henry and Samantha had adored him with an intensity they'd hitherto reserved for one another, and the child had slowly became the most important fixture in their lives. They'd built up such great dreams for him, relished the time they'd spent together each day and had even begun planning for a second child.

Sometimes, though, things fall apart. Completely.

—wʌʌ—wʌʌ—

Henry's grip on the steering wheel tightened till his knuckles went white. He still couldn't think of that night without growing distressed. Devastation of that kind knew no limits. Time and space could not restrain it, and even now, a year later, when he recalled finding his son unresponsive in his crib, the wound was opened afresh. His heart would begin to race, his jaw would clench, his eyes would invariably widen. The small, bluish hand, limp. The stillness. The cutesy print on the freshly laundered nap blanket. The frantic cries for help. The panic that set in when the paramedics arrived. The breathless wait in the hospital. He lived it every day.

The memories never had a chance to rest, a chance to forfeit their newness. Twelve months had gone by, and he was still standing in that nursery, a gasp on his lips, peering down into that crib with utter horror.

They drove on silently, Henry focusing at once on the road and, in his periphery, the form of his sleeping wife. She'd slept the whole night, hardly stirring, so that he could barely believe her in need of sleep. A bump in the road saw her stir. She straightened herself, shooting him a narrow, sidelong glance. There was no grogginess in her eyes as they opened, taking in the grey light. She'd very evidently been knocked from reverie, rather than sleep.

"What's on your mind?" ventured Henry, desperate for some reprieve from the monstrous thoughts that writhed within him. She would lie if she responded at all, and that was fine. Any distraction from the sounds of the road would do. Anything she might say to allay thoughts of that stifling nursery was welcome.

She didn't say anything, merely sighed and combed an unsteady hand through her hair. She was desperately trying to feign fatigue. Henry would not be fooled, however. Though she had worn this mask since their son's death, he still remembered the woman who lived beneath it—and he resolved to find a way to coax her out into the open again.

Samantha had been considered sensitive, once. Her tenderness was something he'd always appreciated, something he'd been drawn to. Twelve months had been sufficient to bury it, however. No outward trace of it remained. That the death of her own son would not incite her to weep or mourn, even in private, was insane to Henry, but from that evening onward, from the moment the two of them had waited in the hospital, this was the look she'd worn.

What went on inside her head when her thoughts returned to Samuel? For that matter, did she ever think of their son? In all the time that had passed, and certainly in the preceding six months or so, she hadn't so much as spoken his name. Henry was beginning to wonder if she even remembered Samuel.

The highway scenery sped by, the windows dripping with fresh rain. The sound of the fat drops striking the windshield came to a crescendo, temporarily allaying the awkward silence that'd grown up between the two of them once more. Henry pursed his lips, foot easing off the accelerator, and breathed in sharply through his nose. In the rearview mirror he caught a glimpse of himself. The past year hadn't been too kind. He was nearing his thirties but looked well into them already. His choice of clothing, a stuffy black cardigan and T-shirt, didn't do him many favors—nor did the greying stubble he wore on his cheeks, or the bags under his eyes.

He rubbed at his jaw, loosing a sigh. Samantha had closed her eyes once more. Outside, the highway offered no sights of interest. There was tall, overgrown grass left a bright green by the rain, a gunmetal sky churning with black clouds and a few far-off trees. The road was theirs. Other motorists were scarce. "It's funny," he said. "I haven't driven this stretch since I was a kid. Not since we went on vacation so many years ago. It hasn't really changed in all those years." This was a lie. Though the scenery persisted, his perception of it had considerably worsened. He wasn't a hopeful, excited kid any longer. He was a grown man looking for some escape from the life that was falling apart all around him.

Samantha grunted and turned toward the window, opening her eyes slightly and watching the raindrops tumble down the glass. From the dash the GPS unit chimed, indicating their progress on the pre-mapped route.

Henry grit his teeth. The trip had only just begun.

Their first night, which entailed a stop at a small inn just past the Mackinac Bridge, was quiet and uneventful. The two of them piled out of the car, sore, and ate a small dinner at a nearby diner before retiring. The rain had taken the form of a mist, obscuring their vision very slightly as the sun went down. Henry hoped it would clear by morning, and said as much. Samantha, unimpressed with the lodgings, settled into one of the two twin-sized beds and was asleep before Henry was out of the shower. It was a strange thing, sleeping in a separate bed from his wife. He laughed aloud as she burrowed beneath the covers, her back turned to him. She didn't crave his companionship, didn't seem to notice he was there at all. It occurred to him that he might walk out the door, wander about town or, perhaps, leave and never return. She wouldn't notice or care, he theorized. But ultimately he toweled himself off, pulled on a fresh set of clothes and climbed into bed.

It was a dingy little place, the sort which hadn't had any worthwhile update in decades. The wallpaper was slightly yellowed and peeling, and the carpet had well-worn trails carved into it from the foot traffic of many decades' worth of tenants. It smelled of dust and the walls were thin. The place had come recommended for its proximity to the massive Mackinac Bridge, and would have been a welcome sight after traversing the entirety of the Lower Peninsula if only it had featured some few comforts. As it was the settings were austere and the beds, though covered in decent-looking linens, proved lumpy and uncomfortable. The night was spent in a fit of tossing and turning. When morning reared its head the two of them did not wait for check-out and merely packed their things, setting out just an hour after daybreak. Neither of them spoke of the place, which suited him just fine. Henry had despised it enough on his own. The last thing he wanted was to hear complaints from Samantha.

Of course, Samantha was her usual, silent self. She moved as one who had slept poorly in uncomfortable quarters but said precious little, except "how much further?" upon entering the rain-flecked SUV. The rain had stopped, but a thick mist remained in the air. The sun would probably clear it, he hoped, or they'd drive out of it once they built a bit of distance between themselves and the Straits of Mackinac.

"Another day's drive. Then we'll be there." Henry tapped a few buttons on the GPS unit, waiting for it to warm up. Slowly, the thing came to life, recalling the coordinates set the previous day. When it was set, he fastened it to the dash and looked over at his wife. "Hungry?"

"Not really," she replied. Samantha clawed at her hair, working loose a few tangles.

The hunger that plagued him wasn't physical. Henry was hungry for Samantha's affection. He wanted to feel like her husband again, wanted to feel loved. He paused before pulling out of the parking lot, toying with the idea of reaching over to her and taking her hand in his. Then, thinking better of it, he slowly backed out of the space and started out onto the open road without another word.

They had no plans at this destination of theirs. As they started back onto the highway, Henry thought about how things would go, growing increasingly agitated at his wife's lack of enthusiasm. She would probably remain somber and silent the whole time, unwilling to take part in the various activities. Hiking, fishing, swimming; no matter what he suggested she was almost certainly going to sit it all out. He wondered why he was bothering at all, why he'd insisted on driving for two full days only to be disappointed.

He caught sight of it in the corner of the windshield, fluttering against the glass sluggishly. It was a moth, bone white, with short, floppy wings. It paused there, clutching the smooth surface and ambling a few paces before taking flight once more, bumbling about as though it meant to break through the glass. It was trapped in the car, and in some small way, the creature seemed to realize it. It could see the outside, the place it called its home, but it wasn't in that world any longer. It was kept apart from that world, locked away from its normal life. Henry wasn't so different, dwelling in the open world but never really living in it, almost as though he were trapped in some glass bubble. He cringed as the tiny body smacked the glass once, twice. It made such a hollow little sound. The sound of futility. To his surprise, Samantha reached out with a tissue in hand and promptly smashed the thing against the windshield. She grimaced, wiped up the mess it left behind, and tossed the wad of paper onto the car floor.

"What do you mean?" she asked, looking up at him with a hint of annoyance.

Henry couldn't help but bask in it. Negative though it may have been, her reaction was the closest thing to genuine interest she'd given him in a long while. Henry ran a palm against his forehead, slowly steering onto the road's edge and parking. He fumbled with the GPS. It came off of the dash with a pop and then beeped wildly as he tapped its screen. With a furrowed brow, he scanned the map, finding large swaths of it blacked out and featureless. He shook his head and repeated himself. "I don't know where we are." Then, carefully, he elaborated a little. "I don't know if the satellites are just out of range or what, but... this thing seems to have taken us on a weird route. We're not on the highway anymore, and... I'm not sure exactly where we are."

For hours they'd been driving down the uncluttered highway, making good time. Just where they'd had their misstep Henry couldn't be sure. He thought he'd been following the device's directions to the letter, and had been surprised when it led him off the highway path they'd been on for the bulk of their trip. Still, he'd persisted, driving down the unpeopled stretch and taking in some rather impressive forest scenery on both sides of the road for more miles than he'd cared to count.

It appeared a newly laid road, though it occurred to him that its newness might be owed to a marked lack of traffic. He couldn't remember the name of the road they were on, and for whatever reason the GPS had seen it fit to keep that information to itself, malfunctioning and leaving the map a pixelated blur. Something had interfered with it, probably, and they would have to drive a considerable distance yet before they'd find a new entrance ramp onto the highway. Henry peered at the gauge on the dash. They had a quarter of a tank of gas left. *Not good*, he thought. He'd planned to fill up at the next truck stop or rest station. On both sides of the road, partially blocking out the hazy sun and wreathed in that selfsame mist that refused to dissipate, were thick trees. Not a gas pump or visitor center in sight. No cell reception, either.

"So, we're lost?" asked Samantha, her breath catching. She slumped back in her seat, hands placed limply over her lap. Her eyes were listless, the lids shuddering a bit, as she scanned the road ahead.

They were lost. There was no other way to put it. He thought to reassure her, to give her a bit of hope, but Henry knew all too well it was pointless. He didn't know where they were and they'd likely run out of gas before he managed to regain his bearings. There was the possibility, if they waited long enough, that the GPS would start to work again. But it was already getting rather late into the day. To make matters worse, the two of them hadn't eaten since the previous evening. Samantha hadn't wanted to stop for breakfast; a decision she was evidently regretting now, if the conspicuous rumblings in her gut were any indication. In the course of some few moments, their unpleasant road trip had devolved into a nightmarish scenario. Depending on the remoteness of the road they were on, it was possible they wouldn't reach civilization with the little gas they had available. And to seek out help on foot would be both arduous and, potentially, dangerous. There were large animals in these parts; bears and cougars, at least.

Still, Henry seized upon the chance to play the role of supportive husband. He reached over and patted her cold hand. "We'll go a little further. The woods are thick here, but I'll bet if we go another mile or two we'll happen upon a break in the woods. Trees are probably just playing games with the GPS reception." He took the car out of park and pulled ahead slowly. "I'll get us out of this mess, don't worry."

The SUV lurched ahead and the pair took to studying their surroundings with great care. They watched as the forest scenery on both sides continued unbroken; indeed, for a mile or so it maintained a dark and uncannily uniform appearance. Henry rested his hands atop the wheel, coasting slowly and looking for some sign of civilization. There was no litter here, no tire tracks. No sign whatsoever of human habitation.

Maintaining her air of annoyance, Samantha interjected. "What is this road even here for if no one uses it? There aren't any houses here, no businesses... who builds a road in the middle of nowhere? We haven't seen another car in hours."

Henry nodded slightly. "Dunno. Maybe they built this road so that trucks could transport lumber. Or maybe they're planning on developing the area." He shrugged, scanning the dense line of trees on his left side. A few birds fluttered about the dense wall of trunks. On the other side of the road, he thought he caught sight of a deer looking out at them cautiously. It was something large, with big, luminous eyes. He peered at the GPS, biting his lower lip and digging a thumbnail into the leather steering wheel. The image on it shuddered but did not improve. Sucking in a slow breath, Henry picked up speed. He wanted to distance himself from this road, to break through the ocean of trees and get back onto the highway. It was late in the day, but the towering trees served to blot out the sun, making it seem later than it really was.

The mist, too, permeated this stretch with an added emphasis. Miles of road would be completely free of it, while others would be so swollen over with smoke-like haze that he was forced to slow down and switch on his headlights. Whenever they entered into a particularly foggy patch, Samantha would always tense up, pressing the back of her head to her seat and narrowing her eyes as though expecting something to jump out of the mist and into the car. She didn't say as much, but her body language told Henry enough.

Samantha reached out and took his arm, giving it so firm a yank that the car was thrown momentarily from its path. Henry loosed a gasp, punching the brake and looking over at her, wide-eyed. Then, his gaze drifted to her window, through which he caught sight of what appeared to be a large property, recessed within the wall of trees. Samantha looked at it breathlessly, her fingers still pressed into Henry's arm as she studied it. It was a tall house, painted nearly the same bone white as the fog that circulated through the air. Two stories. An imposing black door with two small windows in it looked out at them dimly from deep in the shady property. Stumps of trees formed a makeshift path leading up to the house. The sprawling yard, wildly overgrown, basked in a powdery sunlight, whereas its borders steeped in the black shade of the surrounding woods.

She was an ancient habitation with sparse, narrow windows. A squat, red chimney jutted out from its roof, half-obscured by the mop of tree cover that encroached from every direction. She was ensconced, this old house, in a nest of gnarled, centuries-old trees; the one and only sight indicative of humankind to be found in this expansive wilderness save for the road they'd traveled. It had a peculiar, standoffish air about it like that of an individual much averse to interruptions. The house was a thing engaged in sleepy, brooding contemplation and had probably been engrossed in such for longer than Henry, or anyone he knew, had been alive.

Of architecture Henry knew vanishingly little, so he could judge neither the house's age nor the stylistic intent of its long-dead makers, except in the most general of terms. There could be no question of its being an ancient thing. It was in its decrepitude that the lonely tenement confessed its impressive tally of years. The house was a large, boxy thing, with a smaller box stationed atop it and a slanted roof; it was so unremarkable in shape that it could not have been ascribed to any but the most simplistic schools of design. Even in its heyday Henry imagined it must have been homely and austere, though it was understandable that the settlers of a region so untamed as this should have eschewed beauty and sought practicality in their constructions.

Clearing his throat, Henry nodded toward the house. "Interesting," he began, "to find a house all the way out here." He looked at it reservedly; at the dusty, unbroken windows; at the tall, robust grasses. There was no driveway or garage to be seen. Or tire tracks. The grasses appeared pristine, untrodden, in their wildness. "Think anyone lives there?" He couldn't decide whether the place was inhabited. On the one hand, the windows and door all appeared intact, and the house did not look to be in complete ruin. On the other, there were no outward signs of any occupant and it was singularly unthinkable to Henry that someone might survive in so remote a location without a car. Perhaps it was a vacation home, something used only one season out of the year by out-of-towners, he theorized.

His question was answered forthwith by an almost eerie occurrence. The black door of the house was thrown open as the two of them watched, and a small, bent woman hobbled out into the grainy light. Henry and Samantha both startled at her emergence, and laughed awkwardly as the woman came into view, standing at the edge of her porch and surveying their car with a curious smile. Her features were not to be clearly distinguished from this distance, but from their car they could tell that she was a very *old* woman. Her skin was pale, her hair a shocking sort of white that mingled with the daylight and made her into a kind of beacon as she stood against the black door. Ambling out, the woman extended a hand, waving at them.

"Should we... should we go out there?" asked Samantha, wrinkling her nose and turning away from the window.

Henry parked the car and hurriedly removed his seatbelt. "Of course, yeah," he replied, opening his door and stepping out. "Wait here if you want. But this is probably our only chance at directions.

She'll know where we are." Pausing a minute, he waited for her to join him. She began from the car nervously, fiddling with her hair.

Standing close to Samantha's side, Henry led her up from the road into the tall grass of the property. Stumps of varying heights littered the swath of untended lawn, posing a hazard. Samantha stumbled over one, nearly losing her footing and reaching out to steady herself on Henry's arm. Fighting his way through the grass with a hesitant Samantha in tow, he finally marched up towards the patio, constructed of chipped and seemingly rotten wood. It had looked a hardier construct from the road; up close, it was unstable, worm-eaten and robbed of color by the elements.

At the foot of this dilapidated patio, whose black, cavernous spaces were abundant with mist, the pair got their first proper sight of the woman. She was miniscule. What could be seen of her limbs about the borders of a black shawl suggested a thinness and varicosity indicative of tremendous age. She was a thing of weakness, supporting herself against a rotting post and peering down at them with a heaving chest. Breathing did not come easily to her. The woman continued to wave at them even as they came within a few feet of her. Her smile was largely toothless, her thin lips pulled back to reveal a mouth whose only remaining teeth were touched by black rot. Her eyes were recessed and small. One of them, if Henry saw it right in the shade of the repulsive porch, appeared cloudy, aimless, blind.

Placing a hand upon his wife's shoulder, Henry put on the warmest smile he could, glanced stealthily about them, and gave the old woman a nod. From this proximity the disrepair of the property as a whole was entirely more clear to him, not at all relegated to the rickety-looking patio. The paint was chipped, and the boards that comprised the exterior of the leaning tenement were considerably warped so that pests of all shapes and kinds could conceivably have made their homes there. In the earth-scented breeze, Henry thought he could hear the house groaning to him. The building's inner parts braced against the gust, moving in their ancient sockets with a pitiful creak. "Hello," he offered. "I was wondering if you couldn't help us. You see, we're a bit lost."

To Henry's surprise, the old woman picked up the conversation at once, and with an incongruous liveliness. "Oh, lost are you? Tourists, I presume, from out of town?" She nodded emphatically, her ancient eyes squeezing shut for a moment and her face trending upward. "It happens from time to time, yes."

"Our GPS went crazy," he added, smiling sheepishly. "We thought we were on the right track, but suddenly we lost our signal and weren't sure where we were." He felt Samantha stir uneasily beside him.

Again the woman nodded. "The woods here play all kinds of tricks on electronics," she said, her voice steady, clear and bafflingly youthful. While she seemed in every aspect rather advanced in age, her voice and manner of speaking were in keeping with someone a good deal younger. "Please, come in. It has been so very long since I have had company in this old house. I shall prepare you something and get you on your way with detailed directions, once my appetite for company has been sufficiently whet." She grinned, turning slowly and motioning to the black door of the house. In stark contrast to everything he'd hitherto seen of the place, the door appeared to Henry the only rugged fixture.

He peered at Samantha, who had remained silent throughout the brief interaction with the old woman. Now, with the woman shuffling slowly through the threshold of her home, Samantha's eyes were wide and her legs appeared tense with the intention to run. She glanced back at the SUV parked along the empty road and mouthed a silent wish to return to it. Henry, however, pointed to the house. "Let's go, it'll be quick," he assured her. Samantha's range of emotion had been muted for a long while now, so that to see her communicate fright or anger was an exciting thing to him. In this particular case however, he couldn't much understand her sudden trepidation. Taking an exploratory step onto the patio, he bore half his weight upon it and found it surprisingly sturdy despite appearances. Then, looking to Samantha, he motioned toward the door.

Gulping, Samantha lowered her gaze and followed close behind him, up the three worn steps of the patio and to the yawning black door where the old woman waited with that same, toothless grin, her bleak little eyes glimmering in the light of the open doorway. A lamp flickered just inside the door, and a dark entryway rug could be seen upon the floors of stained wood. The pair entered the foyer and the old woman closed the door with surprising spryness.

Tchotchkes were rare. The space just inside the doorway featured only an empty coatrack and a small structure meant for housing shoes. Henry's eyes wandered about the walls, finding only naked and pock-marked plaster. Moving through the foyer, with its dim light, he noticed that the lighting situation did not improve beyond it. Large glass fixtures, their nooks and crannies grown dusty, sat in the ceiling of every room in his immediate view; that is, the kitchen and a small room of unknown purpose attached to it, providing each with unreliable, whitish light like the glare of an autumn moon. Wooden floors creaked with each step no matter the weight or gait of the walker. He could feel the boards give slightly against his soles. The aromas of food and dust-girdled antiquity competed against one another in this place, and it was only in the kitchen that the former could be said decisively to win out.

"Welcome to my home," said the woman, the knot of whitish hair upon her head trembling as she went. "My name is Louise Hillard."

—wᐱ—wᐱ—

Except for the kitchen, where Samantha and Henry sat at the table over steaming cups of coffee, the remainder of the house seemed stuffed with an otherworldly darkness. It was not that any great pains had been taken to keep the abode dark; rather, through uncurtained windows the silhouettes of massive trees could be made out across the floors, blocking out all but a few strands of the feeble sunlight. Henry palmed his cup of coffee and thanked his hostess profusely as she joined them at the table, extending a plate of biscuits. The kitchen was warm and smelled of cooking meat. Louise was in the process of preparing dinner when she'd heard their car stop on the road outside, she explained.

Samantha managed to overcome her reticence, the hunger in her too great to pass up the offered food. She ate two biscuits with evident relish and then accepted, to Henry's surprise, a gracious offer to stay for dinner. With food in her stomach, Samantha's mood was much improved. She almost seemed like a new woman, sitting up pleasantly in the old wooden chair and smiling with what Henry could only deem a natural warmth. He was taken aback at the sight of his wife, the wife he hadn't glimpsed in roughly a year. He didn't voice his awe at her change and did his best not to look too closely at her for fear that she might suddenly change back.

"I'm afraid you're still quite far from your destination," said Louise, sipping noisily from her cup. She set it down unsteadily, her arthritic hand quaking till the cheap porcelain vessel met the table. The coffee sloshed around inside, nearly overcoming the lip. "You're near Gulliver. Unincorporated town, Gulliver. You can go miles and miles without ever seeing another living soul." Her bony fingers sought out the edges of her shawl, pulling it more tightly around her. "I suppose this house is situated in what was once called Winfield Township, but... that was a long time ago."

Henry listened politely, merely thankful for the opportunity to rest and for the changes in Samantha's demeanor. "How do you mean, unincorporated?"

Louise continued. "Well, this isn't a formal town. Our Upper Peninsula is littered with little places like this; settlements that have fallen out of fashion." She broke off a small piece of biscuit and ushered it to her mouth with a quivering hand. "People used to live here, many people." She smiled warmly, the creases in her cheeks bunching together and the blackened ends of extant teeth revealed. "Probably before your time. The two of you look very young. Newlyweds?" she ventured.

At this, Samantha chuckled, coughing on her sip of coffee. "N-no," she said. "We've been married three years now."

Henry was heartened to hear her say it. The past year had been a miserable one that had seen his wife transformed into a stone-faced caricature of her former self, but the details of their life together hadn't been forgotten after all.

Louise threw up a hand. "Oh, three years." She laughed. "*Practically* newlyweds." She smiled to herself for a time before drawing in a long sigh. "Come back to me when you've been married forty-three years."

Henry chuckled. "Forty-three years? Quite a marriage. Is your husband in?"

At this, the old woman shook her head, appearing wounded despite the smile that lingered on her aged lips. "I'm afraid not. Passed on some years ago, the stubborn man. I told him to stay, but he wouldn't have it." She shrugged, giving a weak laugh. The room was steeped suddenly in a sort of melancholy with which Henry was all too familiar.

"Very sorry," he said, lowering his gaze to the off-white tablecloth.

"No trouble at all," Louise assured him. "But ever since Roger passed on, it's been awfully lonesome here. I don't get out much these days, and as you can imagine, visitors are rare in a place this out-of-the-way."

Henry had some trouble visualizing what life in this area must have been like for an old woman like her. There was simply no way she could live unassisted here. How did she get her food? What about medical care? He wasn't prepared to pry, and figured that some of these rare and unseen locals probably helped her out. It was the only way a woman of her condition could still be living on her own. And even then, it hardly seemed safe. He cleared his throat. "So, you've lived here a long time, then?"

"Practically my whole life, yes." Louise looked over at Samantha, who was digging into her third biscuit hungrily. "Poor dear, you seem hungry. Please, help yourself and I'll have dinner ready as soon as I can." She stood and made her way slowly toward the oven, a large, iron thing unlike any oven Henry had ever seen before. The oven door had a large, black handle on it like a coil, and the old woman took hold of it weakly, barely managing to wrench it open to peer inside. The room was flooded with warmth as she looked at the cooking food. "Almost finished," she said, letting the door slam shut. The appliance groaned and shook as Louise returned to her seat, panting.

"Don't trouble yourself," said Henry, giving Samantha a sidelong glance.

"No trouble at all, dear. Quite a treat, having visitors." She looked again to Samantha. "So, what brings the two of you here? Sight-seeing? Anniversary?"

Samantha mulled it over a few moments before taking a swig of coffee and leaning back in her chair. "Well, actually, we're on a mini vacation of sorts. Henry wanted to go on a trip." She cocked her head to the side, chuckling uneasily. "We've had some difficulties and this seemed like a nice break. Our..." She frowned a little. "Our son died. Almost a year ago now."

Henry was floored, and literally steadied himself against the table to keep from falling off his chair. "Samantha, please," he began, looking to dissuade her from continuing. "I don't think Louise here really wants to hear about that." It wasn't good manners that incited him to interject however. He was stupefied at her willingness to talk about their past, and was almost hurt that she was opening up to this old stranger rather than to him. Those very words coming out of her mouth were something that Henry had not managed to wrest from her in a year's time. Now, here she was, casually discussing the trauma of the previous year with Louise. He felt his heart race, his vision go somewhat spotty. He was stunned. They'd had twelve months and more than a day of silent driving and never once had she uttered a word about this burden they shared.

Louise reached out and placed a bony hand upon Samantha's, shaking her head and frowning terribly. "My goodness, I am so sorry to hear that. So, so sorry," she kept repeating, looking awfully distressed. "I can't even imagine."

"It's all right," said Henry. "It's not... it's not something we talk about much." He turned to Samantha, who lowered her gaze and toyed with the rim of her cup.

Louise shook her head. "Well, you ought to. Something like that will eat you up inside if you don't take it out for a walk now and then." She gulped at her coffee pensively, her old eyes scanning the inside of the cup as she set it down. An awkward silence reigned until she saw it fit to speak again. "This house was once a bed and breakfast, if you can believe it. We hosted many happy couples over the years. When my husband passed I had to close up shop. A shame, that, as there's nowhere else to stay for miles around." She looked to them, her eyes smiling. "It sounds to me as though the two of you could use a break from your day-to-day lives, so if there's anything I can do for you, please don't hesitate to ask."

Henry raised his cup. "You've been very generous already, inviting us in for dinner." He laughed. "Running into you has been the only good thing to come out of this trip so far. Up to this point we'd been doing a whole lot of monotonous driving."

Samantha perked up, chiming in. "So, what was this area like, when there were more people?" She leaned forward, demonstrating a marked interest in the old woman's reply.

Louise looked up at the ceiling and sighed. "Oh, it was your typical small-town atmosphere, I reckon. Having spent most of my life here, I don't much remember what life is like in the bigger cities. But being so close to the shore of Lake Michigan and getting to know the locals I found I rather liked it here. It was a warm place; everyone knew each other."

"So, why did people move away?" asked Samantha.

Louise had to ruminate awhile before she could answer this. She seemed almost unprepared to reply, continuing with many a ponderous half-starts. Finally, she continued. "It's a long story. There isn't any one factor, I don't think." The old woman's frame stiffened noticeably, and she began to stir uncomfortably in her seat. She looked longingly at the oven, then took a hurried sip of coffee, draining her cup. "It was a nice place to live, many kind people called this home. It wasn't so lonely back then. I know a few local folk... people who didn't leave. Others just went to the bigger cities and..." She shrugged. "You know, these things happen. Nothing lasts forever. People meet and people part."

Samantha nodded, but her questioning did not abate. "Sure, but why did they leave? This seems like a nice area, perfect for development. I'm surprised there aren't loggers working out here. And you said there were other cities like this all throughout the Upper Peninsula. That doesn't make sense. Why not modernize places like these? Other spots in the country are so crowded."

Louise didn't have an answer, and her discomfort only grew more palpable with every passing moment. Henry smiled to his wife, trying to get her to cease her line of questioning, but before he could get his point across, their hostess decided to reply. Her hand shook as she pushed her empty cup away and her skin took on a sort of grayness in the light of the kitchen. A hanging lamp over the aged, rust-worn sink turned on its chain, which was clotted with spider's silk and dust, as a draft coursed through the room. "The reasons were manifold. You're quite right that it's a fine place to live. On the surface, it makes little sense that areas like this one should empty out." She wet her lips, stuttering a little as she went on. She was very obviously distressed. "W-What I think is that the people here were mighty superstitious. A rather gullible crowd who were willing to read malignity into all manner of... of common occurrences." Louise crossed her arms in her lap. She didn't seem to want to continue. But then, she launched into a short diatribe, unsolicited, and with such intensity that the thick, bluish veins in her neck could be seen to writhe:

"It was the turn of the last century, I think, that people started to leave. In dribs and drabs. It wasn't an overnight exodus. It was slow-going, generational. By the time I moved here, things had slowed. It was nice enough, though. Roger and I married young and settled in. I suppose we just saw something here that the others didn't. And our business didn't hinge on natural resources like others did. I mean, to start with, the mines in this area were supposedly depleted of ore. Lots of miners took off around 1900. Loggers, too, went off to find better areas with richer forests and more accessible routes. This area never was considered good for logging, though I can't for the life of me say why, when we've got so many trees." She cleared her throat, her cheeks reddening and a polite smile peeking through. "There was, well... there was something else that happened in this area. It was a big deal in the local news and it occurred over a stretch of many years. I don't... I don't particularly want to talk about it. It's not the sort of subject that you'd likely wish to discuss, but suffice it to say that some harm came to a few children in this area, and the superstitious folk in town took it as a kind of omen." She cast a dour glance at Samantha. "I'm so sorry, I don't mean to talk about dreadful things like this. Not in front of you, especially."

Samantha, who was apparently quite interested in the woman's story, urged her to go on.

As though she were discussing something that left a bad taste in her mouth, Louise clicked her tongue and frowned. But, after a time, she fidgeted and went on. She'd seemingly waited an age to divulge what she knew. She was a lonely, restless woman, and the discussion of such gossip as this was likely rare for her.

Louise continued, her voice dropping in volume. In a voice just above a whisper, her age was much more apparent. "I don't mean to upset you, dear. Of course not. But this area was known for one thing many years ago. A series of abductions." She wet her lips again, tapping a single finger against the table. "I tell you, the first time it happened it was a minor sensation. People would talk of nothing else. But then, it wasn't really considered much more than one of those unfortunate things. There are bad people in the world and sometimes even innocent children get caught up in their wickedness. But then the second kid went missing, and then, shortly thereafter, a third. That was when their imaginations started running wild, ascribing it all to some... to some legend of theirs." She sighed, fanning herself lightly with her hand. "It all started about thirty years ago, I think. It must've been. And once a year, or once every few years, a child would go missing. You can imagine that, by this time, there weren't a lot of families left. Mostly stubborn old locals who'd been born and raised here. Their houses are still out there if you go looking. Sitting empty now, swallowed up and reclaimed by the woods. But they're still standing, those old houses. Anyway, there was an old story, a local story, which started long before I was even born. A story from the first settlers in this region, about some witch. The Gulliver Witch."

The light above suddenly flickered as Louise paused. Their surroundings seemed to darken very slightly for the utterance of this name, and Henry and Samantha both gave a shudder.

"The Gulliver Witch, that was what they called her. An old hag out in the woods there." Louise motioned about the room. "Now, I'm not saying there was anything to the myth. Find me an old town, even one, that doesn't have some sordid little story like this one. But the folk of this town, well, they found themselves grasping for answers in light of these tragedies. A fourth child, a fifth, a sixth... they went missing over the years. The concern and frenzy would wear off, a few seasons would pass, and then another would just up and disappear without cause. No trace. And the paranoid people took to this old story for whatever reason. They didn't suspect one another, no. They'd come to some sort of consensus that this was the work of an ancient witch hiding out in the woods." Louise shook her head. "It was unbelievable how easily they all came to believe this story, how easily they dismissed likelier explanations. And in a panic, they began to leave town. One by one, the families took off, eager to protect their children. The future generations of this region, the town's lifeblood, were lost when they left. Some stayed a while longer, but when ten children had disappeared in the course of years even the most obstinate families were shaken."

Louise had worked herself up a great deal. She took up a corner of the tablecloth in her thin hand, working her fingers against it and unable to meet the astonished gazes of her guests.

Henry and Samantha weren't quite sure how to react, though now that Louise had divulged so much, the pair could not help but be drawn in. Curiosity had gotten the better of them, and though it might have been ill-advised to do so, Samantha found herself prying further. "This legend… of the witch, that is. What made them think it was really an evil witch that was responsible?"

Louise's old eyes hardened and she stood up. Without a word she marched, with more vigor than before, across the kitchen. She sucked in great lungfuls of air through her flared nostrils and busied herself in the oven, plucking a large dish of meat, carrots, potatoes and more from inside. Setting it atop the stove, she examined it and seemed pleased with its doneness. The air of the room was oppressive now, stifling. Louise busied herself by plating up hefty portions of the roast for her visitors. She did not, however, prepare a plate for herself. While Henry and Samantha began to eat, she returned to her seat, downcast, and picked at the edges of her shawl. She did not react to their compliments on the meal and only spoke some minutes later after the cry of a bird in the woods drew her from a brooding daze.

"It isn't talk suited to dinner-time," said Louise, glancing up at the pair before her. "I don't enjoy talking about ridiculous old stories like these. It gives them life. Disseminates nonsense." She gulped. "But the story *is*, regrettably, a part of this town's past. And since you asked..." Louise cleared her throat, her eyes wandering along the table before settling on Samantha. "The Gulliver Witch supposedly lived in these woods before the first settlers came. Where she came from, how long she'd been there or how she'd even gotten there to start with is all a mystery." She chuckled, but not out of amusement. "Isn't that ludicrous? An old woman living in the middle of the woods before any of the settlers. Just living off the land, wandering, like a ghost. They spoke of her as a creature who fancied children, and who would prey upon them if they ventured into the woods near dark.

"The Gulliver Witch sought to collect—that is—to kidnap thirteen kids," Louise continued. "In the woods somewhere, she had a vessel, a cauldron, perhaps, which she would fill with the blood of these children." She paused, her forehead dappled in fresh beads of sweat. Her nose wrinkled. "Macabre nonsense. Utterly distasteful, all of this. The story went that she would soak an acorn in this cauldron of blood. And, finally, when the thirteenth child was bled and the acorn had steeped in his blood for the winter, the acorn would be planted in the forest, giving life to an oak tree that would go on to bear strange fruit." She dabbed at her forehead with her fingertips, sighing. "Only twelve children ever disappeared, so there's no reason to believe that this old story actually had any bearing on reality. But that didn't stop the locals from losing their minds and declaring the Gulliver Witch a real person."

A wisp of smoke crawled through the air from the stove like a grey tendril as the thing powered down. Henry worked over a bite of roast beef, peering down at his plate. He struggled to hide his disgust and wished Louise would change the subject. Everything on his plate seemed unsavory now, somehow repugnant to him. He wanted to thrust it away, to take Samantha by the arm and leave the old house. Surely an aimless drive along that lengthy road would be preferable to conversations like these. He hadn't saved up money to spend their trip this way, sitting in on dinners with strangers and listening to their grotesque fairy tales. A curious anger welled up in him.

Samantha speared a carrot on her fork and brought it to her lips thoughtfully, apparently more intrigued than horrified. Stories like these had been enough to make her squirm in the past; horror films and novels had never appealed to her. To see her listen intently to Louise's ramblings was unnerving.

After some quiet moments, Louise seemed more like herself. She smiled, cleared their plates and brought out some tea. She apologized for ever having broached the subject of the old story and for quashing Henry's appetite. Talk transitioned to more commonplace subjects after that. She asked them what they intended to do, whether they'd ever visited the Porcupine Mountains in the past. Henry touched briefly upon the fact that he'd been to the Upper Peninsula a few times as a child, but declined to elaborate, his mood effectively ruined by the previous topic of conversation.

Languidly, as though concerned with other, internal things, Samantha inquired after sightseeing opportunities in the locality. On this Louise had little to offer, except for the existence of a long-abandoned apple orchard a few miles from her property. "The place was owned by locals until some years ago. They moved away, abandoning the orchard. It was a wonderful little place, producing the sweetest apples I've ever tasted. You might consider seeking it out for a little tour. It is, of course, overgrown by this point in time, the woods having encroached upon it a great deal. Last I heard however the apple trees still grow there, and they should be ripe for the picking this time of year. Might be worth a look if you're a fan of good, pesticide-free produce." She smiled.

"Why did they move away?" asked Samantha, her eyes widening. It was clear from the look on her face that she was drawing sinister connections to the story of the Gulliver Witch—connections that Louise was quick to deny.

"Oh, no... it's nothing to do with that other business," replied Louise with a chuckle. "The people who owned that orchard were childless. They packed their things one day and departed. Didn't tell anyone, just abandoned the land. A shame, really. I'd heard rumors that they were struggling in business. It's understandable; by then the population had declined and there wasn't enough out-of-town business to keep it profitable. They probably left in search of something more lucrative. Got out of town and never looked back. Kind folk, they were. Well-liked in the area."

"Perhaps we'll check it out sometime," said Henry, standing up and smoothing out the front of his shirt. "Thank you so much for your hospitality, Louise. If you could set us up with some directions to the highway, it'd be great. We should probably get going."

"Oh, of course," said Louise, standing and hobbling about the kitchen in search of paper. "You'll want to keep on this road for about ten more miles. Then you'll come to a fork. The left side will take you straight to the entrance ramp. Shall I write it down for you?" She rifled through a small box on her kitchen counter.

"No, that's all right," replied Henry. "Sounds simple enough." He looked to his wife, who remained seated at the table, hands in her lap. "Samantha, you ready?"

Without turning to look at him, with her eyes fixed in a distant stare, she replied. "You know, it's getting quite late."

Narrowing his gaze, Henry peered over at the nearest window. Much to his surprise, darkness had begun to creep over the property. How long they'd been guests in Louise's home he couldn't quite say, but they'd apparently been there past sunset. He stifled a curse and looked down the hall towards the dense, black door they'd come in through.

"The two of you are welcome to stay, if you'd like," said Louise, pacing over to Henry and looking up at him with her feeble smile. "I've fresh bedclothes and will set the two of you up for the night, no problem. This was once a bed and breakfast, after all." She peered over at Samantha. "Your wife seems tired and, besides, there's little sense in driving out here at night. The roads are just miserably dark after sunset, especially with all the trees. It's too easy to lose one's way, even on a straight shot like yours."

Henry was prepared to politely decline her invitation, however Samantha spoke up before he could reply. "That would be lovely, thank you. We owe you one, Louise."

"Please, think nothing of it," said the old woman, shuffling across the kitchen. She entered into the next room, turning on yet another feeble light and elucidating a rickety-looking staircase that led up to the unlit second story. Turning to her guests, she waved them over. "Follow me. I'll show you to a room."

The tips of his fingernails dug into the flesh of his palms. Henry remained cemented in the kitchen even as Samantha followed Louise. He wanted nothing to do with this ancient house or its equally ancient owner any longer. Though he couldn't say with exact certainty just what had unsettled him, the place felt decidedly unwholesome, and the prospect of spending even a few more minutes there, much less an entire night, was enough to set his heart racing in protest. It wasn't so late yet; if they set off now, they could likely find a motel to stay in. But as he watched Samantha approach the foot of the stairwell, her hand resting upon the chipped bannister and her gaze meeting his, he lost his fight. To insist on leaving would be to upset her. Samantha had come out of her shell. Inexplicably, she'd begun to speak and act freely. Something about this house, this experience, had been therapeutic for her. Gritting his teeth and swallowing back the dread that rose up his throat, he buried his hands in his pockets, relaxed his fists, and started towards the stairs.

Louise led them slowly, her flimsy frame shifting to and fro with each step and her talon of a hand gripping the rail tightly. The stairs were made up of warped planks, which curved inward as though under some invisible load. Debris had found its way into the well-worn grooves in the stairs, and as Henry took his first step, the wood squealing beneath his foot like a shrill rodent, he almost lost his balance. He supported himself against the powdery wall, following closely behind Samantha. It didn't seem safe for the three of them to ascend at once, but the staircase held and the trio found themselves standing at the entrance to a long hall lined with doors. The darkness in this stretch was utterly primordial, the doorways and fixtures appearing rough in the shadow, almost as though they'd been carved out of stone. With some difficulty, Louise located a switch on the wall and flipped it. From the opposite end of the hall, one of the ineffectual ceiling lights in the spirit previously described flickered on, burning briefly in a state of wavering dimness before brightening very slightly.

The three ambled along the hallway, their steps echoing loudly throughout the house. They passed the doors one-by-one, their hostess guiding them silently. Just what dwelt beyond those doors was a mystery. Certainly there were only commonplace things there; the belongings of an old woman, the clutter amassed during several decades of secluded living. And yet, the doors of flimsy, darkened wood, bowing out somewhat and adorned in tarnished, brassy handles, hinted at something more dire. His imagination had already been piqued by dark talk that evening, so that it was simple enough a thing for him to imagine the rooms inhabited by various backwood horrors. Were they alone in this house, the three of them? Indeed they must have been, Henry assured himself. But as they passed through the hall, the dull, coppery glow of each door knob registering in his periphery, he found, to his dismay, that he could not be wholly certain.

They turned a corner and, soon thereafter, three doors from the hallway's terminus, Louise stopped and smiled. "Here we are," she said, pushing open a door with visible difficulty. The thing swung open, the darkness within unmoved by the weak light in the hallway. Standing aside, Louise offered to fetch them some fresh bedclothes and waved them in. It was Samantha who braved the first step into the room, completely obscured by blackness.

There was only a lamp within it, and a frail one at that. Its bulb blinked to life and took on a periodic glimmer soon thereafter that called to mind the flickering of a fire. Samantha stood in the threshold, looking at the bare mattress, the dust-covered chest of drawers, the mirror draped with an old sheet. A dreamy smile came to her lips, the only thing in view that Henry could take even the remotest comfort in. She paced into the room, breathing a sigh of relief, and accepted the neat pile of linens that Louise brought in. She seemed relieved to have a place to rest, excited. She hadn't looked half this happy at the hotel the previous night. Carefully, she began to make their bed.

Off-put by the room, Henry walked in reticently, thanking Louise half-heartedly and giving things a closer look through narrowed eyes. To begin with the corners were matted in cobwebs, the owners of which stirred sluggishly at sensing the new inhabitants. The air here reeked of dust and moisture, as though the door had not been opened in a very long time. Brown spots along the ceiling highlighted areas where the slanting roof had failed. Small holes marred the plaster walls where decorations had presumably been hung and, curiously, the bed frame appeared slightly crooked, as though bent—though, this latter detail might have been due to an unevenness in the floor, which featured many unruly planks jutting out from their original positions. All told, it was a sorry excuse for a room. He thanked his hostess, but his apprehension was impossible to veil.

Louise left them with another of her trademark smiles and promised of a fine breakfast in the morning. She bid them a good night and closed the door as softly and securely as her weak arm could manage. Now, with the door closed and the two of them sealed off from the cavernous hallway, this little pocket of a room took on a most disagreeable quality for Henry. In a word, the space became tenebrous, the flickering lamp at the bedside serving to stagger the available light and render the sparse fixtures in a vaguely charnel shadow. Louise's footsteps vanished to the lower story, leaving the floorboards in the hall squeaking and settling for a time. But then all was still. *Impossibly* still. Locked away in this little chamber, the smells of moisture and dust thrust into their nostrils with every breath, the two sat upon the bed, regarding the sepulchral silence.

Unmoved by their settings, Samantha yawned and reclined in bed, her brown hair falling across the stiff pillow. How long, Henry wondered, had it been since someone had rested their head there? He was more discerning than this wife, picking up the pillow, patting it down, making sure the pillowcase was free of pests. When the dusty thing was as clean as he could get it, he set it back down on the bed, stretched out and placed his head upon it with hesitation. At Samantha's behest he reached over and shut off the light. The bulb died away slowly, the element within glowing orange for some time thereafter like a match-head. His limbs shifted uncomfortably beneath the starchy linens. He hadn't undressed, couldn't bear the thought of exposing any more of his bare skin to the ancient bed than was necessary. As he stared up into the surrounding blackness, attempting to slow his breathing and calm his mind sufficiently for sleep, he fancied he heard a noise issuing from the mattress below, a subtle kind of scraping or picking, as of insects. He pictured a mass of jet-black vermin trapped inside the confines of the mattress, their polished carapaces clacking against one another, their needle-thin legs searching amidst the springs and stuffing.

Henry was startled by Samantha as she rolled over in bed and placed an arm upon his chest. She snuggled up to him, embracing his side, in a way she hadn't done in ages. He nearly jumped out of bed, in fact, wondering if he hadn't been caught up in the menacing embrace of some stranger. Her even breathing and soft voice reached his ears from nearby however, and his heart was instantly calmed. "I'd like to visit that orchard tomorrow," she said quietly, her words punctuated by a small yawn. He could not find it in himself to deny her, and cradled her in the crook of his arm. He felt her warmth, basked in it, and even dared to kiss her forehead. She did not pull away. Samantha remained firm, pressed against him. This was the closest the two of them had been for nearly a year.

The visions of insects and damp caves were drowned out by an intense appreciation for his wife. He held her tightly till sleep overcame him, and replied to her request with a sleepy smile on his lips. "We'll visit the orchard first thing after breakfast."

Samantha had already fallen asleep.

—wᐱw—wᐱw—

The windowless room gave no indication of day, so that it was only by the groggy semi-wakefulness that washed over him that Henry knew it was time to rise. Samantha had been up before him, sitting at the side of the bed.

"Did you sleep well?" asked Henry, catching the slightest glimpse of her in the faint bands of light that came in through the seams of the door. He switched on the lamp, the flickering glow stabbing at his eyes. He palmed at them, then shot up from the bed, suddenly remembering its foulness. Patting at his hair and clothing, he surveyed the spot he'd occupied and then looked to his wife.

She had her phone in hand and was checking the time. "Just past ten. Wonder if we're too late for breakfast," she wondered aloud.

Smoothing out his hair and pausing momentarily in the upstairs bathroom, which he found by means of furtive snooping, he relieved himself and made his way down the stairs with Samantha. The house was quiet, with only the familiar creaking of the massive oven registering. The two paced confusedly about the lower level in search of their elderly hostess, but found no sign of her except for the place settings at the table. Plates of bacon, eggs and toast had been prepared for the two of them, covered so as to keep them warm. Butter, jam and a glass jug full of orange juice also sat upon the table.

"Maybe she went back to bed. Or maybe she stepped out," ventured Henry, dropping into a chair and eyeing his food hungrily. Precisely where the old woman could step out to, however, was beyond him. Louise scarcely seemed the kind to go for long walks in the dense woods. The house was large and unexplored; likelier was the possibility of her dwelling in another room, busying herself with some chore or another.

Samantha shrugged pleasantly and began eating almost at once, nibbling on her toast and eggs with great relish. She seemed in a hurry to finish and drained a glass of juice in a series of long gulps.

The food had cooled considerably, but was still warm enough to eat. Henry cleared his plate quickly and made small-talk with his wife as she ate. Things were turning around for the two of them. The start of the trip had been uncomfortable and unpleasant, but happening upon this old house had been a very good thing for them, despite appearances. Sleeping in dusty old beds, meeting the curious old woman; this experience would make for a great story in the years to come. Recounting the events of the previous day, he could hardly believe that Samantha had come out of her shell. There'd been no mechanism behind the change that he could perceive. One minute she'd been cold and unexpressive, the next a marked thawing had occurred. She was herself again. It'd been a long time coming, but she'd actually recovered. Her smiles were the real thing, and he found himself not a little distracted by them. She looked more beautiful to him that morning than on the day they'd met.

Finishing their meal rapidly, Henry recalled the promise of the previous night. "So, you wanted to seek out that orchard, yes?" He carried their empty plates to the kitchen sink, setting them in the deep basin.

"Oh, yes," replied Samantha excitedly. "I'd like to try the apples there." She sat up with all the pep of a schoolgirl ready to depart on a field trip. "Think it's far?"

Henry shook his head. "Louise didn't make it sound that way. I imagine it's fairly close by. Within a few miles." He nodded towards the nearest window, where an oppressive shadow crowded the glass. "Of course, we'll have to do some hiking through those ominous woods to get there. Sure you're game?"

Samantha grinned, standing up and walking over to him. "I trust your navigational skill," she said, planting a kiss on his cheek.

Henry's face reddened. He felt foolish for it, but couldn't keep the blush from invading his cheeks at the gesture. Sweet, intimate deeds of that kind were alien to him after a year of discord. He was a shy kid again, unaccustomed to romance.He returned Samantha's kiss before pacing through the kitchen in search of their hostess. "We'll get out of here in a bit. I just wanted to find Louise first, thank her for everything."

But after a few minutes, he turned up no sign of the woman. The house sat quiet, the air in the hallways still. Henry was careful not to venture far, the vague apprehensions of the previous day rearing their heads once more at the prospect of entering the house's many unexplored chambers. After a short jaunt through the kitchen, adjacent storage room, staircase and foyer, and a few half-hearted calls of "Louise", Henry returned to his wife and shrugged. "I don't know where she got off to. Let's go. We can stop in again after we're done at the orchard."

Samantha was agreeable to this and made a beeline for the door. With visible difficulty she pulled the massive thing open, its hinges creaking slightly, and stepped out into the cool morning. The tall grasses were heavy with dew and a light breeze whisked away the last remnants of that awful mist. The day was clear and bright just beyond the ramshackle porch. With Samantha's hand in his, Henry closed the door of the old house behind them and led the way down. From there they navigated the sprawling lawn, careful to avoid the the densest patches and the occasional tree trunks. They did not, however, make their way to the SUV, still parked along the road, with its misted windshield. They turned instead toward the back of the property, toward the expansive and darkened woods that had, just the night before, given Henry grounds for unease. The trees towered thickly over the cusp of the property, their tops hanging down about the roof of the house and teasing the worn-out shingles. Their limbs quaked like long, reaching fingers in the breeze.

Hand-in-hand the lovers began their trek, leaving the white house behind them and entering what seemed, at once, a completely new world. Where the road and house could have been said to be rather silent places, the silence that reigned in the woods was of an entirely different class. Birds soared above the treetops and dashed about the forest floor, but not one loosed so much as a chirp. It was almost as though the fauna here dared not rupture the membranous quiet. Henry thought to remark on the awesome quietude but, in drawing breath enough to speak, was quickly dissuaded by the prospect of shattering the stillness himself. The two stepped deeper into the knotted growth of forest, leaving the rear of the white house to their flank.

He noticed something that unsettled him as they wandered on—something that made a chill run up his spine even as he held Samantha's hand and reveled in her company. The old house appeared to stare at them from behind the wall of trees. Its lengthy, slender windows, uncurtained, bore down upon them like so many bleak eyes, and in one particular window on the second story, Henry saw, or thought he saw, the impression of a small, pale face in the glass. He did not look again, did not dare to, and convinced himself that it was merely the face of their kindly hostess who'd been too preoccupied with some chore to see them off.

The line delineating Louise's property from the wilds was not at all clear. Though trees had been sheared away to make room for the house many years before, the remainder of the wood appeared virginal and robust, untainted by human agency. Fed by primordial, nutrient-dense earth, the growth here ran rampant. So immense and crowded were these woods that Henry could not but feel claustrophobic. There was only sun-shaded and gnarled greenery as far as his feeble sight could take him. He doubted very much that the orchard still existed as a separate property.

He was roused from his thoughts by Samantha's musings. "I've been thinking a lot," she began, "about what Louise told us yesterday. About that story."

"The Gulliver Witch?" mumbled Henry without amusement. He stepped over a tall, sprawling fern and steadied himself against a tree trunk.

Samantha slowed down, combing a length of hair behind her ear and peering up at the canopy. The trees threw shade upon her face, obscuring her expression ever so slightly. In the dim autumnal light she didn't quite look herself. "Louise seemed to take it rather seriously."

With a smirk, Henry pushed ahead. "That old woman lives alone out here. It's only natural that her mind should cling to old tales and bits of local gossip. What else has she got to busy herself with? What else could she possibly discuss with strangers?" Something like a shudder wormed its way down his spine, but he did his best to mask it with a quiet chuckle. "Don't pay her any mind. She was very kind to let us stay, but she's not quite right in the head."

Samantha considered his words thoughtfully, advancing with a dream-like expression. Though her eyes were focused on the woods ahead, they seemingly cut deeper than the nearest impregnable cluster, to some point of remoteness that ordinary eyes could never hope to glimpse. He noticed a postural change indicative of determination as she continued forth. She assumed a stance of confidence, shoulders back and head somewhat higher, displaying a subtle certainty that they were on the right track. She even took the lead, walking more quickly and acting as though they could not possibly lose their way.

Henry did not question her, but instead followed with quiet consternation. Samantha steadfastly carved a path in these woods where none existed. He peered to his back, finding no trace of

Louise's home. They'd ventured deep into the woods now. At the realization, his heart began to pound. Even if they found the orchard they sought, there was no guarantee that they'd be able to find their way back to the property. They'd been out for a short while, but already the terrain, with its slight changes in elevation and restrictive flora, were wearing on him. He wasn't in the best of shape, and wondered how much longer he'd be able to keep up with his wife, who seemed charged with a mysterious and hitherto unseen energy. For someone accustomed to spending her days milling about the house, she walked with unbelievable vigor.

It was more than a half hour into their trek when Samantha halted abruptly beside the ridged trunk of an enormous tree and pointed, silently, to something just ahead of her. Henry, his face dotted in sweat, jogged toward her and had a look. There, just beyond a patch of high-grown weeds, were the remnants of a large, wooden sign. And just beyond it, a curious contrast against the other trees he'd seen up to that point, were rows of tall apple trees, many of them teeming with ripe fruit. They'd arrived.

Marching toward the sign, Henry pulled away some of the obscuring weeds, hoping to read it. The thing had been partially effaced by the elements however, and only the word ORCHARD, written in large, black letters, could be made out. "How about that," he said, wiping his brow with the back of his arm. "Guess it wasn't so far from the house after all."

A thin smile teased Samantha's lips. She took a few steps forward, passing the sign and looking up at the trees whose heights were crowded in ruby red fruit. "Look at them," she said. "So many apples. It's like our personal orchard." A few fallen apples, somewhat rotten, rolled about her feet as she shuffled ahead. "Let's pick some."

It was with some difficulty that Henry procured an armful of apples. With no knack for climbing, he was forced to search for smaller trees with lower-hanging branches. From these he managed to knock a few apples by extending a long stick and agitating the boughs. One by one the stems gave way and fresh fruit tumbled to the ground. He picked them up as they fell and handed a few to Samantha, who eyed them hungrily. They were large and brightly colored, almost unnaturally so. When he'd knocked down nearly ten of them, the two settled down against the trunk of a tall oak and munched.

"Whoa," said Henry as he took his first bite. "These are amazing." The fruit was delicious, the sweetest he'd ever tasted. Though he'd never been especially fond of apples, these were in another class altogether. He ate them voraciously, tossing aside the cores haphazardly after cleaning them of their flesh. Samantha watched on with a grin, nibbling on one of her own and remarking at their incredible sweetness. "I guess Louise was right," he said, wiping at his lips and polishing off another apple on his shirt. "These really are great apples. I'm glad we made the trip. Want to knock down a few more? We can take them with us on the road."

Samantha nodded. "Definitely." She continued eating her apple, her pearly little teeth carving into the red skin. She ate with the same enthusiasm she'd eaten at Louise's the day before. Without realizing it, he neglected his own apple and took to watching her from the corner of his eye, a dumb smile crowding his lips. He still couldn't believe how happy and normal she looked. After their year of silence and indifference, he hadn't been sure things would ever return to normal. But now things were improving, and rapidly. Just what this rustic setting had provoked in her he wasn't certain, but he hoped that the positive feelings would persist for the remainder of their trip and beyond. She munched and chatted in precisely the same way she had when they'd first met, her eyes possessed of that lively spark he'd been enamored with back then. She was by no means old-looking, however when she carried on in this pleasant manner she appeared the very portrait of alluring youth. Her cheeks were rosy for the hike and her hair was tousled slightly by the breeze as she sat in the shade.

The orchard had not been completely overrun as he'd suspected, with some pockets boasting only grasses of enormous height and apple trees. Some of the apple trees appeared young and did not bear fruit. Here and there the commoner oaks did encroach, but the density of the orchard was lesser than that of the forest as a whole. The sun was more visible here, the air less stifling. It was comfortable, and Henry wasn't looking forward to leaving. He worked over a sliver of apple peel between his teeth, wondering if they wouldn't get lost on their way back out of the woods. "How did you know where to find this place?" asked Henry, turning to his wife. He was hoping that she'd know how to find her way out again, as well.

To this, Samantha did not reply. Instead, she stood bolt upright, casting her half-eaten apple aside, and peered curiously at the yet untapped orchard beyond. In a voice just higher than a whisper, a voice so breathy it could scarcely compete with the whistling of the breeze through the leaves overhead, she said, "Let's go deeper."

Henry choked down a bite of his apple. "What for?"

Her eyes widened as she turned her back to him and stared, with longing, at the miles of orchard ahead. "I want to find that tree." Her shoulders quivered ever-so-slightly as she said it.

Gulping, Henry cocked his head to the side. "What tree?" A minor dread climbed up from the pit of his stomach however, for he already knew.

"*The Witch's tree.*"

The breeze died down at once as she breathed her answer. Though it was likely due to the shifting of the sun behind a wall of clouds, the orchard grew suddenly darker by a few shades.

"Samantha..." he began, chuckling incredulously. He was glad that she was not looking at him, for his face had grown a bit pale. "Still going on about that ridiculous story? Let's pick a few apples and go, yeah? We need to set out, get back on the road."

Samantha didn't budge, however. Apparently she meant what she'd said, and in realizing it, Henry's dread was doubled. With nary a word she took a step forward. Then another. She walked slowly into the mess of apple trees ahead, looking straight out into the distance with that same intensity Henry had noticed earlier in their trek. The ends of her brown hair trembled in a small gust that saw the sweat on Henry's body turn to ice. He was taken aback, positively repulsed at her insistence, but did not speak up to dissuade her. Everything else had been going so well for them up to this point. He couldn't bring himself, despite his unease, to pull her away from this search of hers. The last thing he wanted was to upset her, to ruin this peace that was budding between the two of them after a year of harsh frost.

And so he followed. He found himself chattering nervously, mostly for his own benefit. Samantha did not react to his words if she heard them at all. "That story of Louise's is just that; a story. We're not going to find some... some... *demonic* tree out here in the middle of nowhere. That's just silly, Samantha. You and I both know it." He wet his lips, finding that the sickly sweet aftertaste of the apples upset his stomach. "We can have a look, of course. It's a nice orchard, and I guess it would be a shame to leave after we've just arrived, but..."

Without a word, Samantha struck past the tangled rows of forgotten apple trees, past the swaths of untended, swaying grasses, and focused her search instead on the knotty and night-anointed woods from whence they'd come. Beyond a certain point, the orchard grounds became difficult to discern from the general forest; only by the species of nearby trees could he guess where he stood. To his harried mind, the oaks represented darkness and fear; the apple trees indicated comfort and light. This battle raged on in his head as the two worlds overlapped. Here the apple growths were more sparse. There, the oaks and sprawling, shadow-loving weeds seemed on the wane.

And then something changed. In keeping up with his wife's dim silhouette in the ever-darkening woods, he noticed that they had completely left the orchard grounds. There was not a single apple to be seen in this stretch they now walked through, only darkness-tinged foliage and disfigured trunks older than any living man. "Where are we?" he asked as they ventured deeper into this wilderness. Samantha, who walked some feet ahead of him, did not reply. Instead she pushed on with that same stubborn insistence, that same uncanny confidence, that had seen them stumble upon the orchard. To see her navigate this expanse blindly chilled him to his core. It was like she was being led by the hand; and now and then, when her movements and the shifting of the shadows about her were just so, he seemed to glimpse a stirring of her hand, as though her wrist was being tugged upon by some unseen agent.

He didn't want to walk. His legs didn't want to take him any further. It was as though his body was bracing itself in anticipation of some horrible discovery. He disregarded his instinct and followed only because the thought of letting Samantha out of his sight was even more terrifying to him. He called her name a few times, hoping to get her attention, but found she answered him only half-heartedly, through mutters and cryptic gestures. She was fully devoted to the quest for this supposed demon-tree, and would not be bothered.

"I think we've gone far enough," he said, his voice wavering. He glanced up at the shaking limbs all about him, the sea of green worked into a roil by an unexpectedly forceful wind. His words were swept away along with a cloud of leaves and dust. "We should turn around," he said a few times. "We should stop here and head back to the car. Samantha, we need to get back." She didn't respond, which caused his pleas to grow all the more frantic. "We need to leave, Samantha. Please, let's go. Forget about this nonsense. We... please, let's... let's go."

How far they walked into those uncharted woods he couldn't say. To him the march seemed aimless, but to his taciturn guide, whose small hands reached out quickly now to clutch the trees so that she could pull herself forward with even greater speed, their progress was anything but directionless. As though she were on the verge of some momentous breakthrough, she refused to slow down. She could be heard to pant, to loose a series of audible grunts, chillingly bestial, as she took furiously to the unmarked path of her fevered devising. He expected her to break into a sprint at any moment, and wondered whether he'd be able to keep up, his legs already burning in pursuit of her, his heart thrashing in a mixture of fatigue and mounting terror.

And then Henry stopped, his stomach seizing and its contents very nearly lurching out of his gut on a wave of bile.

It was neither the prodigious girth of its trunk, nor the strange, spectral fruit that hung from its distant boughs that alerted Henry to the sight of the massive, aberrant tree. Even as Samantha stopped, her thin form quivering and her eyes drawn up along its gigantic length, Henry walked on, his breath catching in his lungs and his heart galloping sloppily. It was in the marked lack of vegetation surrounding the accursed thing that he first came to notice it. A nearly perfect circle of dead grass encompassed all the land wherein the monstrous growth had lain its roots.

"What in the—" Henry clenched his teeth, his eyes brimming with terror. The tree was monolithic, of a size and appearance the likes of which he'd never seen. It would have been a picturesque oddity well-suited to the pages of a nature magazine if not for its utter grotesquerie. He staggered forward, into the ring of dead grass, past the knobby roots that stuck out of the ground like fat veins. His legs trembled as though they might give way. He steadied himself against the thing's enormous trunk, but let go almost immediately when the bark's odious texture registered against his fingertips.

He wanted to tell Samantha she'd been wrong, that this tree was merely some hideous and titanic anomaly. But intuition told him otherwise. An abomination like this could only be borne from wickedness; nothing save for real, tangible evil could account for it. There was a malevolent air about this colossal tree, whose deep ridges carried about them a marked softness not unlike that of aged human skin. There was a special kind of darkness superadded to the shade this monstrosity cast, and it was possessed of a great warmth despite the absence of sunlight. Aside from the large, spherical fruit it bore in great amounts, the tree's tangled extremities were weighed down also with the ponderous burden of myth.

Samantha's reaction was quite the opposite of his own. She laughed, walking up to the tree and touching its bark with tenderness. "I think this is it," she said, admiring the tree with apparent fondness. "Isn't it amazing? This tree is unlike all the others. And look, there's fruit, too! I told you it was real! Don't look so sore about it," she needled.

Henry glanced at the fruit hanging above. There was only one thing he could be sure of where those strange and fiery fruits were concerned. They were *not* apples.

"Will you pick one of those fruits for me?" asked Samantha, tugging on his arm.

The stimulus was jarring, drawing him out of his private panic attack. Sickened at the thought of Samantha holding such fruits, he refused. He paced around the thing, giving his heart a few moments to calm down, and regarded the tree afresh. He tried to do so with a steady mind, but the sight of it so inspired fear in him that it was all he could do not to run into the woods.

"Please," said Samantha with a surprising bit of firmness. "I want that fruit. Give me a piece."

He grit his teeth to keep them from chattering and backed away from the tree. "I don't..." He had some difficulty in finishing his sentence. "I don't really want to go near it."

Samantha would not take no for an answer, and marched solemnly over to him, taking hold of his arm and pulling him back toward it. "Just one piece," she said, her ordinarily soft hands possessed of an unfamiliar strength and roughness. She pressed his palm against the tree, forcing him once more to take in that strange, skin-like texture. His senses revolted and he loosed a groan, but with a monumental effort he managed to rein in his fears and appraise the tree once more.

Just before him, some ten feet from the ground, was a low-hanging bough. Upon it there grew one piece of the strange red fruit. It was reminiscent of a pomegranate, but was brighter in color and a bit larger. Its exterior, too, was polished and flawless. It looked too perfect to be natural. With Samantha prodding him ardently he gave a feeble jump and reached for the fruit. To his surprise and horror, the limb seemed to dip of its own volition, and the tips of his fingers succeeded in knocking the fruit free of its stem. It dropped down into his quivering hands and he looked at it, frighteningly, before Samantha snatched it from his grasp. The fruit had felt especially warm, as though it'd basked in the light of the sun all morning. The broad, waxy leaves of the atrocious tree served to blot out the sun in its entirety however, so that such basking was an impossibility. He couldn't help but suspect that its warmth originated from *within*.

Samantha squealed in delight. Without the least hesitation, she brought it to her lips and ate. From the very first bite, a thick, reddish liquid that could easily have been mistaken for blood in the scarce forest light oozed from the inside of the strange fruit. An unsightly bead of the stuff trickled down her chin and stained the grey sweater she wore. The flesh gave way with a crisp snapping, reminiscent of the apples they'd been feasting on, but the color of the fruit was all wrong. It was a light pink on the inside, and it appeared partitioned into different chambers by thick, translucent vessels that reminded him of an orange.

Henry cringed as he watched her eat, then backed away a few paces and turned. Still the sounds of her feasting met his ears. "Don't eat that," he warned. "You don't know what it is, what's in it..."

His words fell on deaf ears.

He heard the way her tongue dashed about, slurping up the reddish juice that seeped from the ruptured flesh, the sounds of her gulping down large mouthfuls of the pale inner meat. The savagery of it all had disturbed him. This was not mere hunger; it was something else entirely. She was cramming the fruit into her mouth like her life depended on it, as though it might otherwise escape. Her progress was rapid; everything but the very inner core of the thing was consumed, including the small, black seeds that lined the ridge closest to the hard center.

When Samantha was done, she dropped the inedible core and looked down at her hands, stained with red juice. Red smudges marked the corners of her lips and dotted her chin. The madness had left her eyes and reason had at least partially returned there, but into her expression there stole something of real confusion. The imp that'd compelled her to consume the fruit was evidently gone. Licking at her lips, she exhaled and turned to Henry, suggesting that they return at once to the car. Her fingertips explored the seams of her mouth, resting weakly on her chin and leaving behind yet more red stains. With each passing moment, as he stood there in a mix of fright and anxiety, her eyes seemed to grow wider, bespeaking a mounting urgency.

The request left him flabbergasted. "Y-You want to go back to the car? *Now?*" He laughed incredulously. "I don't even know where we are," he continued, hands outspread. She had led them to this tree in a seeming trance. Where they were or how they would ever get back was a mystery to him. It was possible that a few hours of confused wandering could lead them back to the house, or to some road by which they might reach their car, but in all likelihood he could walk through these woods for miles without ever finding his way out. He looked around, the scenery feeling somehow impenetrable. He was in a bubble—trapped, helpless—like that moth in the car had been.

All the while, the hideous tree loomed large in his field of vision. While she'd eaten he'd thought he'd seen it sway as though in silent celebration, its coiled trunk shifting imperceptibly and its many limbs creaking in applause. Its presence now was even more oppressive than it had been during the moment of its discovery. Its branches seemed to hang lower, its waxy leaves seemed to obscure the sun with more effectiveness and its height appeared somehow increased. He wanted to build as much distance between himself and the wretched thing as possible, but wondered if moving even half a world away was enough. He'd seen the tree and it would live on in his memory. There could be no expunging it from his mind.

Samantha gulped, her wide eyes drawn suddenly to something in the woods at her side. If in fact her vision had tracked something in that dense growth of trees, it had been positively discrete and soundless in its entrance. Her feet dug into the dead, yellowed grass and she appeared on the verge of running. Holding her breath, she surveyed the woods for a time and then extended a reddish finger, motioning to the distance. "It's not far, come on." She began to lead him again, striking deep into the woods with quick steps. Henry could do little but follow, keeping always the sight of the grotesque tree in his periphery until the surrounding woods mercifully obscured it from view. Even then, it was not until they'd emerged from the woods completely—finding their way by what seemed to be mere chance onto the road in front of Louise's—that the presence of the tree was no longer felt.

Samantha pleaded to stop into the house and say goodbye to Louise, but Henry would have none of it. He guided her to the car, urged her inside, and was down the road not a minute later. As he drove, the woods flying by on both sides, he cursed silently the sight of the ancient white house, of the trees that surrounded them, and rejoiced at the discovery of an entrance ramp some miles later. Samantha cleaned herself up and sat quietly in the passenger seat, looking dazedly out the window as they picked up speed along the highway.

Even as they drove Henry couldn't seem to rid himself of the unpleasant taste on his tongue. The sweetness of those apples lingered until his next meal some hours later.

One thing had especially disturbed him as they'd started the SUV and pulled away from the quiet old house. Samantha had utilized a canister of wet wipes, cleaning herself up and seemingly forgetting the trek through the woods and everything they'd experienced. She was quiet, thoroughly normal, her expression betraying a quiet confusion at the state of her hands and face as she looked herself over in the sun visor mirror. When she'd nearly cleaned away all of the stains, she turned to Henry, laying a hand upon his forearm, and said something quietly. In the next moment, she'd returned to the task of cleaning herself up, so that Henry couldn't be certain if she'd intended it as a joke.

"Drive faster," she'd said, a wet wipe pressed to the corner of her mouth. "She's following us."

When next Henry found himself at the easel, he couldn't keep himself from painting trees.

It always started the same way in those first days after they'd returned home from the trip. He'd announce his intention to go down to the studio to work. Samantha would wish him luck and he'd hunker down in front of a blank canvas, seeking to create something. Anything. After stalling out and starting into something hodgepodge, an exercise meant to loosen his creativity, he'd invariably start selecting from the browns and greens with more and more frequency. And before long, without even having realized it, he'd thrust upon the canvas a number of trees in a dark, scarcely detailed landscape. It was occurring with such prevalence that it was beginning to scare him.

Their trip had been peaceful. A week in a cabin had seen the two of them relax, passing their time as pleasantly as could be imagined. No longer did there exist between the two of them those barriers of silence and coldness. They were truly together now, carried on like a loving couple should. Henry was thrilled when improvements in Samantha's mood continued even after they'd arrived home. She was talkative again, loving and supportive.

But something in *him* had changed. In passing, he'd mentioned to his wife that he'd hoped to find some new artistic inspiration while vacationing in the Upper Peninsula, but he had never expected that inspiration to come from these particular subjects. His most recent doodles *always* took the form of trees. This may not have been a problem if not for the look of the trees he was painting. Henry's landscape work was well-regarded, and his paintings of trees had always been remarked upon for their thoroughness and realism. This, however, was precisely the problem with these newest works of his. Though only half-realized, the realistic look of these trees, which always took the appearance of something dark and terrifically gnarled, roused in his mind memories of the forest, of the orchard, that he'd have preferred lay dormant. It was in that setting, in that silent, unwelcoming wood where the monstrous tree had grown, that his creative mind still dwelt. The trees he painted always had about them a knotted and dark bark, and without any conscious effort on his part he'd seemingly bestowed in these slapdash paintings small, hateful faces, borne out in the textures of the trunks and in the masses of thick leaves. He'd inspected them with equal parts dread and annoyance, tossing away a great and many canvasses and burning through his stock of blanks.

One night, a week or so after their return to the house, Henry had felt the pangs of inspiration and had holed himself up in the studio. There, he'd begun to paint with great fervor; broad, curving lines had come to him, and he'd felt himself on the verge of creating something important, something of great magnitude. The image had seemed to issue from some untapped subconscious space. Up until the final stroke, he'd felt assured of its greatness.

Upon stopping to take in the completed picture, Henry grit his teeth and began to shake, however.

His mind had betrayed him. Dashed upon the canvas in true detail, was the hideous nightmare tree from that accursed wood in Michigan. It was all there; the great trunk, the gnarled branches that hung down like claws, the broad leaves. He'd even begun to outline the ring of dead grass around it. His brush quivered in his hand, fell to the floor. He was not quick to retrieve it. Henry had half a mind to destroy the canvas and retire for the night, but ultimately talked himself out of it. It might be therapeutic in some way, he thought, to purge these diseased memories of his on the canvas. Perhaps, once painted, he could rid himself of the nagging dread, of the constant and frightening reminisces. As he resumed his painting however, he knew it would not be so. Stroke-by-stroke, moment-by-moment, his fears only grew and his apprehension came to imbue the scene on the canvas with yet greater life. When he took the time to study it in odd intervals throughout the night, he found it so realistic that it very nearly appeared genuine to him. It was realer on the canvas than it was in his own memory. Realer, perhaps, than it had even been in the flesh.

Henry had very nearly completed the painting, incorporating a number of grotesque flourishes within it, when his courage finally fled. White in the face and weak in the hands, he hurriedly tossed a sheet upon the canvas and stomped up the stairs to bed, thankful that the morning sun had reared its head. He slept uneasily and held his wife, promising himself that he would burn the painting when he awoke. It had not been therapeutic in the least, and its presence in the house was sure to incite in him only unease.

He woke up in bed alone that afternoon, a powdery, grey light flooding in through his bedroom window. Sleep had somehow dulled for him the enormous terror he'd felt at the painting and as he crawled slowly out of bed, venturing downstairs in search of his wife, he was surprised to find the basement door open and the familiar twinkle of his studio lights glimmering just beyond the cellar stairs. It was then that he recalled the horrible painting and sprinted downstairs, very nearly tumbling. He found Samantha staring with wide, watery eyes at his rendition of the demon-tree, the white sheet clutched in her still-whiter hand. Henry ran to her side, pulling the sheet from her grasp and caressing her face with quivering fingers. "Don't... don't look at that," he urged, pulling her away towards the center of the room.

As though betrayed, Samantha's eyes welled with tears and she fought to get away from him. She stormed up the stairs, stopping half-way up to look back at him, her face bone-white in the studio light. Her jaw could be seen to tense as she bounded up the final steps and slammed the door, leaving him down there with his sinister work. Henry regarded it cautiously, lips trembling. He felt on the verge of tears, fearing that he'd just decimated the new calm they had nurtured, when something caught his eye and buried all feelings of sadness beneath a mountain of chest-pounding dread. He about lost his legs, and steadied himself against the nearest wall of cold concrete before he finally found the courage to look more closely at it.

There was something new on that canvas, something in that nightmarish scene that he could not for the life of him remember painting. He could hardly bear to look at it, but the longer he did, the more terrified he became. He clutched at his upper arms, his fingernails leaving deep indentations in the skin. Henry took a step forward and bent down, narrowing his gaze. His eyes weren't fooling him after all; the feature was genuine. To the left of the easel, on the small table where he kept his supplies, he found fresh paint on the palette; dots of the very colors necessary to create the new, fearful addition spread upon it and traces of the same dwelling also on the tip of one of his brushes. It was too skillful a flourish to have been painted by Samantha, he tried to tell himself. She'd never had even the remotest skill in painting. But then, if not Samantha, who had been responsible for this small, dark, but positively insidious figure in the background of his painting? He himself had not painted it, would not have dared to. Any other explanation only served to invite more fear however, and he glanced hurriedly about the dim cellar, as though expecting to catch some rogue artist crouching beneath the stairwell.

Henry was alone; alone in the cellar with that figure in the painting.

He had only ever glimpsed its like—and at that, only very briefly—in the foulest of dreams. It was a person, or a suggestion of a person, painted in a series of quick but precise strokes that created a very specific effect. The humanoid outline was done up wholly in black, while the smaller features, vague, but just detailed enough to arouse repulsion in the viewer, were a pasty off-white. Still other colors impinged on the design; touches of red, in particular, caught his eye around the face and in those narrow strokes where hands were hinted at. The crooked figure lurked behind the shape of the great tree, standing out from the doubtful background even as it seemed to melt away into it. To look at it too closely, in the light of the unsteady hanging lamps that were often toyed with by stray drafts, was to almost discern movement in it.

It was, in a word, *terrible* to behold, and it was only a perceived unwholesomeness that kept him from picking up the canvas and throwing it out. He didn't even want to touch it. He backed away from it slowly, edging his way up the stairs as though he were keeping his eyes on a dangerous intruder, and let himself out of the cellar. He closed the door and bolted it.

From then on the desire to paint was much diminished in him.

In the days to come, neither of them entered the cellar, nor did they speak of the hideous painting it contained. To Henry's great relief the sordid work of art did not much interfere with their dynamic, and within a day it seemed altogether forgotten.

Samantha, always a voracious reader, had brought one of her books with her to the breakfast table one dreary morning, and pawed at the pages pensively while nibbling on a toaster pastry. After watching the raindrops smack against the kitchen window listlessly for a time, Henry leaned in over his coffee and asked her what she was reading. She murmured a reply, apparently too involved in her book to converse, but lifted it off of the tabletop just enough for him to glimpse its title. It was a library book, a long, laminated sticker clinging to the uppermost edge of its greenish spine. And just below it, Henry caught the title. *Trees of the Midwest.*

Henry couldn't articulate just why her choice of reading material proved distasteful and unsettling to him. She was known to read widely, over many genres. Nonfiction wasn't uncommon in her catalog. But a book on the topic of trees struck him as strangely inappropriate considering the nature of their most recent quarrel and the still unpleasant memories he harbored about their trip north. He nursed his lower lip and peered into his coffee cup, stealing the occasional glance at the yellowed pages of her book. The margins, he found with no little curiosity, were crowded with notes in Samantha's recognizable hand. Just what had been cause for such interest, why she felt the need to so intensely study the topic of trees at such a time, was beyond him, but it was sufficient to make him wary.

This, he was to learn during a brief perusal of her most recent library borrowings, was but one of many such books, all of them dogeared and filled to an almost ludicrous degree with detailed, somewhat manic notes about trees. Once, when she'd settled down for a mid-day nap, he'd flipped through a few of them, finding the notes within hurried and sometimes illegible. There were notes about certain structures in trees, about types of soil and other minutiae. Crude pictures of different leaf types had been drawn and then viciously crossed out as though they didn't meet the description or need of their maker.

Pressed between the pages of one of these many books Henry found something that truly frightened, rather than baffled him. It was a leaf, broad and waxy, and the book that contained it fell from his grasp at its discovery. It was a leaf of that demon-tree, apparently collected by Samantha in secret and placed in the book as a kind of keepsake. If approached about it, Samantha was sure to furnish some story about how it was simply a memento of their trip, unthreatening and not worthy of anxiety. But as the book slammed shut and only the edge of its stem protruded from between the yellowed pages, Henry couldn't help but feel otherwise.

It was around this time, when she became steadily more absorbed in her reading, that Henry first noticed the look in her eye. Her usually warm and inviting eyes were possessed of a strange, distant trait, but it was markedly different from the look of distance she'd worn prior to their trip. Then, she'd merely looked washed out, ambivalent, numb. Something else dwelt there now where indifference had previously existed alone. Something he couldn't put a name to, but which he disliked without question. It wasn't always there, either, this look. It stole into her gaze only during those moments when she seemed most focused on her studies. Because of this, Henry thought himself merely imagining it. He figured it was simply his nerves, or that he'd mistaken the look in her eye for something ominous.

Slowly, though, Samantha's habits began to change. The alterations in her behavior were subtle to begin with, her daily patterns trending more and more toward nocturnalism. She would shuffle around the house, talking very softly to herself after having read for several hours. This would continue even in their bedroom, while Henry struggled to sleep. Just what she was saying or why she spoke with such vehemence he couldn't guess, and in those rare instances when he asked her why she was doing it, she would fall silent.

The changes didn't stop there. More than once in the days that followed, Henry found her awake in the middle of the night, standing at their bedroom window and looking out with a kind of longing at the tall oak tree that grew in their yard—the branches of which reached very nearly to their window. Her lips would quiver as if in silent speech, and no quiet remonstrations on his part would interrupt her. Eventually she would return to bed of her own volition, tucking herself in and sleeping peacefully till the next afternoon. When questioned about her behavior, she was consistently evasive.

Then came the whimpering. Henry awoke one night to find Samantha standing once more at the window, the curtains drawn back and her tear-stained cheeks bathed in moonlight. She cried and cried like he'd never heard before. She sounded like a little girl, lost and frightened. Immediately concerned, he sat up in bed and pleaded with her to join him, but she remained in place, looking out the window and crying her eyes out. Between sobs, her lips would sometimes move subtly, as though she were mouthing words to someone standing below, in the yard, but upon inspection Henry found there was no one there to receive her silent messages. When this episode continued for more than a few minutes and she did not react to Henry's concern, he was forced to stand up and guide her gently to the bed, where she broke down and clutched at his arms.

In a shaky voice that was robbed completely of strength, she asked, "H-Henry, do you think that Samuel was the thirteenth child?"

In his groggy state, Henry wasn't sure what to make of this cryptic query and rubbed his eyes. The utterance of their son's name grabbed his attention and held it. "What do you mean?" he asked. It was not long before he realized the full extent of her question however.

Leaning forward so that her nose nearly met his, she grit her teeth and elaborated, fat tears rolling from her eyes and down onto her T-shirt. "Do you think that Samuel was the thirteenth child who was taken by the Gulliver Witch?"

Henry's heart seized violently at the question, and without thinking he fastened a hand around Samantha's mouth. He pulled it away quickly, embarrassed at having silenced her, but could not hide the paleness of his face when she looked up at him pleadingly. "Samantha..." he said after a time, slumping down onto the floor.

"That's... that's utter nonsense. I don't even... how could you possibly say such a thing? How could you think that stupid story could possibly..."

Samantha stormed off soon thereafter in a flurry of sobs, slamming doors as she went and sequestering herself in another room till morning drew her out. Henry spent a good portion of the night trying to reason with her, pacing about in the hall outside the guest room and listening as she slammed her palms against the walls and cried out. She flung curses at some adversary for perceived slights, demanding that the witch "return" her child. Eventually she fell silent, exiting the room and joining Henry in bed well after sunrise.

They did not speak for nearly a day after this episode.

Henry was worried about her. The trip had served to unseat her, mentally. There could be no other explanation for her change in behavior, for her delusions. He asked her if she wanted to visit a doctor, if she felt well, and even went so far as to compile a list of local psychologists. Each time, she turned him away.

She came to him with her good news during one evening when he'd emptied the better part of a bottle of wine and his nerves were ratcheted in anticipation of the oncoming night. "I'm pregnant," she told him, approaching him with a hand to her belly. It appeared somewhat distended in the white cardigan she wore.

Henry wasn't sure how to react, looking her over and giving a slight grin. "W-What?"

"I'm pregnant," she repeated.

This, of course, was not possible. There had been no marital embrace between them in a long while, and what's more, she had looked her thin, normal self just hours before. The change in her belly had been sudden—*too sudden*. Nevertheless, she continued rubbing at her abdomen thoughtfully, smiling with evident pride. "Did you... did you take a test?" he asked.

Her expression soured and she looked down at him firmly. "I know how my body works, and I'm pregnant," she declared. "I felt the baby move just now."

Lowering his gaze, Henry set aside his glass and sighed. "Honey, that's... that's not possible. There's no way that you could—"

Samantha grasped his wrist and guided his hand to her belly. Within her, he felt a persistent roiling—but it was not that of a child. Her gut undulated, her insides making a sort of croaking noise. As he looked up at her, her face became somewhat ashen.

And then the retching started.

"Samantha, are you all right?" he asked, standing up so quickly that he knocked over his chair. She looked awful, her face growing sleek with sweat and her eyes squeezed shut as though in tremendous pain. She didn't cry out, her throat stopped up by a welling bolus. Doubled over and scrambling back against a wall, Samantha began to heave.

In the dim light of the kitchen, the shiny linoleum at her feet was marred in a pool of scarlet. A stream of brightly colored blood poured from her lips, coming in waves. Her arms were gathered up against her abdomen and every time she managed to draw breath, another small torrent escaped her throat.

Henry, panicked, took hold of her shoulders and tried to keep her steady. The blood ran across the floor, meeting his socks and seeping into the woolen fibers. He glanced around for the phone, finding it across the kitchen and out of his immediate reach. "S-Samantha!" he said, holding her tightly. A groan escaped her lips and she grew weak, sluggish.

Barely managing to sit her down in a chair, Henry stepped into the kitchen and prepared to call an ambulance. As the 9-1-1 dispatcher answered and asked him the nature of his emergency, he couldn't seem to form the words, wasn't sure where to begin. "Please, we need an ambulance... My wife... my wife is..."

While awaiting the ambulance, he inspected the spot on the floor where Samantha had vomited. There, he found a number of small, round objects mixed in with the blood and bile. In the moments before paramedics ushered her out on a stretcher, he knelt down and examined them despite his disgust.

Acorns.

—w√—w√—

The emergency room doctor straightened his glasses. He was not a kind man, curt and stone-faced. "Does the patient have any history of mental illness?" It was the same question he'd been asking for the bulk of their interaction, but Henry still hadn't come upon a decisive answer. It was true that one of Samantha's relatives, an aunt of hers, had succumbed to some mental illness later in life. A kind of schizophrenia, he thought. Samantha herself had never exhibited symptoms of mental disease before this. At least, he didn't think so. But then, her demeanor *had* changed significantly after Samuel's passing. Did that count?

Henry shook his head and wet his lips. "Uh... I mean, no. I don't really think she's ever suffered from any mental illnesses. Nothing diagnosed, anyway. And it's not especially prevalent in her family, either."

The doctor sighed and made some quick notes on his clipboard. "Tell me again about this thing she ate," he continued, arching a brow. "This... fruit?"

Henry blanched. In the hopes of helping his wife, Henry had spilled everything he could think of to the unfriendly doctor. He'd detailed the passing of their child, the trip they'd just returned from, even the strange fruit she'd eaten from the hideous tree in the woods. This particular detail had interested the doctor, but when Henry insisted he didn't know what type of fruit she had eaten, he proved irate.

"There's no telling what was in that, and it was probably unwise for her to ingest it. All sorts of things out there, mushrooms and the like, that people shouldn't eat. They contain dangerous compounds, you know? A wild fruit could make one very sick. This episode may have been caused by whatever it was she ate, or else it could be some psychological issue rearing its head. And you said that she vomited up, eh..."

"Acorns."

The doctor arched a brow. "That's what I thought you said." He massaged the bridge of his nose. "Certainly in line with a compulsive psychiatric disorder. Who knows why she did it, but I can arrange for a consultation with a good psych doc who can lend more insight into that." He cleared his throat. They were the only two people in the hallway. Samantha was in the nearest examination room, strapped down to the table. The doctor had insisted it was for her own safety, but Henry could hardly stand to look at her in such a state. "I want to put her in observation at a particular facility. A mental ward. They'll get to the bottom of this, figure out if it's a toxin or just a mental break. Either way, she looks medically stable. Tore up her digestive tract a little with those acorns, but the scope results indicate the bleeding has stopped. I'll be putting her on liquids for a few days." He forced an unconvincing smile before walking toward the nurse's station.

The emergency room, with its long hallways lined in doors and impersonal staff was profoundly unwelcoming to him. From the other rooms along the hall he heard the moaning and weeping of patients, hidden only by starchy-looking white curtains. The pitter-patter of tennis shoes against the polished floors and the jingling of keys filled his head as he paced back into Samantha's room and closed the door half-way. Walking past the curtain, he appraised his wife sullenly, finding her absolutely morose and fractured-looking. Her eyes were a brilliant red. The doctor had attributed this to the rupturing of multiple capillaries during her retching. Her skin, already rather pale, had grown only whiter over the course of the evening. Her limbs were limp, arms perched atop her unmoving abdomen. She stared up at the ceiling, lips slightly parted and parched. They trembled whenever she drew in breath.

She hadn't said a word since they'd left in the ambulance, and Henry preferred it that way. The thought of her speaking frightened him. He was ready for the nightmare to end now, ready for things to return to normal. Even the silence and coldness she'd regarded him with for the bulk of the previous year was preferable to this madness that'd suddenly taken roost.

But normalcy only ventured further out of his grasp.

The move to the psychiatric hospital downtown was fraught with delays owed to mountains of paperwork and the observance of obscure regulations. Henry, having no experience with such bureaucracy, was appointed her power of attorney, but was forced to abide by the same rules as any common visitor when the transfer was complete. It took three days to get her to the psychiatric facility, and in the interim she'd been admitted to a medical-surgical unit at the hospital, where she'd been granted a private room and a patient-sitter who stayed at her side whenever Henry couldn't be there or his body demanded sleep. The sitter, a stern middle-aged woman, said nothing and spent most of her shift leafing through magazines. For Samantha's part, she was silent, staring, very much the same spiritless creature she'd been ever since first landing in the emergency room. She did not sit up of her own volition, but was helped to a recliner once a day by the nurse. This was the only walking she did on a daily basis now, the narrow, three-foot stretch between her bed, which was festooned with all sorts of restraint devices "just in case", and the sticky, rickety recliner.

By the time she was transported to the other facility, her already slight figure had been whittled away further, a marked hollowness coming to haunt already gaunt cheeks. Her eyes, once hazel, were obscured by darkness. She didn't seem to sleep much. No sedatives affected her, and she demonstrated no interest in food or water.

That she was in a bad way Henry understood, however it was the scenery of the mental facility that really drove the point home and served to instill in him a kind of panic. Glimpsing for the first time the rigid, bolted doors, the armed security guards who marched solemnly about the complex, the panes of scuffed bullet-proof glass that enclosed the nurse's station, Henry began to realize that he might never truly get his wife back. She was lost to this world now, the world of mental illness and institutionalization. Maybe, he thought, she'd always been there, barely managing to keep herself in check, barely resisting the plunge into madness. Samuel's death, probably, had planted a seed in her. The trip to Michigan, the weird experiences they'd shared there, had served to water it. Now things were coming to fruition. Like that awful tree in the Michigan woods, Samantha grew into a gnarled, terrible thing, a caricature, a grotesque parody of her kind. And like that tree, she too was bearing fruit in the form of twisted ideas. Samantha was two days admitted when she first began to speak.

The visiting hours were terribly restrictive. It seemed almost like the staff didn't want Henry to visit his wife, allowing a space of just two-and-a-half hours a day for visitations. After going up the elevators, submitting to a pat-down by a pair of guards and getting buzzed into the common area by way of a locked door surrounded by cameras, Henry checked in at the nurse's station. Though the staff already knew him by sight, regulation dictated that he give his name, declare his intention, and be led to the patient's room by an orderly. He detested the rigid policies and wondered how such a setting could possibly be therapeutic to individuals of wounded mind, but nevertheless obeyed because he wished to visit Samantha. No amount of rules-lawyering would deter him, and as he started down the carpeted hallway, the orderly making polite chit-chat as they went, he recognized Samantha's door, the door to room thirteen. What's more, he heard a familiar voice on its other side. He couldn't parse precisely what was being said, but knew the voice was his wife's.

"She's been acting up today," the young orderly said, nodding toward the door. "If you need anything, hit the call-light and we'll be right in. Doc was talking about trying a new tranquilizer or maybe a vest-restraint. She still hasn't slept."

Henry had nothing to say to this bit of news and nodded, an appreciative but forced smile contorting his lips. With that, he pushed open the door, finding Samantha sitting upon the edge of her bed, arms stretched across her lap. She rocked forward and backward, cradling herself and looking frightfully bedraggled. What was once a mane of well-loved hair was now a tangle of unseemly knots. Though he couldn't be sure in the dimness of the room, whose only light came from a well-reinforced window fitted with recessed, half-open blinds, her hair appeared dull and greyed—a far cry from its rightful brown. Her eyes retained their reddish color. In fact, the hue had only deepened since his last visitation; the whites of her eyes teemed with what looked like rust. She did not react in any conspicuous way to his presence, glancing at him briefly before returning once more to her hushed rambles. She appeared deep in conversation with herself, the intensity of her speech corresponding to increases in her fidgeting.

"Hello, Samantha," said Henry quietly, removing his jacket and dropping down into the uncomfortable plastic chair stationed near the door.

She didn't react, except to dive deeper into her fevered whisperings. Her eyes narrowed and she made strange signs with her hands. It occurred to him that *she* was the trapped moth now, relegated to this little prison. For two hours a day, he would enter this little world of hers and share it in an effort to bring comfort where he could not hope to bring freedom.

Leaning against the back of his chair and taking in the sights of the austere room, Henry choked back tears. Though he was sitting in the room with her, sitting right before her, she didn't even appear to recognize him. She didn't speak to or acknowledge him, but seemed permanently entrenched in some other world, a world of madness that her injured mind apparently found preferable to the sphere of reality they'd once shared. Why she'd fled there, what in particular had incited this precipitous change in her, he could only guess; but that she would never return to him he felt somehow certain.

The realization pained him more than he could express. He threw a hand over his mouth and wept, stifling his sobs and leaning forward so as to shield his face from view. His life had gone to pieces. For a brief while things had seemed on the mend, but their trip and the few moments of peace they'd enjoyed at home afterward had only been a calm before this tempest. Everything and everyone he loved was gone from him, and already he was wondering how he would go about the rest of his life. Was this what awaited him now? Scheduled, two-hour visits in a psych ward with a patient who could not be aroused from her delusions long enough to even notice him? He wiped at his eyes, his vision blurry, and shuddered.

It was unkind of him, selfish perhaps, to dwell on his own sadness. He was in to visit Samantha, the one who was truly suffering through a prolonged mental break. But then, as she was lost in her muted mutterings, could she really have been said to suffer? Perhaps, but she seemed passively oblivious to her situation, already too far-gone to question anything that approached reality. It was Henry who would be cursed to watch her slow decline; it was he who was in the thick of it, with the worst suffering and grief yet ahead. His mind was still intact. It might never give way and award him the same merciful insanity that'd left Samantha a bumbling, murmuring mess. He would have to live with these memories every day. The pain of loss, the pain of watching his once-happy family torched to ruins, was his alone.

That was when he saw it. Looking up from his teary palms, he noticed that Samantha had quieted down. In fact, her attentions appeared focused directly on him, and in her red eyes he spied some vague trace of familiarity where the madness had been not a moment before. "H-Henry," she breathed, her lips forming the words soundlessly a few times before she managed to speak aloud. He stood up at once, staggering toward her, and knelt at the bedside. Her hands felt cold, entirely unfamiliar. Had he not been aware of all that had happened, had he not been looking her in the face, changed though it was, he would have thought these the hands of a stranger—and an ancient one, at that.

"Henry," she repeated, leaning in, her eyes widening and the little red spheres quaking in their sockets. She appeared reticent to continue, glancing for a moment about the room before finally speaking once more. "The Gulliver Witch... The Gulliver Witch took our baby." She cleared her throat, eyes widening further as she doubtlessly glimpsed the incredulity and distress in Henry's gaze. "Samuel was the thirteenth child. The Gulliver Witch took my Samuel..."

What happened next Henry wished he could block out of his memory forever. With a level of strength a woman of her small frame and evident weakness should not have possessed, she cast Henry aside, into the flimsy nightstand, and stood up, her thin legs carrying her across the room to the corner nearest the window. Balling up her pale, vein-ridden fists, she smacked at the walls with all her might, raising her face up to the ceiling, and screamed, "The Gulliver Witch stole my baby! She stole my baby! The Witch... Gulliver Witch... stole my... my baby!" The screams that left her lips between these shouted declarations struck him as fearsomely savage and inhuman, and he was frozen in place, cowering as her knuckles dug into the inoffensive wallpaper. She knocked and knocked against the walls, the sound of her impacts reverberating throughout the building and drowned out only by her piercing cries. The drywall was indented by her efforts and her knuckles began to bleed, leaving small, blunt streaks on the wallpaper.

Unable to rouse up the courage to stop her, the strength and will completely gone from him, Henry watched as a pair of orderlies rushed into the room to restrain her, and watched still while they attempted in vain to wrestle her back onto her bed. The two men, large though they were, struggled to contain her. Samantha's thin limbs shot out from their holds and struck their bodies with great blows so that the men cursed and groaned. Another orderly bounded in and ordered Henry from the room, and the nurse informed him that the visitation was over. Henry was forced to leave, white-faced and shaking, the sounds of his wife's thrashing still ringing out from the doorway of room thirteen and the other patients along that stretch growing audibly agitated for the commotion.

Henry limped out into the daylight, tears stabbing at his eyes and heart racing.

That was the last time he would see Samantha alive. Not one day later, a grave call came in the night from the nursing supervisor at the psych ward, informing him that "something" had happened in the night and that his wife had passed. He was asked to come in and make arrangements for the transport of the body. The whole call consumed less than five minutes and was conducted without the leanest sliver of consolation.

This news signaled a closure to the most recent chapter in his life. The era of suspense was over now. All of his fears, all of his suspicions were proven true. He never would manage to wrest Samantha from the clutches of madness. The madness had won out in the end, claiming her for itself.

He realized then that Samantha hadn't really been with him for quite some time. In losing Samuel, he'd actually lost them both. He just hadn't known it then.

Funeral arrangements were simple enough. The plot beside Samuel's was chosen and the body was interred with little fanfare.

Family members convened for a small service, and throughout it Henry acted as graciously as he could.

But the process was not so smooth as the quick ceremony made it seem, for there had gone into it a fair bit of work; work the likes of which he'd never performed and would never care to repeat. He'd been forced to visit the psychiatric hospital, had been admitted via buzzer and escort to the small morgue in the basement level. It'd been a claustrophobic space, lined with a few full-length refrigerators and a metal examination table. It'd reeked of foul chemicals, and Henry had brought a sleeve to his nose to keep from growing ill. His nerves had subsequently picked up where the chemicals had left off however, and as a local physician and the nursing supervisor had led him into the chamber lit in fluorescent bulbs, he'd felt his stomach churn.

From one of the metal-doored chambers, his wife's body had been drawn, set down with some effort onto the examination table and covered in a white shroud. Henry had then been called near to examine her body. Doing so wasn't a necessity, but was simply one of those things that people were supposed to *want* to do when a loved one had passed. And so he'd stepped up to the examination table, his palm meeting the polished edge and its coldness provoking the first in a series of shivers.

The creature on the slab, with its faded hair, eyelids stubbornly hanging half-open, chapped lips obviously forced shut post-mortem for the efforts of a morgue worker, had not been in any proper way his wife. Oh, it'd called to mind certain familiar characteristics, of course. He'd recognized in the corpse some particular beauty marks and other small details of that kind. But as he'd peered more closely at her—studied those beauty marks—he'd discovered in them tiny, hateful faces. This had called to mind that painting of his, still locked in the basement, whose minor features had had a similar effect on him. He had been forced to admit that the body was, in fact, Samantha's, but even as he'd signed on the dotted line that it was so, the alienage of the corpse had only filled him with doubt.

Samantha was laid to rest in the cemetery plot beside her deceased son; that is, if so disfigured and wretched a body as hers could ever be said in any capacity to rest. But it wasn't until after the service, until after he'd entered into his period of bleak mourning, milling about the house soullessly, that he was plunged into a new, uninvited terror.

An autopsy had been done, and its results gave new life to something that Henry wished had died with Samantha. The cause of death was determined to be an aneurism of some kind, a bleed occurring during one of her fits and the resultant spike in blood pressure that came with it. More interesting—or perhaps horrific—however, was the coroner's survey of the deceased's small intestine, wherein he found a number of oddities implanted directly into the tissue. The report claimed that a number of seedlings had been found in her digestive tract. Scattered along the lining of her gut, small black seeds had given life to rather robust seedlings with deep green stems and lively roots that, curiously, appeared to have wormed their way into her tissues and remained anchored there.

The seeds of the devil-tree had taken root in Samantha's body. They'd grown, had been nourished by her. Perhaps, after her burial, they would continue to grow, to draw sustenance from the decaying tissues, until some day her burial plot—and their son's, by extension—would be consumed and overshadowed by a monstrous growth like the one that haunted Henry's dreams. He lost a good deal of sleep for having read that report. Perhaps there was a more commonplace explanation for the presence of such saplings in his wife's body, but Henry was at a point where commonplace explanations no longer pleased him. He was well beyond the territory of rationalism, the strange and inexplicable events of the previous weeks piling upon one another and looming large in the background of his thoughts like a black, insurmountable mountain.

The image of the hideous demon-tree waxed dominant in his thoughts during those next days. It'd never really left his mind, had simply been obscured. But when he dared to look upon it in his mind, he found it there still, its limbs swaying, the knotted bark furrowing into a sort of leering face.

He decided, at least superficially, that Samantha had died of grief. When their son had died she'd taken the loss horribly; more horribly than anyone had known. And the grief, in time, had eaten her up till nothing was left. The thin thread of her mind had given way, and when it'd snapped she'd been left an incoherent mess, clinging to whatever explanations her fancy had led her to. Perhaps in meeting Louise up North, in hearing the old story of the Gulliver Witch, she'd found a scapegoat, a means of off-loading the guilt she may have felt in Samuel's passing. With Samantha's death, the Gulliver Witch was lent a sort of credibility. Perhaps the crone of the Michigan woods had never existed at all, but it had still managed to claim a victim in Henry's wife.

In the days that followed, Henry was possessed of an intense rage. He wanted badly to expunge every trace of that story from his memory. His dreams were clouded with visions of knotted trees, of gnarled growths, and it became so that he could scarcely conceive of anything else. His obsession became so great, his anger so powerful, that he began weighing the possibility of a return journey to those remote northern woods, to the site of that myth-wreathed demon-tree and to the orchard where he and Samantha had flirted, briefly, with happiness before their lives had fallen into ruin.

It seemed utterly mad to think of it. What was he to do? Drive for two days to the Upper Peninsula and seek out the ugly tree? What would he do if he managed to find it again? The more he thought about it, the more the tree took on the form of a specious boogeyman, of a thing often hinted at, but which he could not, in the light of day, dignify with genuine belief. At night however, when the moon rose into the sky and he found himself alone in that quiet house with nothing but dark thoughts, he saw the reason in it, and he felt certain that his memories of the tree were genuine.

The monstrosity had killed his wife; or, at the least, it was the only tangible part of the responsible myth-cycle that he could focus his rage upon. The tree was the one thing he could lash out against in retribution. His thoughts wandered to the old woman in the white house, Louise, but for whatever reason he couldn't find it in himself to bear her any ill will. She'd shared the story of the Gulliver Witch, it was true, but it had not been until the two of them had set off through the orchard in search of the titular witch's tree that everything had gone to rot.

Henry wasn't sure that he could find his way back there, but early one morning before the sun rose, he purchased a good axe, packed the car with a small suitcase of personal effects and drove to the nearest highway entrance ramp that would send him North.

—wʌ—wʌ—

He re-traced their original route with all the exactitude he could muster, utilizing the same GPS unit and loading it up with the coordinates for Winfield Township; the name Louise had given to the very specific region where they'd stumbled upon the white house. The trip was a lonesome one, and Henry missed his wife intensely. He'd glance often at the passenger seat, catch himself very nearly starting conversations with her, only to find her nowhere in sight. Where rain and mist had obscured their way the first time, now Henry's vision was hampered only by bleariness. Tears would well up in his eyes as he drove, sometimes for seemingly no reason at all, and without warning.

Tirelessly he drove, passing over the Mackinac Bridge and continuing on, past the cheap little motel both he and Samantha had stayed in the first time. He drove despite his fatigue, shoving it off obstinately and stopping the car only once every few hundred miles, for coffee and gasoline.

Samantha hadn't made a great traveling companion during the start of their trip up north. He recalled the way she'd sat in the passenger seat, lost in thought or pretending to sleep. It'd upset him terribly in the moment, but as he looked back upon those times he was overwhelmed with sadness and wished that she would reappear. She'd been gone but a short while, but already he was forgetting her beautiful face, her smiles. He cursed his memory, ran a hand through his messy hair and gave it a tug out of frustration.

But he was going to set things right. Even if it was strictly symbolic in nature, he was going to lash out at that evil thing in the woods. He was going to trudge through those wilds as bravely as he could and strike the tree down. And when it was down, its filthy trunk laying at his feet, he would be pleased. He didn't care how long it would take. He was prepared to give all his strength just to mar its awful body.

He thought himself delirious when—well into his marathon drive—he arrived at a spot where the GPS fizzled out and presented him with black pixels. The sight of this malfunction stirred real excitement in him, and his sleepiness was banished forthwith. He was in the right place. He'd entered into nightmare country. Recognizing the long, pristine stretch of road in the dim light of the early morning, he picked up speed and roared further, keeping his eyes peeled for the old white house amidst the trees. It was from that property that he would find his way to the orchard, just like he'd done on that day with Samantha. The sun was not fully risen, seeming to struggle in its ascent. The abundant, towering growth kept the light at bay, making it difficult for him to study the treeline with any thoroughness.

He found the house by mere chance, for he'd very nearly missed it in a careless perusal of the woods. Henry slammed on the brakes and looked out at the property bleakly, his eyes clouding over with confusion. That this was the place there was no question, however the state of the property had changed tremendously since their last visit. So radical was the transformation that he felt he couldn't believe his eyes and began inching forward along the road. This must surely be another house, he thought.

But it was the right house. He saw it in that black door with the two small windows, which stared out at him from within a nest of shadows, just beyond the crumbling patio. The house was of the same size, the same make, but in inexplicably shabbier condition than he remembered it. Though not at all attractive or stable-looking during his previous visit, it had somehow aged. No, it'd more than aged. It had begun to *fester*, leaning to one side like an arthritic old body pinioned amidst the network of trees which had, somehow, completely overcome the property. That was why he'd almost missed it on his first pass; where during his first visit the land in front of the house had been cleared of trees, the forest had now reclaimed that stretch of the property. Seemingly new trees had sprung up in place of the stumps that had previously been there—and, though he knew it to be impossible, they'd grown in within the space of some few weeks.

He shut off the SUV, ambled out onto the road and leaned against the car's cool carapace as he inspected the property. Windows had been shattered, the mighty door sat ajar. Within there was only darkness to be seen. There were no signs of habitation; no indication whatever that an old woman lived there, or could possibly live there, or had lived there in a very long time. So, how was it possible? How could the degraded property have slipped into a state of such advanced decrepitude in so brief a window? There was no accounting for it, and to attempt to do so only gave Henry a bad headache. He was awfully tired, but the curious appearance of the house incited dread that continuously beat back the torrents of sleepiness that threatened to encroach upon his waking mind. Taking an exploratory step onto the property, whose grasses were every bit as overgrown as he remembered them, he tensed.

He'd forgotten his axe.

Fetching it quickly out of the passenger seat, he held it firmly in his hands and was emboldened. He remembered now why he'd come, what he intended to do. What did it matter to him if the house was new or old, standing or completely demolished? The house and its ancient tenant didn't figure into his plans in the least. He was there only so that he could find his way to the apple orchard that was located some miles beyond the property. The sun peeked out somewhat from behind the tips of the trees as he sucked in a deep breath, tugged at the collar of his denim jacket and started into the woods.

The trees were accepting of him, cradling him at once as though inviting him deeper still. He dwelt in the shade of the repulsive old house only a moment, bypassing it and marching half-aimlessly into the denser barrier of the woods. He was without a guide this time, and recalled with a shudder the spectral form of his now-deceased wife who had led him with surety through these same trees not so long ago. At turns, when the light of dawn intruded upon the forest from small breaks in the trees above he thought he saw her still, the sight of her flashing for an instant in the eye of his mind like some bright, airy beacon. She had been herself led by some sinister presence; though she had never told him as much, had never so much as broached the subject of their trek toward the orchard in the subsequent weeks, he somehow knew it to be so. For what, save a diabolical presence in these woods, could possibly have led her to the very threshold of that old orchard?

Henry's right wrist felt suddenly numb as he marched on. He flexed and twisted it but could do nothing to banish the slight cold that'd taken hold there. Though his eyes revealed nothing of the kind, he could have sworn that small, chill fingers had been closed around his arm and some insubstantial figure, visible perhaps to keener eyes, was leading him now to where he wished to go. Small spots in the undergrowth ahead appeared vaguely trampled on, left in a state of unrest where the surroundings appeared pristinely wild. Were these the tracks that the two of them had left during their initial visit, lit up for him and highlighted plainly by the rising sun?

The axe was heavy in his hand. The hefty handle grew damp with his sweat, and the blade threw off slight flashes of metallic color whenever it caught the light of day. He took to dragging it behind him, hoping that the trail in the soil and underbrush might help to lead him back out of the woods when the job was done. Here and there he spotted the remnants of a thick mist hanging about the lowest reaches of the trees and in the small, dark places near his feet. The further he went, the more pervasive this mist seemed to become, till he reached a point when the sunlight was engaged in battle with this diffuse cloud and his sight was severely limited. Thankfully, he had not far to go.

Looming darkly ahead, outlined in a winding tendril of mist that was disturbed in his approach, Henry saw the wooden sign, its bleak old letters reading ORCHARD. The ridges in the edematous wood seemed swollen with rain, and he wondered that the whole thing still stood at all, a goodly portion of the signage effaced by years of abandonment to the elements. Invigorated by the sight of the sign, Henry charged past it.

Slinging the axe over his shoulder, his pace increased and he broke through the wall of undisturbed fog into the orchard proper. All about him the apple trees appeared less robust than previously. The fruit upon the trees was shrunken and spoilt, and upon a few apples he spied large, curious insects. Strange, he thought, that the trees should all have died within the space of some few weeks. He remembered the way he'd eaten from those trees, the way the sweetness of those apples had lingered for far too long.

With no path to go off of and working solely through intuition, Henry pressed on through the orchard, finding himself eventually in a stretch where the native oaks and apple trees intermingled. He'd broken through the bounds of the orchard now, was heading to that dark area where the two of them had faced the monstrous tree. His feet were beginning to ache for the changes in terrain and the constant hindrance of jutting roots. Still he went on, and with no little quickness, in the hopes that he might very soon stumble upon his target. That he was closing in on it he felt somewhat sure. He could feel the hideous pull of the towering thing working upon him from somewhere in the woods.

Suddenly, the mist cleared out immediately before him. The underbrush directly at his feet was transformed into a dead yellowish-brown and, standing darkly some fifteen yards beyond, was the gnarled shape of the demon-tree. Its every contour had been etched faithfully into his memory; as he glimpsed it in the flesh for the second time, he was chilled at just how perfectly his mind had captured it. The boughs still carried loads of spherical red fruits, and the broad, waxy leaves still flourished along its branches. There was not a drop of water on the thing, no trace of wetness on its trunk or leaves, despite the pervasive mist. The haze seemed to avoid the tree as though it were much averse to going near it.

The ridges in its thick trunk seemed to shift as he took his first step toward it. Henry took the axe, gripping the handle in both hands. He approached the tree from the side, pacing slowly as if wishing to sneak up on it, his pulse shooting up with every step. And then, without the least provocation, he reared back and took his first swing, the blade meeting the side of the massive trunk and resulting in a deep cleave.

Henry grit his teeth, but a cry erupted from his lips as the blade sank into the wood. The handle vibrated in his hands, the shock coursing through his palms, up his arms and terminating in his shoulders. He felt somewhat numb after that first swing, and paused just long enough to get his feeling back. He looked up at the tree, whose upper reaches appeared to sink lower now. It was like the canopy was looking down at him, exhibiting curiosity. Henry placed a foot against the trunk and grunted as he loosed the blade. Then, weighing his next cut, he reared back again and took a swing.

The crying began around the third or fourth swing. Up to that point he'd been making regular progress, the dark wood giving beneath the new blade, splinters flying with each of his forceful strokes. But at some point while he weighed the position of his next strike, he heard something that chilled him to his core and nearly saw him drop the axe so that he might stop up his ears.

From somewhere, seemingly *inside* the tree, he heard the anguished, blood-curling screams of an infant.

Henry's skin took on the color of the fog, his heart dropping down into his stomach. His fingers trembled against the handle of the axe and he struggled for a long while to free it from the trunk where it was now deeply embedded. When finally he loosed it, he fell back onto the dead grass, and was terrified at the volume of the crying that seemed to erupt from the very cut he'd just made. It was incessant, explosive, ear-rending. Gritting his teeth, his shaky frame steadied in anticipation of another swing. He cut once more into the tree, more weakly this time, and to his horror the crying only intensified. It reached new limits of volume, the sound reverberating through the material of the axe and rattling his bones.

He'd heard that crying before. In his terror, that was the only thing he could be sure of. That was Samuel's crying. There could be no question. It followed the very same pitch and character that paternal instinct had taught him to recognize. This was his son's crying, and the pattern of the cries followed, with uncanny exactitude, the cries of that fateful night, one year prior, when the child had died. Of this he was equally sure. The child's pained, gasping cries were something he could never banish from his memory. Tears came to his eyes as he listened, stunned, his mind revisiting that night for only a moment before he gingerly placed his hands once more upon the axe and prepared to continue.

The child had cried incessantly that night one year ago. Samantha had been out for a walk, entrusting Henry with the baby. He remembered how quickly his patience was worn out by Samuel's cries that night; the way the child had yelped and writhed as though trying to express some unimaginable pain. Losing his temper, he'd marched the child upstairs and left him in his crib, slamming shut the door to the nursery and stomping angrily down the stairs to the basement to work on one of his paintings. He'd closed that door, too, in the hopes of drowning out the obnoxious crying. The tantrum, he'd told himself, was nothing but a colossal bother. The child was always getting in his way, always throwing fits that interfered with his work.

Eventually, there'd come sweet, perfect silence. Henry had sighed with relief, resumed his painting and announced to Samantha upon her return that he'd successfully put the child down for a nap. That'd been a lie, of course; he'd left the child to his own devices, let him shriek till he'd given in to sleep. He'd never mentioned the maniac crying, the child's inconsolable fit. It'd stopped. It hadn't mattered. He'd kissed his wife and climbed the stairs to peek in on the child, no longer angry. Those warm, paternal feelings had returned in anticipation of glancing in on his sleeping boy.

But he had not found a sleeping baby.

He had found Samuel's tiny body twisted up in one of his blankets, skin tinged in blue, eyes glassy.

Henry sobbed as he pulled the axe from the tree. He staggered back, wiping at his eyes and nose with the upper sleeve of his jacket before loosing a terrible scream and lunging at the monolithic growth again. His ears rang with the sounds of separating wood and the spectral screaming; a screaming that issued from either the darkness of memory or, inexplicably, from the growing wound in the trunk.

The tree's strange bark, whose texture had felt so much like human skin to him, had begun to seep profusely with a deep red liquid. Henry told himself it was sap, but in time the leakage became so profound and its color proved so alarmingly red that he could not deny the truth. Blood from the tree crept along the blade of his axe, running down the handle and staining his hands. He looked at them with terror, wishing, praying, that this was but a perverse hallucination. All the while the screaming continued.

Henry could do nothing but focus on the next cut. And the next. With every swing he felt an enormous pain course through him. Snippets of memory burst out of the darkness of his mind, parading for an instant before melting away. A part of him was isolated in that nursery again, hands gripping the rails of the crib. And then he was in that morgue, the white sheet pulled away and Samantha's corpse revealed to him. That sinister analogue to her face, its features led astray from their recognized shapes and forms till the whole came to represent, without doubt or question, something undeniably profane and other. Horror after horror passed through his mind now.

The blade sank in. A trickle of blackish blood erupted from the tree's center and pooled in the dead grass below. His ears rang with Samuel's deafening cries. He was fifteen, twenty whacks into his assault and still the abomination conjured up fresh streams of blood, purging itself through the ever-growing opening. His hands were drenched in it; somehow, he retained his shaky hold on the axe.

The tree fell. Even as the titan crashed to the ground, the delirious Henry prepared to take another swipe, his arms burning and his lungs on the verge of bursting for the exertion. When the forest quaked for the weight of the fallen tree, Henry fell to the ground, sobbing, and let the axe, slick with blood, fall beside him. There, in the dead grass, he dazedly examined his kill.

A near-perfect silence took hold of the forest. The crying had stopped the moment the tree had fallen; only Henry's wild exhalations filled the air. There was no sign of the strange fruits anywhere on or near the felled tree, and as he surveyed the length, crawling on hands and knees to get a good look at it up-close, he noticed that its bark had changed. It seemed to him thoroughly ordinary, like the bark of any old oak. The leaves, too, were different now. Not at all waxy or broad like they'd been just moments before. He stood up, supporting himself on the handle of the axe, and walked around the fallen tree a few times, taking stock of its various features.

It made no sense. The tree on the ground was a normal oak, of the very kind he'd seen all throughout the forest. He shook his head, rubbed at his eyes. Still the sight was the same. Acorns littered the ground all around him. He'd been hacking at the demon-tree, he was positive, but there was no arguing the fact that it was a normal tree that'd been cut down.

Feeling a mixture of confusion and despair, Henry paced about the woods, looking up into the dark canopy, at the pervasive mist, and wondering what'd just transpired. Was he going mad? Had he not just lashed out at the hideous tree that'd borne strange, red fruits? The tree that filled his nightmares, and that Samantha had eaten from? The tree whose shape he had painted? He leaned on his axe and dried his eyes.

Then, to his sheer terror, he saw it in his periphery.

A towering, blackened trunk, bent in seemingly hostile posture. Waxy leaves of a deep and odious green, and littered with an array of large, red fruits. A ring of dead grass surrounding it.

Henry chuckled uneasily. Somehow, he'd focused his attentions on the wrong tree. Either that, or the demon-tree had escaped destruction by trading places with this common oak at his feet. This, of course, was impossible. He sucked in a deep breath and appraised the enormous, nightmarish thing. It'd escaped him once, somehow, but it would not escape him again. This time, he felt quite sure, he would succeed. Hoisting the axe up with no little difficulty, Henry started toward the demon-tree. Panting, he broke into a run and made a wild swing at it.

As before, the entry point erupted into splinters, and from within there broke out a cacophony of familiar-sounding screams. Tensing as Samuel's cries once again filled his ears and a trickle of dark blood worked its way down the length of his axe, he shook his head violently and went in for another swing. And another. Another. *Another*.

Henry's throat burned with tears and pent-up cries. His palms were damp with blood and swollen for the jostling of the axe handle at every strike. But he persisted, chopping at it again and again till gravity won out and the thing began to crumple. The monster tree crashed to the ground, flattening a swath of undergrowth. Henry nearly collapsed upon it, dropping to his knees and letting go of the axe.

"There," he muttered, mouth dry, cheeks stained in tears. "I've done it." He reached out before him, giving the thick trunk of the fallen tree a shove. He appraised it from behind bleary eyes, looking for the broad, waxy leaves, the reddish, alien fruits, the repulsive, skin-like texture of the bark.

What he found instead was a regular oak tree, just like the last.

Henry wasn't sure what to make of this, and crawled over the thing, inspecting it with thoroughness. Sure enough, it was a mere oak, not the monstrosity he'd set out to destroy. That thing, with its towering, darkened bulk and repellant air, engaged in a quaking and shuddering of its uppermost limbs from nearby, as if in a silent laugh. It had seemingly escaped him again, trading places with the next tree over as it'd done before. How had the evil tree managed this move? Was such a thing even possible?

Henry did not concern himself with such questions. He stood up, axe in hand, and began marching toward the demon-tree.

This time, he felt quite sure, he would succeed...

THE UNCANNY

He's been following me for hours now. I'm sure of it.

I first noticed him when I parked my car in the back lot and started walking toward the cafe. A cold rain had just begun falling, sending me and everyone else on the street into a mad dash for cover. We sought shelter beneath awnings, scrambled into open shops along the strip. Those of us with the foresight to bring along umbrellas hoisted them high with a certain smugness. But that man—the tall one with the black eyes I found leering at me from across the parking lot—did not seem to notice the rain. He stood out on the sidewalk as the skies opened up and centered me in his sights, a cruel smile cutting into his mottled cheeks.

I could not help looking at him as I darted into the cafe, and was unsettled at the grayish hue of his skin and the two obsidian eyes planted in his odd, shrunken face. He was wearing a tattered corduroy suit and shoes of black, scuffed leather. Not wanting to be rude, I looked away from him, gripping my umbrella and trudging across the street toward the cafe.

That was when I first heard his heavy tread behind me. His large feet clopped on the wet pavement like a horse's hooves, and I turned to find his whole jagged form lumbering toward me with surprising speed. That he was intending to approach *me* was never in the least doubt, for I saw him raise a withered hand in salutation when I turned to look. Something about the way he moved, the way he beckoned, set me ill at ease, and I broke into a jog, eager to distance myself from him. Within moments I had arrived at the entrance to the cafe, and I barged in through the glass doors, pant legs dripping. Before starting inside, I turned back to the rain-soaked scenery and sought out the man, finding that he had ceased giving chase directly across the street. The sidewalks remained virtually empty as pedestrians remained cowering beneath awnings, but the man with black eyes was still in the open, still smiling and staring as I gawked at him from the cafe entrance.

I did my best to strike the chill his dark gaze had imparted and made my way to the counter, where I ordered an Americano. I sat deep within the establishment, apart from any street-facing windows in a booth with my head low. There, I nursed my drink and waited for the rain to cease, and eventually made casual conversation with other patrons seated nearby.

While bantering with a pair of university music students I pretended to be an avid listener of classical music when an easily identifiable Vivaldi tune came on overhead. I sought to impress a studious twenty-something wearing a pencil skirt and glasses by saying that I, too, had begun reading Proust. I passed an hour engaging in the fraudulence well-known to those who haunt coffee shops in college towns, and then bowed out when I could no longer hear the thrum of the rain on the roof.

To my surprise—and horror—I found the man with black eyes still stationed across the street. He hadn't moved in all that time, was still facing the cafe, and at sighting me through the glass doors the cruel smile returned to his lips and I knew that he was merely waiting for me to exit. I had no idea what he wanted with me. Was he looking for something in particular? Had I offended him in some way?

I retreated back into the cafe and ordered another Americano, sucking it down nervously while chatting up the middle-aged barista whose teardrop tattoo afforded a whole ten minutes of awkward conversation. Driven to the bathroom by the ache of my teeming bladder, I rid myself of those two Americanos and then looked myself over in the mirror, certain that I mustn't allow myself to be intimidated by this bizarre stranger. I toweled the perspiration from my brow and decided I would leave the cafe without worry, marching down the main strip heedless of whatever odd characters saw fit to follow me.

Instead, I slipped out the back entrance of the cafe and slunk against the building's brick facade like a cartoon character, hoping to give the weird old man the slip. The rain had quit, but everything in sight was sodden, and before very long my careful climbing through manicured hedgerows and creeping through back alleys left my shoes full of water. I returned to the main road, feeling quite clever for having evaded my stalker, and prepared to continue about my business.

But as it turned out, my spur of the moment escape had been fruitless, for the clopping of heavy feet met my ears and across the street I saw now that the black-eyed man was rushing toward me, more than keeping pace. Panic stole over me and I once again sought shelter, staggering down the boulevard and studying the signage of nearby shops. I chose for my savior the Mattress Depot, barreling in and being apprehended at once by a sweaty salesman who evidently hadn't earned a commission all day. He led me by the sleeve to an assortment of thousand-dollar mattresses and urged me to lounge upon them despite the damp and grime clinging to every inch of me.

I besmirched many a bare mattress with the mud on my shoes and was interrogated by the desperate associate, made to divulge my preferences as to the softness or hardness of my sleeping surface. He insisted on inspecting the alignment of my spine so as to steer me toward more ergonomic options and, at one junction, joined me on one of the mattresses, stirring vigorously in an effort to showcase the stability of the frame. He confided in me that he sometimes rolled around on these beds when customers were few, and, unbeknownst to his superiors, had spent no few nights sleeping in-store.

I left him some time later, admitting an affinity for the denser models with memory foam toppers, and barely escaped his lecture on financing. When I walked out, the sun had begun to set and the air was still thick with the stench of rain. What's more, my relentless pursuer with the black eyes had not yet relented. The grotesque apparition in the corduroy suit was still stationed across the street, grinning, and at seeing me he started once more into that hateful gallop, his wizened fingers quaking in a come-hither motion.

I am now faced with one of two prospects. Having left my car parked in the opposite direction, I might try and run past him, toward it. The only other option is to continue my flight through the labyrinth of shops and alleys, hoping to lose his scent and regain my peace. This latter plan strikes me as the less feasible option, for many of the shops have locked up with the setting of the sun. Even so, I can't bear the thought of meeting the man. Something has changed in him—something has entered into his withered countenance, his bony frame, that repels me more forcefully than anything previous.

With every glance, his supposed humanity becomes less and less apparent. The magnetism of those eyes, drawing in all things like two minuscule black holes, is probing and weighty even from afar, and the sagging of his heavily lined flesh smacks of a rapidly degrading covering merely worn to obscure the true horror that exists underneath. His legs bow out with each of his great strides and his upper body is craned forward, arms raised stiffly like the forelimbs of a mantis. The closer he gets the wider his eyes seem to become and the deeper the creases about his wild grin.

I can't risk a collision. I decide to run for it; surely, being several decades younger, I can outrun him? I break into a sprint, racing down the sidewalk. *He'll give up soon enough,* I tell myself. *There's no way he can keep up!*

Not a minute into my maniac flight I feel a sharp pain in my abdomen; my lungs are on the verge of shriveling and I can't help but lean against the stony facade of a nearby building to catch my breath. Suddenly I find myself wishing I actually used my gym membership for more than bicep curls and sports talk with local grandfathers in the sauna.

From very close-by, I hear the clip-clop of that man's feet. He's almost upon me. It's all I can do to limp around the next corner and search for some place to hide. Cutting to my right, I make it a few steps down the street, finding it empty. Parked cars are few and the sun is nearly gone from the sky. There's a narrow alleyway leading to a small parking lot, and along it are peppered the entrances to tiny shops—a video store and arcade among them. Having no alternative as the steps draw nearer, I rush into the alley and station myself in the recessed doorway of the video store. Pressing my back to the door of the closed shop, I hold my breath, listening for the black-eyed man's advance. I hear his steps slow for a moment. Then, I hear him enter the alley. His tread has a certain confidence to it now; he knows I'm nearby, that he's just about got me. I press myself into the crook of the doorway as tightly as I can, make myself as small as possible, shutting my eyes and hoping that he doesn't see me.

The steps have just stopped.

The alley is silent.

Do I dare open my eyes? Can I breathe a sigh of relief? Will the man turn away from here and leave me be?

Taking a slow breath through my nose, I open my eyes.

And there, standing before me, is the man. In the dimness of the alley his eyes—empty sockets—seem to smolder with an infernal darkness, and I see now that the creases in his stone-like face are actually cracks beneath which squirm legions of insects. He extends his bony hands, taking hold of my shirt and pulling me toward him till my nose nearly touches his own. His jaw makes a harsh grinding noise and his mouth falls open. Without the movement of his crumbling lips, he begins to speak—to scream the message he has trailed me all over town to deliver:

"SIR, I AM CALLING TO INFORM YOU THAT YOUR CAR'S WARRANTY IS SOON TO EXPIRE—"

MORE CHILLS FROM VELOX BOOKS

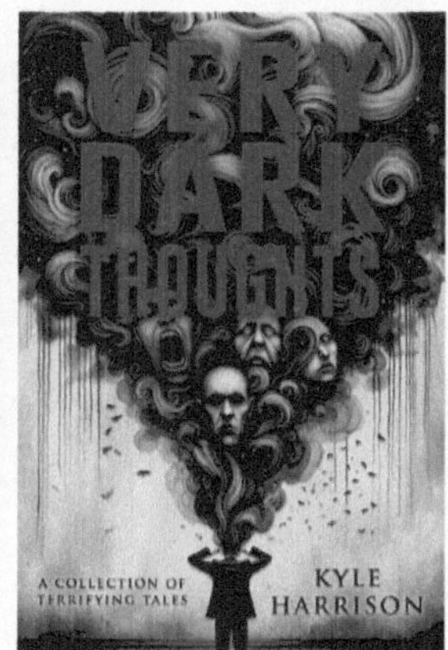

MORE CHILLS FROM VELOX BOOKS

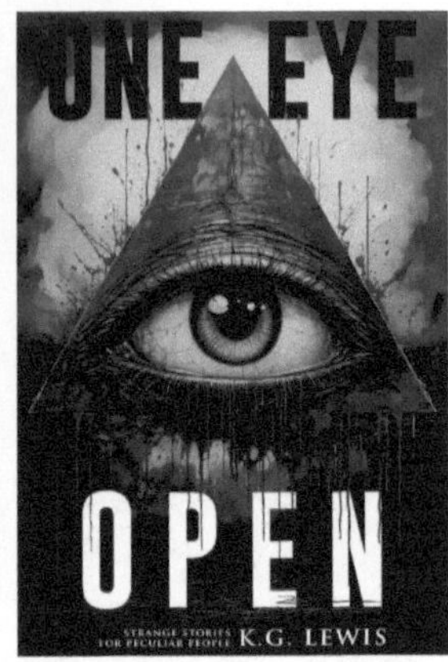

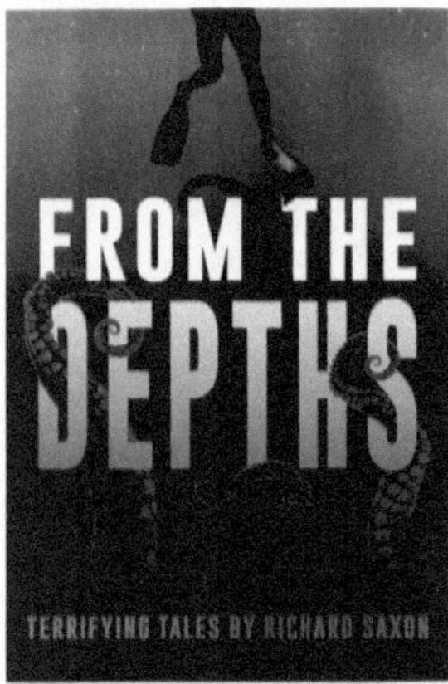

MORE CHILLS FROM VELOX BOOKS

www.ingramcontent.com/pod-product-compliance
Lightning Source LLC
Chambersburg PA
CBHW030132010826
48973CB00002B/531

* 9 7 8 1 9 6 3 1 0 7 2 5 8 *